The Lasso Part 3:

Castle Island

Dave Bair

A very special thanks to my beta readers, who continue to keep it light and real while helping me to stay on track.

John Limbach
Gladys Bennett
Sherry Mullet
Rena Thomas
Marilyn Uzzle

Gladys —

Thank you So

Much for Everything!

Chapter 1

"I don't want to go home today Buck," Karma said, softly as she lay with her body draped over her husbands, with not a stitch of fabric between them.

"I know, love," Jesse whispered. "Neither do I."

"I have thoroughly enjoyed our time together here, Jesse. Our walks on the beach. Our naked, midnight swims in the ocean. The exquisite cuisine. I have loved everything."

"Even the sex?" Jesse asked his wife with a smirk.

"Especially the sex!" Karma replied crawling on top of her man and kissing him on the lips. "I could never get enough of you, Mr. Buck".

"Good," Jesse replied while wrapping his arms around her "because I want you again right now, Mrs. Buck!"

One week later…

"Tell me, Jesse, are we going to miss our flight again today?"

"Karma, we really need to get back to Eureka," Jesse told her while getting out of bed and heading for the shower. "We have a business to run, a house to rebuild and all kinds of stuff going on."

"I know we do, Buck. I guess you're right," Karma agreed as she got out of bed and headed into the shower where her man was.

Three days later…

"Okay, love," Jesse said to Karma as he pinned her to the mattress and climbed on top of her. "I have to touch you one more time," Jesse whispered softly while nibbling on Karma's ear. "Then we *really* need to get in the shower, we have a plane to catch…"

Noon the next day…

"How many times is that?" Karma asked in a playful fashion.

"How many times is what?" Jesse asked, sitting up in bed. "How many times have we missed our flight? Three I think, maybe four."

"You know what I'm talking about!" Karma said, grinning from ear to ear. "How many times have we…" *Wham, wham, wham!* was heard on the entry door of their floating bungalow.

"Mr. Buck."

Jesse and Karma looked at each other, recognizing the voice coming from the other side.

"I am tired of waiting for you to come out. You have three minutes to cover yourselves before I come in."

"It's the Kaiser!" Jesse and Karma said to each other as they jumped out of bed and scrambled for some clothes.

"Two minutes, Mr. Buck," the Kaiser said with his deep, baritone voice, waiting on the other side of the door.

"You will wait until I answer the door!" Jesse fired back sharply. "I don't report to you, Kaiser!"

Jesse and Karma, now dressed wearing only shorts and t-shirts, calmly made their way to the main quarters of their bungalow. Karma headed for the sofa as Jesse headed toward the door.

"You smell like sex!" Karma shouted in a whisper.

"That's not me, love, it's you!"

"Really, Buck?"

"Shh, shh," Jesse told Karma along with a hand motion to sit for he was about to open the door and let the Kaiser in. When Jesse unlocked the door and opened it, the Kaiser was standing right there. He was wearing khaki colored cargo shorts, with a Hawaiian style shirt that had parrots and palm trees on it. His sunglasses were as black as night and his feet were bare. He looked like a fish out of water standing there.

"Trying to blend in?" Jesse asked as he moved aside to let the Kaiser in.

"I'm in disguise," the Kaiser replied unamused. "I suggest you sit, for what I have to talk about won't be pleasant to your ears."

Jesse sat next to Karma on the sofa and picked up her hand to hold it.

"Whatever it is you have to tell us couldn't wait until we got back?" Jesse asked with a bit of attitude. "We're still on our honeymoon."

"I told you I needed Camper alive and you deliberately killed him," The Kaiser started with an angry voice.

"Things got a little…" Jesse started to reply

"Jesse didn't kill Camper," Karma immediately interrupted. "I did!" Karma fired back with just as angry a voice as the Kaiser had.

6

"You broke a direct order!"

"You weren't there Kaiser; how would you know?"

"You deliberately disobeyed the rules!" the Kaiser shouted at Karma.

"I thought there *were* no rules," Jesse replied softly, eyeballing the Kaiser, calling him out on his own words from the previous meeting.

"Then you destroyed a casino on the Las Vegas strip! What in the hell is the matter with you?! You killed more than thirty people!"

"That's crap and you know it," Jesse answered very calmly, doing everything he could to maintain composure.

"How many innocent people died in that explosion, Kaiser?" There was silence in the room while Jesse and Karma waited for the answer.

"You are missing the point!" The Kaiser shouted at the couple.

"None," Jesse answered calmly. "There were no innocent civilian lives lost. The only people who died in that explosion had it coming. They were the criminals that were untouchable to the rest of the world. Drug lords, kidnappers, human traffickers and meth cooks. My team did the world a favor and you know it. My team Kaiser, completed their mission."

"YOUR OPERATION CROSSED THE LINE, BUCK!" the Kaiser shouted at the top of his lungs.

"What are you here for, Kaiser?" Karma finally asked in a relatively calm fashion, bored with the shouting match. "You need to tell us why you are here because you're fouling up my chi."

"Your chi is not important."

"Are we in trouble, Kaiser? Are you here to relieve us of our duties?" Jesse asked sarcastically. "If you are, we'd…"

"That's enough, Mr. Buck," the Kaiser interrupted holding up his hand for Jesse to stop talking.

Wham, Huh! With one smooth motion, Doc grabbed the Kaiser from behind and dropped him to the floor, landing him on his back.

"Does this guy live, Commander?" Doc asked while pointing a Colt .45 at the Kaiser's head and keeping him planted on the ground with his foot on the Kaisers chest. "I say we feed him to the fish," Doc continued. "I don't like the way he was talking to you."

"I suggest," Jesse started talking to the Kaiser as he slowly got up off the sofa, "that you start to address your team with a little more respect." Jesse held out his hand, offering it to Karma, helping her off the couch. Karma stepped up to her man and put her arms around him, smiling at the Kaiser pinned to the floor the whole time.

"Now, if we let you up, are you going to play nice in the big boy sandbox?" Jesse asked the Kaiser with a very sarcastic attitude.

"I can make your life…" The Kaiser started speaking to Jesse, nearly foaming at the mouth.

"Don't threaten me!" Jesse interrupted. "I don't answer to you. Do you understand me? I will never answer to you. If you have something you want me to look into, then from this moment forward you will ask me if my team and I are interested in helping you out. You will ask me with respect, and you will DAMN SURE respect my wife!" Jesse paused for a moment while looking straight into the eyes of the

Kaiser, showing no fear and demonstrating complete control.

"Nod your head if you understand me." The Kaiser nodded his head, cautious not to nod too fast.

"Nod your head if you still want my team to be part of your bigger picture." Again, the Kaiser slowly nodded his head.

"Let him up," Jesse instructed Doc. Doc removed his foot from the man's chest and slowly de-cocked his pistol.

"Now," Jesse continued with a normal talking voice, "tell me, us, exactly why you are here."

"You have 45 days," the Kaiser replied as he got up off the floor and dusted himself off, "to get your affairs in order, Mr. Buck."

"Why?" Jesse asked taking a step towards the Kaiser.

"In 45 days, I would like to meet with you and your team regarding your next assignment." There was a pause with the Kaiser's request, and after a moment he followed up with a struggled "please."

"Where will this meeting be held?" Doc questioned the man.

"Same place, at the Lasso," the Kaiser replied, looking at Jesse almost as if he were asking for approval.

"Done." Jesse answered back. "Fine tune the details with Pastor. Will there be anything else right now?"

"That is all." The Kaiser answered, leaving through the door with a disgruntled look on his face, certainly not happy about how things went.

"If we get out of here in an hour, we can still make our flight." Doc informed the group.

"Let's move," Jesse instructed.

Chapter 2

"Where am I?" Darren Beaver muttered through his bandages. "Why can't I move? Why can't I move!!! SOMEBODY TALK TO ME!!!"

"Dr. Nola, please report to the trauma room immediately. Dr. Nola, to the trauma room immediately." Cindy announced over the 'immediate assistance needed' intercom. Like he fell from the heavens, Dr. Nola magically appeared in seconds, worried that this urgency was for the mystery man in critical condition.

"Dr. Nola, your John Doe is awake."

"Is he really?" Dr. Nola questioned in disbelief and fearful of what he might be walking into.

"I thought he was in a medically induced coma?" Dr. Nola darted into the room where Darren Beaver was and immediately tried to communicate with him.

"Sir," Dr. Nola spoke softly and walked cautiously as he further entered the room where Darren Beaver lay. He was completely wrapped up in bandages. He looked like a mummy; he was a mummy… with a pulse.

"Sir, can you hear me?" Dr. Nola asked carefully, trying to stay calm, knowing his patient could be experiencing uncontrollable fits of rage and anger from the severe nerve damage caused by the burns.

"Are you a doctor?" Darren Beaver asked. His voice was charred and rough. His vocal cords must have been damaged in the explosion for he sounded like a monster.

"Yes, sir, I am a doctor. My name is Dr. Nola and I have been looking after you."

Unlike his brothers, Darren Beaver was not a stupid man; he could connect the dots. If he really was where he thought he was, then something bad must have happened and instead of asking a bunch of questions up front, he needed to hear exactly what was going on from the doctor.

"Will you please tell me what you know?" Darren asked, fearful of what he might hear about his condition.

"Sir," Dr. Nola started to speak as he pulled up a stool to sit next to 'Mr. Doe,' "I don't know what your name is. Do you remember your name?"

"My name is Darren."

"Do you remember your last name?"

"Beaver. My name is Darren Beaver."

"Okay Mr. Beaver," Dr. Nola continued, "I don't know where to start…"

"Start at the beginning," Darren insisted. His words came slowly, with a monstrous sounding tone. "Tell me what you know. Tell me everything." Darren's words were so slow to cross his lips, and his voice was so rough it was very difficult for Dr. Nola to make out what he was saying. He truly sounded like Satan when he talked.

Knowing the state of his condition was severe by the sound of his own voice and the fact that he was strapped to a bed, Darren deemed it was in his best interest to hear everything the doctor could tell him *before* he freaked out and did something stupid, like demand to leave.

"Before we start, I need to know, Mr. Beaver, are you experiencing any pain at all?"
Darren gently shook his head. "I can't feel anything. I can't feel anything at all. I'm actually a little scared."

You have every reason to be scared, Dr. Nola thought to himself. *You are not far from death.*

"Mr. Beaver," Dr. Nola started, "what I am about to tell you isn't going to be any easier for you to hear than it's going to be for me to say."

"Just say it, doctor. Just start at the beginning and tell me what you know. Tell me everything. I just need to know."

"You have been in my care for over a month now…" Dr. Nola spoke slowly and clearly, making sure his words were clean and sharp, explaining the situation as he came to know it. Dr. Nola was sure to give details while not being too graphic at the same time. He started at the minute the medics brought him through the door to the current moment in time. It took Dr. Nola over an hour to tell his version of the story and when he was done, there was nothing but silence from Darren.

"Sir?" Dr. Nola asked. "Mr. Beaver? Mr. Beaver, can you hear me?"

"Leave me be," Darren finally replied.

"Mr. Beaver, there are…"

"Leave, now." Darren interrupted.

"There is staff here for you 24/7 when you are ready to see us," Dr. Nola replied before leaving the room.

You're gonna pay for this, Buck, Darren thought to himself as anger started to build from the deepest depths of his soul. *YOU'RE GONNA PAY FOR THIS WITH YOUR LIFE!!!*

Chapter 3

"I know this is going to sound crazy, Buck," Karma said with a very spirited attitude as they neared the property on Flathead Lake. "I can't wait to get you home and have my way with you!"

"Whoa, Karma love!" Jesse fired back in a chuckle. "Where did that come from?"

"Hey, conversation police," Doc yelled out from the back seat. "I'm sitting right here, remember?"
Jesse and Karma chuckled at the comment and heeded the hint.

"I'll get you later," Karma whispered to Jesse with a wink.

When the trio pulled down the dirt road to where the trailers were sitting, they were stunned with what they saw. The trailers had all been moved down closer to the lake and instead of there being two of them, there were now four! Everyone was there to welcome the return of Jesse and Karma. Recon and Savannah, Hack and Barbara and Pastor and Georgia-Jean were all there welcoming the return of their beloved friends. Erin and Meo were wearing aprons that boasted the Lasso's name across the front, and Desi was, of course, pouring Champagne into chilled Champagne flutes. The group was lined up cheering and clapping as Jesse stopped the truck.

"This looks fairly interesting," Jesse said to Karma as he put the truck into park.

"What are you talking about, Buck?" Karma replied with a light smack to Jesse's arm. "Haven't you ever seen a welcome home party before?"

Karma was the first to jump out of the truck and run over to see her friends. Meo was the first to give her a hug, followed by Savannah and then licks and kisses from Bourbon the pup.

"You're getting big, Bourbon," Karma said cheerfully as she knelt to love the puppy all over.

"It's good to have you back, Commander," Recon said as he and the group of men walked up and greeted Jesse with a man hug.

"Good to be back, Recon."

"You know you're nearly two weeks late, don't you?"

"Too much of a good thing," Doc chimed in, pointing to Karma.

"Didn't think I was going to see you again, Doc," Pastor threw out, just to make his presence known.

"You'll be seeing a lot of me, Pastor."

"Are you telling me you'll be coming to Sunday morning service?"

"No," Doc answered with a chuckle. "I sold my bar; I'm working with Jesse again."

"I don't know if Jesse is going to have a job after the debacle in Las Vegas," Pastor responded, making eye contact with his friend. "Sounds like you screwed the pooch while you were there."

"I don't know what you're talking about, Pastor," Jesse told him reaching for his suitcase from the bed of the truck. "It was a perfect mission."

"Jesse."

"Yeah, Doc."

"Is one of those cribs over there mine?" Referring to the trailers.

"Yeah, Doc, but I'm not sure which one yet. Check with Recon."

"And Jesse…"

"I know, I know – you need to go pick up Sue. Keys are in it. Fill it up on your way back."

"Who's Sue?" Pastor asked with perked up ears.

"Sue is the flight attendant that Doc met on our way to Fiji. She's flying in tonight."

"Ahhhh – SINNERS!!!" Pastor shouted while pointing two fingers towards Doc.

"She's already coming to see you?" Recon asked his old buddy.

"She's moving in with him – hence the reason for one of the two new trailers you see," Jesse added with a smirk.

"Moving kind of fast aren't you, Doc?"

"Recon," Doc fired back with a look of disgust on his face. "How long did you and Savannah know each other before you moved in together?"

"Yeah, baby," Savannah commented as she walked up behind her man and wrapped her arms around him. "How did that work out for you?"

"That's not the same thing, honey," Recon replied, defending himself. "You and I were destined to be together."

"Bwhahahahah!" The guys in the circle burst into laughter when they heard Recon's comment, spoken so innocently.

"Animals," Recon said as he grabbed Savannah by the hand and led her away.

"Keys are in the ignition, Doc," Jesse reiterated with a head nod. "Drive carefully."

Jesse put the suitcases in the trailer and joined the circle of friends by the fire. Champagne was being poured freely and conversation was light.

"Where's your old man, Meo?" Jesse asked, a little surprised that Rod wasn't around.

"He's been working a lot lately," Meo responded with a bit of a sheepish voice.

"What's going on, Meo?" Karma asked directly. "Sounds like there's trouble in paradise."

"It's not that, Karma," Meo responded, looking up from her glass of bubbly. "Apparently, some guy in town owns a Christmas tree farm, and when Rod told me where it was, I mentioned to him that Chippewa legend has it that at least part of that land is sacred ground and he flipped out on me."

"What do you mean exactly, when you tell us it's sacred ground?" Jesse asked with his ears perked up, not knowing really anything about native Americans and what they refer to as sacred ground.

"I mean exactly that, Jesse; part of that land was a burial site for the honored. It's still sacred ground. Just because the white man stole it from us and *we* don't own it anymore, doesn't mean that it's not sacred." Meo continued to speak with passion in her voice about her native heritage. "Our culture honors our dead. When we put them to rest, that ground becomes a private place for those who have earned it. It becomes a sacred place. There are plenty of ghost stories and taboo about Indian burial grounds that just aren't true. We are not a creepy, evil people that come back

16

to haunt you because we can, Jesse." Meo paused to take a sip of her Champagne and then continued with her story.

"I will tell you this, some older generations do believe that when you are going to be buried, you need to be put to rest properly. If you are not put to rest properly *or* you have died before your time, your soul *could* be lost in purgatory for all of eternity, never even getting to final purification so you can ascend into heaven."

"There's your ghost story." Erin said with a chuckle, trying not to think about it too much.

"Why would Rod act so uneasy about that?" Karma asked.

"I don't know," Meo responded with a solemn voice. "Maybe because it creeps him out knowing that he has to go onto that land."

"Well," Jesse said to Meo with a very calm, non-suspicious voice, "I don't think the guy that owns it is alive anymore". *I would know.* Jesse thought to himself, *because we hog tied him and burned his place down with him in it!*

"Are you and Rod okay, Meo?" Karma asked, a little concerned about her friend. "Let's go for a walk," she said as she got up and grabbed Meo by the hand, leading her off towards the water's edge so the two friends could talk in private.

The rest of the afternoon and evening were spent catching up. Doc eventually returned with Sue and introductions were made. After the guests left, the four couples, Jesse and Karma, Recon and Savannah, Hack and Barbara and Doc and Sue talked a little more about what was what.

They talked about the awesome pay they received from their first mission, more money than any of them had ever dreamed of. Not all missions come with jackpot size paychecks, but this one did and, with nine zeros to the left of the decimal point in their bank accounts, there were nothing but smiles to be had. An added bonus that wasn't mentioned before is that GHOST agents are 100% tax exempt for life. The only tax they pay is local sales tax, ever. It's tough to pay taxes when you don't exist.

"Jesse," Hack asked as he held Barbara on his lap. "Maybe I'm not seeing the big picture here but, now that we're all filthy rich, are we going to continue living in these travel trailers?"

"We love our trailer," Savannah replied. "Don't we honey?" Savannah asked for confirmation as she leaned over and kissed Recon on the cheek.

"I'd love living in a cave with you, Savannah." The group rolled their eyes and chuckled as Recon and Savannah seemed to be lost in their own little world.

"I like the thought of us being this close," Karma chimed in. "There is something appealing about our little compound here at the lake."

"Karma and I talked about that a little bit on our honeymoon," Jesse answered. "This is a great piece of land, but it may be better suited as a resort rather than a compound. We're trapped on the peninsula if something bad happens, and we're further away from the Lasso than I want to be."

"So, what's your solution, Commander?" Recon asked, hoping Jesse was thinking what he was thinking.

"Karma and I were thinking about building a custom home on Lost Lake where the other one burned down, and we should find three more home sites for you all, strategically positioned so we all have our privacy yet no one can sneak up on us."

"Are we heading out there tomorrow?" Savannah asked with what seemed to be a little bit of urgency in her voice.

"Jesse and I have a meeting with the contractor at the Lasso tomorrow morning, but we can certainly head to the lake after that," Karma replied.

"What's your urgency, Savannah?" Doc asked, digging for info. "You already pregnant?"

A smile slowly crept across Savannah's face as she stared back at Doc. The group started to get excited and asked Savannah for confirmation.

"No, Doc," Savannah answered in a very sensual manner, repositioning herself on her man's lap. "We don't want to get pregnant until we're married and our house is built. Until then we're just going to enjoy practicing!"

"When is the wedding?" Barbara asked entering the conversation.

"Well," Recon started, looking over at Jesse. "Savannah and I have talked and we're going down to Kalispell sometime this week to get rings made and we'd like you, Jesse, to marry us as sometime after that."

"Something quiet, here by the water with only our closest friends," Savannah added, looking at Karma. "Much like you and Jesse had."

The group jumped up and burst into emotional joy! Hugs and congratulations were shared by everyone. Recon and Savannah were a great looking couple, and they did have an instant connection. Jesse was very happy for his closest friend. Savannah was a good woman and after everything she'd been through, she deserved a man like Recon.

"One more thing before we all head our own ways for the night," Jesse said, settling the group down. "We have a meeting with the Kaiser in 44 days at the Lasso about our next mission."

"About that, Buck," Karma said, looking at her man. "I don't want these meetings to be held at our place of business. That's too creepy for me."

"Well, Karma, where would you like us to have the meeting?"

"At my friend Allison's place," Karma answered, intentionally leaving out a few details.

"Well, Karma," Jesse told her with a peck on the lips, "make it happen."

Chapter 4

The next morning dawned with Jesse and Karma excited to see the Lasso and how the rebuild was progressing. Their morning shower together was quick and playful rather than the usual long and intense. Their drive to the Lasso was hurried, with hopes that the building was ready to be insulated. When they pulled up, they couldn't believe their eyes.

There were hundreds of people clapping and cheering, whistling and shouting. The group was showing their excitement, love and support for Jesse and Karma and the grand reopening of their business. There was a massive red ribbon around the building with a giant bow over the front doors.

"Oh my gosh, Jesse, look!" Karma said excitedly, holding her hands over mouth.

"There's no way it's ready for business," Jesse said in disbelief at what he saw.

"It sure looks like it is to me, Jesse!"

Erin was there and pointed to a parking spot right out in front for Jesse to park. As he and Karma stepped out of the pickup the crowd got even louder!

"We have a little bit of a surprise for you this morning, Jesse." Erin shouted over the noise of the crowd with a hug for her boss. Jesse and Karma were overwhelmed with joy. It's not easy to surprise Jesse and this was truly an amazing surprise. Karma had uncontrollable tears of joy falling from her eyes.

"Before we go in, there is someone here who wants to meet you." Erin shouted over the crowd of excited people as she led the couple to the front doors.

"Jesse, Karma," Erin said as a well-dressed man approached from the other side. "It's with great pleasure that I introduce to you the mayor of Eureka, Dick Hanson; Dick, I'm proud to introduce to you the owners of the Lasso, Jesse and Karma Buck."

Mayor Hanson shook hands with the couple and motioned for the crowd to quiet down so he could have a quick word. When the crowd settled, Erin handed Mayor Hanson a microphone.

"Jesse, Karma, it is a pleasure for me to be here with you today." Jesse wrapped his arm around his wife and held her close as the Mayor delivered his speech. "Your restaurant, the Lasso, as it's named, has brought a kind of communion to our small mountain township that has been unsurpassed by anything prior. Your warmth, your kindness and your dedication to us have been nothing short of overwhelming."

"When the construction crews started the rebuild, the people of Eureka were eager to help in every way that they could. Volunteers from Eureka and surrounding areas pulled together and worked around the clock to expedite the grand re-opening of not only Eureka's favorite watering hole, but Montana's favorite watering hole!"

The crowd roared with excitement and approval. The whistling and cheering were almost deafening, and the emotion felt by everyone was magical.

"On behalf of the entire township of Eureka, Montana, it is with great pleasure to not only present you with the key to the Lasso, but also with this key to the city."

Just then a woman handed a large brass key to Mayor Hanson, who in turn handed it over to Jesse.

"May your future here with us be everything you want it to be."

The people of Eureka, roared with approval. "WE LOVE YOU GUYS!" yelled an unknown voice from the crowd. Jesse had a stray tear fall while Karma's eyes were flowing freely. Jesse held the key up over his head with both hands for the crowd to see.

"Speech, speech, speech..." the crowd chanted, wanting Jesse to say something.

"Give them what they want, Buck," Karma said, nudging Jesse while reaching for the giant brass key. Jesse started with a sigh as he took the microphone and looked out over the crowd.

"Ladies and gentlemen, people of Eureka, I am truly touched." Jesse paused for a moment, for his emotions were ganging up on him, making it a little harder to talk than he first imagined it would be.

"I moved up here to live my lifelong dream of building and running the Lasso. I never imagined it would bring as much to the community as it has. Every day I see you, the people, standing in front of me, gathering here, eating among friends, bringing your children to movie night and competing amongst each other with your chili recipes." There was a light chuckle among the crowd.

"I cannot take full credit for the success the Lasso has had, or the energy that has brought everyone together. I have had lots of help. My beautiful wife Karma, whom I met here, and my manager Erin, who most of you know better than I do, have both been instrumental in making this your favorite place. It has truly been a team effort."

The crowd cheered wildly as Erin stepped forward and put her arm around Jesse. The trio, Erin, Jesse, and Karma, in that order, paused for a moment and savored the experience.

"Now, without further ado," Jesse continued, with a chuckle and playful grin, "why don't you all come in and help us celebrate!"

The crowd cheered at football stadium sound levels! Jesse took the key to the city from Karma and encouraged Karma and Erin to cut the ribbon together. Seconds later, the doors to the Lasso officially reopened. Jesse and Karma took two steps through the door only to be greeted by their group of friends. At that moment, the dots were connected.

"You and Doc set this up, didn't you?" Jesse asked Karma while he pulled her into his arms to give her an emotional kiss.

"I don't know what you're talking about Jesse. I'm as shocked as you are!"

"This was mostly Erin's doing, Commander," Recon admitted, giving Jesse a man hug. "We just asked Karma to keep you away for a couple more days. We told her you could use the break."

The *new* Lasso was amazing inside. It was a near duplicate of the first one in many ways; however, the electronics and *special features* were completely new and state-of-the-art, certainly not the outdated equipment that Jesse purchased the first time to keep within budget. There was no shortage of lights accenting everything, all which could be controlled with one of several touch pads. There was a new Steinway and Sons grand piano next to the stage. The piano appeared to be made from salvaged campfire wood and had bullet holes shot through it to resemble its predecessor. The legs on the piano were made to look as if they came right out of a fire pit, it looked really cool. There was also a fog machine mounted inside of it adding the effect of a smoldering campfire with the touch of a button.

There were minor things that Jesse wanted to change in the first Lasso that got changed in the rebuild. The bathroom signs were changed to their original design of reading "Cows" and "Bulls," honoring the lands previous life as a cattle auction.

Erin grabbed both Jesse and Karma by their hands and led them out to the back where the *Party Arena* was. This was the area that was enclosed with the giant tent during the Rodeo; it was now a warehouse-sized building with fifty-foot-tall ceilings. The arena boasted the same kind of wood plank floor that the main building had, except where there were two indoor horseshoe pits.
When Erin turned on the lights in the pavilion, The Hickory Sticks started jamming out. The crowd of people followed behind and swiftly joined in the party.

"What do we do now, Buck?" Karma asked Jesse as she clung to her man with excitement.

"There's only one thing we can do, Karma. Let's find some aprons and get to work!"

Just as Jesse and Karma were about to turn and walk away to get to work, Erin appeared before them with a stack of new aprons.

"Check these out," Erin told them, excitedly handing aprons to both Jesse and Karma. The aprons had "The Lasso" stitched across the front of them with an authentic rope-like thread. The light brownish color of the thread contrasted beautifully against the black apron; they looked really sharp. That's when Jesse's emotions took control and tears of joy started dripping from both eyes. He reached out and gave Erin a big hug.

"How did you do all of this?" he asked her as he let her go.

"I didn't Jesse. Your people did this for you," Erin confessed. "These people love you two," Erin said to Jesse and Karma both." The whole town is crazy about the Bucks and their place called *The Lasso*. Jesse, check the parking lot, all of Montana loves you!"

"This is truly amazing," Karma replied holding onto her man.

"It gets better," Erin said. "Watch this." Erin gave a wave to the lead singer of the Hickory Sticks and with a head nod, the music stopped abruptly.

"Ladies and Gentlemen," the singer announced. "Ladies and gentlemen, I have a special announcement to make." The crowd quieted down and gave their full attention to the man on stage.

"Ladies and gentlemen, this Saturday night, two nights from now, this Saturday, we are having a live Karaoke contest!! The crowd erupted in cheer and seconds later started chanting. "Karma! Karma! Karma! Karma!"

"Sounds like they want you to sing right now, Ms. Karma!" the singer said, pointing to Karma with the mic.

"Saturday!" Karma tried to shout over the crowd.

"They can't hear you, Ms. Karma," the singer continued. "Why don't you come up here and talk."

"Give them what they want, Mrs. Buck," Jesse said to Karma as he nudged her toward the stage. With a big smile on her face, she went. When Karma made her way onto the stage, the singer of the Hickory Sticks gave Karma a hug and handed her the mic.

"I'm not singing today," she started as the people quieted down. "It's already been such an emotional day; I just need time to catch my breath." The crowd went wild again before Karma could complete her sentence. "…I promise…" she paused while the crowd settled down again, "…I promise to sing Saturday…" One more pause before she continued. "…I promise to sing Saturday, if Erin promises to sing, too."

Immediately the crowd roared with excitement and started to chant "Erin… Erin… Erin…!" Getting the hint, Erin hurried to get up on stage next to Karma. Once there, Karma gladly handed over the mic.

"How about a friendly little wager?" Erin asked playfully into mic. With a roaring, cheering crowd, the answer to that question was an undeniable 'yes'. Jesse and his group of friends listened with keen ears as the two women had everybody's attention.

"What do you have in mind, Erin?" As the conversation continued, Karma and Erin shared the microphone between them.

"Well, Karma," Erin answered back with a very deviant smile. "Since we never got to finish our competition the last time we sang together, I'm thinking that we have a sing-off between you and me."

"Oh no!" Jesse said out loud to himself with a chuckle. "Don't do it Karma, be strong."

"Game on!" Karma answered back before anything else was said.

"Okay then," Erin continued, "we each sing three songs by the artists of our choice and the crowd picks the winner." The crowd was now cheering so loudly that they were literally rattling the windows.

"I accept that challenge," Karma answered playfully. "What do I get when I win?" Karma continued, deliberately egging on the crowd. "What's my prize?"

"You, Karma," Erin stabbed back not missing a beat, "will be handing the winner, that would be me, the trophy for the first annual Karaoke contest and sing-off.

"I'll see you Saturday!" Karma answered back. The two women hugged each other and left the stage, letting the party get back into full swing.

Chapter 5

Erin and Pastor insisted that they had things under control at the Lasso and encouraged the four couples to go tend to their business at Lost Lake. On the way to Lost Lake, Jesse and Karma rolled up to their accident site. It was the first time they had been there together since the night of their near fatal crash.

"Do you want to stop?" Jesse asked Karma as he took his foot off the gas.

"We don't need to, Jesse. We'll drive past it every day for the rest of our lives," Karma answered back as she squeezed Jesse's hand.

When the caravan of friends reached Lost Lake, it looked desolate. Overgrown foliage and debris from the fires littered the property. It was almost heart breaking to see it in this condition. Jesse instructed the others to walk with Recon and scout out three other building places. Bourbon the pup was quick to head over to the other side of the lake and see if there were any more bodies to be discovered, or maybe something else he could get into.

"Over here is where I buried Louie," Jesse said to Karma softly as they walked up towards the knoll holding hands. "I buried him right next to you."

Karma could see the pain Jesse was feeling in his eyes.

"You miss Louie, don't you," Karma asked as she clung onto his arm.

"I do miss Louie, Karma, but that's not why I'm shedding tears."

"Well, then, what's the matter, Jesse?"

"Burying you was the hardest thing I have ever had to do, Rachael."

"But, Jesse honey, you didn't bury me. I'm right here."

"I hope that when it's our time Rachel, we go together," Jesse said holding onto his wife tightly. "I don't ever want to have to do that again. It was really hard to do the first time, and I knew I'd see you again. I can't imagine how it would feel if you were gone forever."

The couple embraced in an emotional hug and cried together, holding each other tightly.

"Well, since we don't need this grave here anymore, why don't we just get rid of it?" Karma asked Jesse as she released him from the embrace. "We'll make that our first project together."

"Would you like to do that before or after you take your new Corvette for a test drive?" Jesse asked with a playful demeanor.

"Is my car done?"

"You bet it is, Baby!"

"Don't call me Baby!" Karma fired back with a hard smack on Jesse's butt. Jesse grabbed Karma by the waist and pulled her toward him. Looking into her sparkling blue eyes, he slowly planted a kiss right on Karma's lips.

"Let's go have some fun."

Karma nearly dragged Jesse to the shop. Jesse unbarricaded the door and let Karma enter first.

"Huh!" Karma gasped, for this was the first time she'd *really* comprehended the condition of the wrecked vehicles. "Jesse!"

"It's okay, love," Jesse assured her.

"Are these our cars?" Karma asked, looking at the piles of Corvette rubbish.

"What's left of them, yeah."

Karma was staring at the vehicles as she slowly made her way around them. "How did we survive that crash?"

"The simple answer to that question, is God was with us." Jesse started, "however a more detailed answer would be, contrary to what most people believe, the Chevrolet Corvette is actually a very safe automobile. If you look at the passenger compartments of both of these cars," Jesse explained while pointing to them, "they are fully intact, protecting the occupants inside them. In this case, that would be you and me. The vehicles are designed to come apart and absorb energy. The more energy the car absorbs, the less energy you do."

"No more racing each other home at night." Karma turned and said with a smile.

"How about no more racing at all?"

"Do you really think that's gonna happen?" Karma asked with her hands on her hips. "I will always beat you home Buck, always."

"C'mon, let's get your car out," Jesse replied, not paying attention to the poke Karma just jabbed him with.

Hearing the powerful ZR1 Corvette start up from across the lake, Recon and Savannah looked up to check it out.

"There they go again," Recon muttered to the rest of the group.

"What's that all about?" Doc asked with his arm around Sue. "What's up with them?"

"They have this *thing*," Recon replied as the Corvette tore off down the dirt driveway.

31

"It's foreplay," Savannah commented.

"Call it what you want, baby. It sure doesn't turn me on!"

"Speed isn't your *thing?*" Savannah asked, smiling.

"Nope! You're my *thing!*"

"Take it easy, Karma," Jesse told her as he grabbed onto the door handle. "It's been a while since you've driven something like this."

"I've got this, Buck," Karma replied while totally focused on road. She drifted the Corvette onto the asphalt and dropped the hammer. With smoking tires and soaring RPM's, Karma effortlessly controlled the powerful beast like it was nothing. She tore down the road completely fearless and in total control.

Drifting through corners and using every inch of asphalt, she piloted the Corvette well into triple digit speeds, Karma was wearing a smile the whole time. Aside from being a little nervous, Jesse was quite impressed.

"Don't miss your turn," Jesse shouted as he pointed to the onramp for the highway.

"Not to worry, Buck. I've got this!"

Karma tapped the brake and hit the gas, sending the car into a four-wheel slide. Turning into the slide, her right foot started to feather the throttle, keeping the back tires spinning and drifting all the way around the ramp. Accelerating hard, 140, 150, 160 the Corvette projected the speed through the heads-up display as Karma kept grabbing gears. A factory perfect Corvette will accelerate faster than most cars will free fall through the air. This one was eye watering fast with what seemed to be infinite amounts of power.

"I'm going for it, Buck!" Karma shouted out excitedly, grasping the steering wheel with both hands.

"You've got this, Karma, go!" Jesse encouraged his wife with enthusiasm. "Turn it loose!"

Hearts pounded as the speeds continued to climb, 168, 174, 179, 181, 183 were the numbers that appeared on the heads-up display. Jesse glanced over and saw the speedometer pass 190. "Your almost there. You've got this!"

"I can't believe how hard this car keeps pulling!" Karma shouted with excitement. "It just doesn't quit!" Karma eased the Corvette over to the left-hand lane to pass a couple of cars. Before they knew what was happening, she blew past them, leaving them in a vapor trail.

"One ninety-seven!" Karma shouted. "One ninety-eight! One ninety-nine!" The roar of the Corvette engine was thunderous and the sound of the wind over the car was like a hurricane. "Two hundred!"

"Keep going!" Jesse told her, loving the ride as much as she was."

"C'mon!" Karma yelled excitedly. The Corvette passed 205 and her foot is still on the floor. Two hundred and eight and still accelerating.

"You've got a gradual turn to the right up ahead." Jesse informed her as he held on to the door handle even tighter. The Corvette passed 222 MPH and was still accelerating. Karma left her right foot planted on the floor until the Corvette reached 227 MPH. Holding the car there for just a moment, she finally decided to gently take her foot off the gas.

"Wow!" Karma said, breathing a little heavy. "That was intense, and there was more to be had!"

"How do you like it?" Jesse asked, still clinging to the door.

"Uncle Bernie would be proud of you, Buck."

"That doesn't answer my question."

"I love it!" Karma replied, gently tapping the brakes, slowing the car down. "This is my kind of car."

"I'm impressed, Karma." Jesse said finally letting go of the door handle and relaxing a bit. "You handled this car pretty well."

"That was a lot of fun. I love the car, Jesse. Thank you."

"You ready to head back?"

"I'm ready for you!" Karma replied, glancing over with a grin.

"You're driving," Jesse replied, smiling while he reached over and placed his hand on her thigh. "Take me home."

Chapter 6

"Lenny, this is Jon Mar."

"I figured you to be dead."

"I'm not, but Camper is."

"I am well aware of the Camper situation, and the Casino."

"I have buyers calling me, Lenny. What do I tell them?"

"Jon, where is the guy with the Christmas tree farm?"

"I don't know, Lenny"

"WELL FIND HIM!" Lenny shouted into the phone.

"Start searching jails, checking obituaries, plane reservations – find him. 'I don't know' is not good enough! The guy's name is Beaver, Darren Beaver!"

"Okay, Lenny, I'm on it," Jon replied a little sheepishly.

"Which buyers are calling you?"

"Florida and Chicago."

"If they call you again, have them call me. I'm in charge now."

Chapter 7

Friday morning.

"The dumpsters are being delivered in about an hour, Jesse. We should really get going." Karma told him as she zipped up her jeans.

"I know, I know." Jesse replied hurrying out the door.

"Let me tell Recon we're leaving. He and Doc are going to start bringing the trailers up."

"Okay – meet me in the car."

Jesse touched base with Recon and gave him the keys to the pickup. Recon and Doc were going to start moving the trailers from Flathead Lake up to the Lost Lake property. Jesse and Hack were going to set them up and the ladies were on clean-up detail, tossing out all the trash, Corvette pieces and debris from the shop into the dumpsters.

It was time to move back to Lost Lake. When Jesse and Karma pulled up to the Lost Lake residence in her Corvette, the electrical and plumbing contractors were already there waiting for instructions. Before they could get out of the car, the dumpster trucks were coming down the drive.

"I'll park the dumpsters and you handle those guys," Karma told Jesse, giving him a peck on the lips.

Karma arranged the four dumpsters perfectly out in front of the shop. There was room to get cars in and out without having to carry debris and trash too far to throw it away. Jesse walked with the contractors to show them where the drop points for the trailers were and where they should be for the future homes. By 10:00 in the morning, everyone was working, and by 12:00 noon, two of the four trailers had already been moved and set up.

"Lunch is here!" Barbara yelled out as she joined the group, carrying a stack of pies from Valley Pizza towards the shop. The group was ready to eat. Hunger had set in from the long morning of hard work and everyone needed a break. Jesse insisted the contractors take a break and join them as well.

Lunch was short and sweet. Before everyone got too comfortable, the group was back at it and working hard. By 5:00pm, all four trailers had been relocated and set up at their desired locations around the lake. Karma's gravesite had been raked out and the black cross that Jesse had made for her was now positioned at the head of Louie's grave.

Jesse and Karma sat on the edge of the rickety pier and shared an ice-cold beer as they finally called it quits from a hard day's work.

"It's good to be back here, Buck."

"It sure is, Karma, it sure is," Jesse replied, reaching over and laying his hand on her leg.

"You getting hungry?"

"Get out of my head," Jesse replied. "I was just getting ready to ask you how you felt about having dinner at the Lasso tonight."

"Can we shower first?"

"You know we can, love."

"Together?" Karma asked with a seductive grin on her face.

"Would I ever tell you no?"

"Why don't you tell the others what our dinner plans are and then come meet me in the shower!"

Chapter 8

"Are you awake?" Jon said to the mummy-like figure lying on the hospital bed. "Darren!" Jon said a little more obtrusively. "I'm talking to you."

"Take caution with how you address me." Darren replied with slow words, still sounding like a monster. "Who are you?"

"Who I am is unimportant," Jon answered. "All you need to know is that I'm from Vegas." After a slight pause Jon asked him "What happened to you?"

"Jesse Buck happened to me. You incompetents from Las Vegas don't know how to take care of business."

"You're obviously, *gravely* mistaken." Jon replied chuckling. "Jesse Buck is dead. Lenny himself killed the man, and the broad. Lenny doesn't make mistakes."

"Then you're both idiots. I don't communicate with idiots. Why am I talking to you?"

"We still have business to tend to, on your Christmas tree farm."

"My deal was with Camper, not you."

"Camper is dead. You work for me now."

"If Camper is dead then Jesse Buck killed him. You are such a fool. The deal is off." Darren said opening one eye to focus on the man.

"Nothing is off!" Jon said, sternly pointing a finger directly in Darren's face. Darren grabbed Jon's forearm and started crushing it with his bare hand. Jon started to scream from the pain. *Snap, snap, snap* broke the bones in

Jon's forearm as Darren continued to squeeze it, harder and harder, crushing it.

"Aahhh!" Jon continued to scream. Darren's rage boiled from within. He tightened his grip harder and harder, effortlessly crushing the bones in Jon's arm like they were nothing. Like his arm was trapped in a vise, Jon was not strong enough to pull it free of Darren's grip. Darren started to twist Jon's arm backwards, nearly twisting his arm out of its socket, bringing the man to his knees.

"AAHHH!" Jon screamed louder and louder from the pain. Darren got out of bed, ripping the IV's from his arms at the same time. He picked Jon Mar up from the floor with one arm and shoved him through the tempered glass window like a rag doll, watching him fall to his death, nine stories below.

Uncontrollable surges of adrenaline now flow through Darren's body. He feels no pain; he feels no physical pain at all. He feels nothing. Only bursts of super-human strength, anger and rage. He headed for the door and proceeded to walk out of his room.

Dr. Nola and staff heard the commotion and came running down the hall. Stunned to see his patient up and walking around, Dr. Nola tried to talk to him.

"Mr. Beaver! Where are you going?! MR. BEAVER!!!"

"I am leaving."

"Mr. Beaver, you can't leave!" Dr. Nola told him with urgency. "If you leave now, you'll be dead from infection in a month, two at most!"

"I'm already dead," Darren replied to the man as he limped right past him. "I'm so charred that the skin grafts won't adhere to my body. If my life is over, then I'll die on my terms."

"Mr. Beaver, you can't leave!"

"You can't stop me!"

"Listen to me!" Dr. Nola told Darren, this time grabbing him by the arm. Darren stopped and yanked his arm free of the doctor's grip asking him, "can you fly?" Dr. Nola, startled with what just happened, slowly shook his head, and then answered "no."

"Think about that the next time you touch me, Darren said to the man with intense aggression. "If you touch me again, I'll throw you out the window."

"Darren!" Dr. Nola begged, "Please don't leave. You will die! I can give you your life back!"

"I'm leaving," Darren replied to the man while walking away. "It's unlawful to keep a patient against their will."

Dr. Nola knew Darren was right. It is unlawful to keep a patient against their will. If they can walk out on their own, by law you must let them leave. Not knowing what to do, and in total disbelief about what just happened, Dr. Nola watched the walking mummy leave.

"What happens when the morphine wears off?" Cindy asked.

"He will experience fits of rage and anger with peaks of adrenaline that are unmeasurable."

"I think he already has."

"We need to call the police," Dr. Nola replied, scared for his patient. "I don't care if we have to shoot him with a tranquilizer, we have got to try to stop him."

Chapter 9

Saturday morning; 6:00am

Jesse and Karma were sitting by the lake sharing a mimosa, watching the sun come up when they heard a vehicle coming down the driveway.

"Look," Karma told Jesse, pointing down the drive, "it's Pastor. Kind of early for him to show up, isn't it?"

"Yeah, especially for a Saturday," Jesse agreed. "He might be here to do some fishing with Recon."

A few moments later, Pastor walked over to where Jesse and Karma were sitting and sat down on the grass facing them.

"You look pretty serious this morning friend," Jesse started. "You doing okay?"

"Jesse," Pastor answered with a sigh, "It seems that we might have a bit of a situation on our hands."

"What situation might that be?" Jesse asked, reaching over to hold his wife's hand. "We have plenty of mimosas."

Pastor looked at Karma and was hesitant to say anything else.

"Whatever it is you have to tell me Pastor," Jesse said to him while looking over to Karma, "you can tell me in front of my wife."

"Do you remember the night of the motorcycle incident?" Pastor asked.

"I sure do!" Karma immediately replied. "That's the night I discovered how crazy my husband is."

"As it turns out, Jesse," Pastor continued, a little nervous with how Jesse was going to react when he heard what needed to be said. "The body found in the debris belonged to Damon Beaver, Darren's son. Darren's body was not found that night."

Karma looked over toward Jesse with a concerned look on her face.

"I'm not worried about that guy," Jesse replied, not paying much attention to the situation. "Why should he be a concern of ours? What does this have to do with anything?"

"Apparently, he walked out of the trauma unit at the burn center in Colorado yesterday, after he threw a man out of a ninth story window."

"Who'd he give flying lessons to?" Karma asked with a smirk.

"One of Camper's thugs, a guy named Jon Mar."

"Pastor," Jesse replied, not really giving any thought to the whole story, "if Darren Beaver wants to pick a fight with a group of Navy SEALS then give him our address."

"Jesse..." Pastor started to reply.

"Jesse, nothing! I'm done with the Beaver family. Besides, Pastor, I thought you were going to take care of it. What happened there?"

"Apparently the blast was so powerful that it blew him completely out of the back of the building." Pastor continued, ignoring Jesse's last comment. "He had enough strength to pull himself out of the debris and crawl another couple of hundred feet. No one knew he was there. A couple of kids skipping school found him two days later, clinging to his life. The state police life-flighted him to

Colorado, where the closest trauma center is for burn victims."

"If he comes close to me, my wife or my team, he's a dead man."

"I think we need to be aware of his presence if he shows up, Jesse. That's all I'm saying."

"Pastor, that guy tried to kill Karma and me. If we see him, we will end him. I promise you."

"He might be coming after you, Jesse."

"He won't come around here, Pastor. Nevertheless, I'll let the team know."

By noon Saturday, the team had moved over to the Lasso. Jesse and Karma were waiting tables and talking with customers. Pastor and Doc were tending bar and everyone else was picking up slack wherever they could. Erin was back and, of course, ensuring a smooth operation of the restaurant. Jesse could never quite figure why she wanted to work if she was already filthy rich, but choose not to dwell on it for Erin had proven her worth many times over. The Lasso wouldn't be the same without her. At 6:00 pm Meo walked in and sat down at the bar.

"Meo," Pastor greeted her warmly, "it's unlike you to sit at the bar, what's the matter?"

"Sometimes a girl just needs a stiff drink," she replied, a little frustrated. Pastor could tell right away that something was eating at her.

"So, what kind of *stiff drink* are you looking for?"

"What would Karma drink?"

"I'd be drinking Johnnie Walker Black, on the rocks" she answered coming up behind Meo, giving her a hug.

"What's the matter girl?" Karma asked her, a little concerned. "Go ahead and pour two, Pastor," Karma told him.

"You want Black or Blue?"
Karma looked Meo in the eye and determined something was definitely wrong.

"Make it Blue."

"Can we find a table?" Meo asked, fighting back the tears.

"Of course, we can honey. Go find a table and I'll come find you." Meo got up and headed toward the back, to the Party Arena where it was a little quieter.

"Looks serious," Pastor mentioned as he set the pair of Scotches on the bar.

"Yeah, it really does."

"If it's anything suspicious Karma…"

"I know Pastor," Karma interrupted. "But I think it's more girl stuff rather than *secret squirrel* stuff." Karma grabbed the pair of drinks and headed off to find Meo.

"Hello there, handsome!" Georgia-Jean blurted out, sitting down at the bar. "How about a club soda on the rocks? Make that a double, on the double." Doc didn't know how to react to the spritely behavior of the spirited woman who just sat down.

"She's talking to me, buddy," Pastor intervened.

"Are you sure?" Doc questioned, *knowing* he is much more of a stud than Pastor.

"Yeah," pastor insisted, "I've got this one."

"How do you know I wasn't talking to that *super fine* Frenchman over there?" Georgia-Jean asked with gusto.

"Were you?"

"No, but I'm just saying," Georgia-Jean replied with a smile, "that man right there is a gift from God."

"Thank you, ma'am," Doc shouted over his shoulder with a grin.

"Here's your drink," Pastor replied as he placed Georgia-Jean's drink down in front of her, feeling a little jealous. "I'm glad you can appreciate the finer things in life, Georgia-Jean."

"I've got eyes on you, don't' I?" Georgia-Jean replied with a playful smile.

"We dancing tonight?"

"I don't know," Georgia-Jean answered, "Are you singing to me tonight?"

"I might."

"Then probably not."

At 7:30 pm Erin got on the microphone in the Party Arena and started prepping the crowd.

"Ladies and gentlemen," pausing for a moment while the crowd settled down before she continued. "Ladies and gentlemen, Karaoke will start in 30 minutes and we'll break for the 'Karma – Erin' sing-off, at 9:00 pm. If you're singing tonight, it's time to get ready!"

"You heard the woman," Jesse poked at Karma, giving her a nudge, "go get ready!"

"I'm not changing yet," Karma nudged back.

"What are you wearing tonight?" Jesse asked, ogling over his woman.

"It's tight," Karma snapped back, giving Jesse a seductive look. "You'll like it!"

Before one could count the passing minutes, the Hickory Sticks were on stage warming up, and shortly thereafter the microphone was passed to a little bitty fella named Harvey West. Catching the crowd off guard, little Harvey West sang with a big booming voice that hit a home run when he belted out *Summer Nights* recorded by Rascal Flatts. It was the perfect way to kick off the event.

Harvey, who made his debut appearance at the previous karaoke night, remembered the *pass the mic rule* and passed the microphone off to a cowboy-looking dude. Vic Rue was this guy's name and he rocked the house singing a tune by Brantley Gilbert titled *Country Must Be Country Wide*. Third to sing was the Hickory Sticks themselves doing a cover from Chris Young titled *Aw Naw*. They sung it with authority. Chris would have been proud.

"Call it, sister," Erin said to Karma flipping a quarter into the air as she approached, dressed in her black leather outfit, ready to kick some ass on stage tonight.

"Tails," Karma threw out as Erin snatched the coin out of the air.

"Tails it is. Who sings first?"

"You're already dressed; go for it!"

"Good luck," Erin replied, holding her hand out to shake.

"You've got this Erin," Karma replied, shaking her hand.

"Erin sure does look good in that outfit," Pastor said to Jesse as he walked up and handed him a Scotch.

"Yeah, she does." Karma agreed walking up right behind. Jesse and Pastor were stunned when they heard that come out of Karma. Looking at each other and then at her, they were speechless.

"What?" Karma said shrugging her shoulders. "She does!"

Erin, just like the last time, started with her back to the crowd and when the drummer counted to four, she was off and running. She opened with *I Love Rock -n- Roll* by Joan Jett and the Blackhearts. The crowd loved her. They were singing along and getting into the moment. Erin was born to perform and controlled the stage well. When the song ended, the lights dimmed and the sound from a single guitar filled the room.

Erin stood there with her eyes closed and slowly swayed back and forth to the music, and when the words started the crowd erupted with cheer.

> *"I've got a girl crush;*
> *hate to admit it but;*
> *I got a heart rush;*
> *its slowing down…*
> *I've got it real bad;*
> *want everything she has…"*

"Who is she singing that song about?" Jesse asked about the *Little Big Town* classic.

> *"I want to taste her lips,*
> *yeah cause they taste like you,*
> *I want to drown myself in a bottle of her perfume…"*

"Recon," Karma answered. "She wants Recon back and now he's consumed with Savannah. She has forever lost her chance and now she knows it."

Erin put everything she had into singing this song. Every bit of passion and emotion she had from deep within her was seeping out. She was doing an amazing job. Whether she was singing about a life experience or not, her real singing talent was shining bright tonight.

> *"I want her long blonde hair,*
> *I want her magic touch,*
> *yeah cause maybe then,*
> *you'll want me just as much,*
> *I got a girl crush…"*

Just as the song was ending and she opened her eyes, the first person she made eye contact with was Jesse. Erin fumbled on a note and nearly lost her concentration. Immediately collecting her thoughts as the drummer led the band into the final song named *Amen*, by the metal group *Halestorm*; Erin regained her composure and took control of the situation, hitting another home run.

"She's *in it to win it* tonight, isn't she," Jesse said to Karma as he threw his hands around her and kissed her on the neck.

"I didn't know Erin was such a rocker. She looks so innocent."

"Doesn't she though?"

"She does sound really good tonight. You have to give her that," Karma agreed, "but I'll be fresh in the crowds' mind when the voting starts."

"You better get up there, love," Jesse whispered into Karma's ear. "You've got this."

"I've got you Jesse, and that's all I need!" Karma replied, spinning around and giving him kiss on the lips. "My turn!"

Making her way through the crowd, Karma headed over to the stage. She was also dressed in a tight pair of black leather pants, but they were open on the sides with a crisscross pattern; like an open seam running up the side held together with shoelaces. Her blouse was blue silk and it was unbuttoned a little over halfway down, exposing her black tank-top underneath. The 4" high heels gave her outfit the perfect touch.

"It'll be fun to watch her dance in those won't it?" Recon said over the crowd so the others could hear him.

"I feel confident she knows what she's doing," Savannah replied, having great faith in Karma's balance.

The band finished with a crash and the crowd went wild, whistling and cheering, screaming and shouting. Erin took a bow and blew a few kisses out to the audience. They loved her. When she turned around, Karma was there to give her a hug.

"That was awesome!" Karma told her. "You're a tough act to follow."

"I'm sure you'll give me a run for my money," Erin replied. "Have fun up here!"

Karma took her place on stage and with the mic in her hand and on her signal, the band started to play. It only took a couple of measures before the crowd started cheering, before a single word was sung.

"I guess I should have known,
by the way you parked your car sideways,

that it wouldn't last...
You're the kind of person that believes in making out once,
loves 'em and leaves 'em fast...."

When Karma got to the chorus, the entire place belted out "*Little Red Corvette, Baby you're much too fast.*" *Little Red Corvette* was a huge, smash hit for the late singer *Prince* in the 1980's and Karma was hitting a home run with it. She moved seductively up on stage and sounded incredible. It was obvious to everyone that she was not only singing to the crowd, she was also singing to Jesse.

"I can't believe she's singing that song!" Savannah shouted out, feeling the vibe.

"I can," Jesse replied with a smile, proud of how well Karma sounded up on stage. "She drives one, she loves them!"

"That's a man's song!" Erin said as she walked up to the group, a little jealous about how good a job Karma was doing singing the Prince classic. "But she does sound really good!"

"Hey, Jesse," Pastor asked with a deviant grin on his face. "You guys didn't drive separately tonight, did you?"

"No." Jesse replied, wondering where that question was coming from. "Why?"

"Just making sure," Pastor said as he started to chuckle. "The last time we did this, you and Karma tried to kill yourselves on the way home."

The group of friends burst into laughter with Pastor's poke. Jesse shook his head and smiled, having to chuckle at the comment. *Little Red Corvette* ended, and the band started into another 80's classic, *Self Control* by Laura

Branigan. It's one of those classics that you don't hear very often and when you do, you fall in love with it all over again. Karma reached up and teased her hair a little bit to give herself a hint of a wild look. The crowd went crazy!

"She's singing all 80's songs tonight." Erin said out loud to herself. *Clever woman,* Erin continued in thought. *Everyone loves the 80's. Very clever woman.*

The crowd was singing and clapping to the beat as Karma gave them what they wanted, pointing to people out on the floor and giving it all she had. Her voice control and octave range were very impressive. She was definitely going toe to toe with Erin. When the second song ended, the band rolled right into the third and Karma never missed a beat.

"Her hair is Harlow Gold,
her lips are sweet surprise,
her hands are never cold,
she's got Bette Davis eyes."

Closing out her trio of songs with Kim Carnes's biggest hit ever, *Bette Davis Eyes,* Karma just sealed the deal with a tremendous performance. Once again when it was time to sing the chorus the crowd jumped right in and sang along with her, *"she's got Bette Davis eyes!"*

As Karma wrapped up her trio the crowd was going insane. The cheers were loud and supportive. People were whistling and clapping; it was like being at a real concert. Jesse and Erin walked up on stage as Karma was taking a bow. Jesse reached for the microphone, addressing the crowd for the results.

"How about another round of applause for both Erin and Karma tonight?!" Jesse asked and the crowd delivered at epic sound levels, approving of the vocal duel they just heard the two women perform.

"Do we have a winner tonight?" Jesse asked, anxious to hear who the crowd will chose.

"NO!" the voices in the crowd shouted.

"NO? How is it we don't have a winner?"

"They both won!" A voice shouted from the crowd. "It's a tie!"

"We love both of them!" shouted another.

"It's a tie?" Jesse questioned into the mic.

The crowd erupted wildly, cheering with Jesse's question. Jesse looked down in front of the stage and there was a man there begging for the microphone. With no better plan in place, Jesse handed it over to him.

"Ms. Erin, Ms. Karma" the man spoke. "Y'all don't know me; I'm just a guy. But I believe I speak for everyone here tonight." The crowd silenced quickly to hear what was about to be said. "Most of us heard you two go for it a few months back during rodeo time, and we loved you then. After tonight, I do have to say that we can't pick a favorite between the two of you. We love to hear both of you sing and when you sing against each other, it's like you both want to win so bad that you both do!"

The crowd cheered wildly, agreeing with every word the stranger said. He then handed the microphone back to Jesse. Jesse turned around and looked at Karma and Erin standing there, in disbelief with what they just heard.

"Ladies?" Jesse asked with a smile. "Any comments?"

Erin snatched the microphone from Jesse. Giving Karma a grin, she commented "looks like we're going to have to do this the old-fashioned way, Karma."

"What way is that?" Karma replied into the microphone. "Gun fight at high noon tomorrow?" The crowd burst into laughter.

"Not exactly," Erin answered smiling. "Looks like we'll have to settle this over there at the horseshoe pit." There was another chuckle among the crowd. The two women gave each other a hug and let karaoke night get back under way. The small group of friends were both stunned and relieved with the outcome of the sing-off between Erin and Karma. None of them would have wanted to pick a winner either; they both sounded fantastic!

Chapter 10

"It's a blessing to see all of you here this morning," Pastor started, wearing a smile from ear to ear. "It's also a pleasure to know that everyone is accounted for after last night's party at the Lasso." The congregation chuckled at Pastor's remark as most of them knew what he was getting at. Pastor made eye contact with Jesse and Karma sitting in the front row, who were both smiling as well.

"Today I want to ask you, the congregation, what you would like to hear a sermon on. Please, shout it out if you will. Anyone?"

Pastor's hands were raised as he addressed the people. He wanted to see if anyone would really throw out a suggestion, or if the room would remain silent. Finally, an unknown man stood up in the back and answered, responding to Pastor's request.

"I love my wife," the man said with a shaky voice. "I love her very much, but I often find myself tempted to do things that I shouldn't, to do things that would ruin my marriage. Can you help me with that?"

"Temptation." Pastor responded nodding his head. "I commend you sir, for standing before us and admitting that to a room full of strangers. I ask the rest of the congregation, if there is anyone in here who suffers from any kind of temptation at all, please stand now."

One at a time, slowly but surely, people all over the room started to stand. No one knew what everybody's story was, but there were many that felt they were suffering.

Pastor was stunned to see two-thirds of the congregation standing when he asked them to be seated.

"Temptation by definition *might* be something like: a desire or an urge to do something, maybe a desire or urge to do something wrong. It doesn't have to be something wrong; it may just be something unwise. Temptation may also be looked at as a desire, or an urge to participate in short term enjoyment that potentially impacts long term dreams or goals. Some might believe that temptation leads to sin or at least to the inclination of sin."

The congregation was silent. Everyone in the room had an ear perked up as they were all interested in what Pastor had to say on this Sunday morning.

"I am going to tell you that there is truth in all of what I have just said. However, to me temptation is greed. Temptation is focusing on yourself regardless of what the consequences or outcome might be. You might be tempted to sneak some ice cream while on a diet, or to drive 70 miles per hour in a 65 mile per hour zone. Maybe it's to cheat on your spouse or have one more drink – I'm telling you..."

Slam! Pastor slammed his hand down on the podium he stood behind and delivered his message with authority.

"...Temptation is all about you!" Temptation is selfish! It is greed filled! As disciples and followers of Christ, we have no time for that! How do we overcome temptation?" *Slam!* Pastor brought his hand down on the podium again, hard. "It's simple." He was now speaking in a normal voice and walking around the front of the sanctuary.

"We can attack temptation with two simple steps. The first is to remember and live by the golden rule. Do unto others as you would have others do unto you. The second rule is to remember the first."

"Do you want to stray from your diet? Do you want your spouse to think about another? Do you want that relative to sneak another drink? If you don't want it to happen to you, then don't put yourself in a position for it to happen and certainly don't put yourself in a position for it to happen to someone else. Here's the other side of that - we all are guilty of encouraging others to make bad decisions."

"If we would encourage others to make the tough decisions, to make the hard decisions, to make the right decisions, temptation would lose every time. We need to be aware of the constant bombardment of temptation and when we see it, we need to turn away. We watch movies and read books and newspaper articles that are filled with adultery, cold blooded murder, drugs, rape, theft, lies, betrayal and more. We've seen so much of it that to many of us that kind of behavior has become the norm. It has somehow become less offensive, or almost okay. We've become numb to it.

People, I am telling you it is not okay!" Pastor paused for a moment and then delivered a powerful repeat. "Did you hear what I just said? Walk away from temptation! It is okay to walk away! It's okay to stop watching! It's okay to stop doing! People, it's time to start living your life like the example and stop living your life like the exception! Do unto others as you want others to do unto you! CAN I GET AN AMEN?"
"AMEN!"

Pastor's sermon was short, sweet and powerful. He really made everyone stop and think about the difference between right and wrong, and how you should treat other people. He left the congregation thinking about what was said and had most of them wondering how they could be better Christians. Another home run from the small-town minister.

Chapter 11

"It sure is great to have our Sundays at the lake back!" Recon shouted as he and Savannah joined the group after church.

"It really is, isn't it!" Karma added as she looked around with a smile on her face.

"Steaks are here," Doc added to the conversation as he carried a large tray of marinated steaks over toward the grilling table. "Here you go, Karma."

"That steak is marinated in a special Filipino family recipe," Sue told her.

"They smell absolutely divine!"

"It's sweet with just a hint of zing. I think you'll like it a lot."

"Wine's here!" Desi shouted as her and her niece Erin showed up each carrying a case of wine.

"Where's Jesse?" Erin asked, surprised that he was not around.

"Jesse went to pick up the new grill and a bushel of lobster with Pastor and Georgia-Jean. They should have been back by now."

The sound of Jesse's pickup was heard just seconds after Karma answered Erin's question. Before Jesse could park the truck and get it shut off, the guys were unloading a new Jenn-Air stainless steel grill. It was big and looked heavy, nothing of course a couple of SEALS couldn't handle. By the time Jesse had the new grill assembled, everyone else was completing the assembly of the new tents and positioned the new patio tables and chairs accordingly. In less than an hour the group of friends was relaxing with a glass of wine, ecstatic to be back at Lost Lake.

"Hot dogs are here!" Sheriff Rodney hollered as he and Meo arrived fashionably late.

"Hog dogs?" Desi questioned, raising an eyebrow. "I don't eat hot dogs."

"We're doing surf and turf today, Rod," Jesse replied, chuckling at Desi's comment.

"I brought the turf then."

"Actually, we're having steak. We can save those for another time."

"Or feed them to the dog," Savannah added.

"Where is Bourbon, anyway?" Karma asked looking around.

"He's over there," Sue replied, pointing to the dock. "He's over there watching fish swim by, doesn't know exactly what to make of it." Bourbon was lying on the dock with his front paws draped over the edge. His head was tilted over, and his ears were perked up as he intently stared into the water, watching, waiting for something, but not sure what, exactly.

"Well, Rodney," Karma started, "It sure is nice to see you again. Meo tells us you've been spending more time investigating the Christmas tree farm than spending time with her."

"Did she now?" Rodney asked while looking over at his beautiful wife. "Sometimes police business is a little more involved than Mrs. Rodney wants to admit."

"Well Sheriff," Jesse said handing him a beer. "It looks like the dust has settled and Eureka has once again become the quiet little, tranquil town it used to be."

"I think we a need toast," Pastor chimed in.

"What are we toasting to?" Barbara asked, breaking her silence.

"To second chances," Pastor replied holding up his wine glass. "To second chances at Lost Lake!"
"To second chances at Lost Lake," the group said together and sipped their drink of choice.

"Something interesting going on over at the Christmas tree farm, Rod?" Doc asked with a rather serious tone in his voice.

"No, not really," Rod answered nonchalantly. "It's just a lot of ground to cover on foot, it takes a lot of time."

"So, who really won the sing-off last night?" Georgia-Jean blurted out with lots of spirit.

"Karma," Erin replied instantly

"Erin," Karma replied at the same time.

"This sounds like a scam," Hack threw out. "Where's the wine?"

"I think the whole thing was rigged," Sue announced, shocking the group with her sudden assertiveness. "There is always a winner."

"I'll tell you want," Karma said, standing up to address the group, but looking at Erin. "Last night your performance was spot on. You sang a classic, a country ballad, and a new metal. You demonstrated incredible vocal control and your performance, Erin, was far better than mine. You were born to perform, girl, and you looked really hot in your outfit. In my mind, you are last night's winner, and you know that doesn't come easy for me to say."

"We sure know that's the truth!" Jesse poked, grabbing his wife from behind and kissing her on the cheek."

There was small talk within the group of friends for a moment, all agreeing at some level with what Karma had just said.

"Well, Karma," Erin replied. "You looked pretty hot up there on stage yourself, if you don't mind my saying so. Your three songs were also very impressive. Prince, Laura Branigan and Kim Carnes? Three totally different singing styles from the same era and you crushed it. You had the whole place singing with you. Very nicely done, Karma. I'm actually surprised they didn't call you the winner. In my mind you earned it."

The group of friends also agreed with what Erin said, making some very valid points. "By the way Karma," Erin added, "That was the sexiest version of *Little Red Corvette* I have ever seen or heard."

"Thank you, Erin, and I must tell you, everyone there last night wanted to know who you were singing *Girl Crush* to."

The group of friends went silent. Everyone's ears immediately perked up as they were dying to hear the response Erin was about to offer.

"No one," Erin replied calmly, sipping her wine, as if it were nothing. "I love that song and I know how to sing it. I wanted to win."

"That was a pretty seductive performance," Pastor added.

"Really?" Georgia-Jean fired right back.

"Yeah." most of the group replied. "It really was."

Conversation for the rest of the evening was light. The steak and lobster were 'melt in your mouth' perfect and there was plenty to go around. Bourbon made short order of Sheriff Rodney's hotdogs, and then spent time on his back basking in the sun with his paws in the air.

"Hack," Jesse said with a head nod, pulling him away from the group.

"Yeah, Commander. What's up?"

"Can you move money around?"

"You're kidding, right?"

"Move money around, hide it – and not lose it?"

"That depends on what's in it for me, Commander?"

"Can you, or can't you?"

"Whatever you want I can do, and if I can't do it, Barbara sure can."

"Here," Jesse said handing him an envelope. "Do it. Keep it between us."

"When do you want it done by?"

"The sooner the better, just get it done. Get it done tomorrow, today, yesterday."

"You got it, Commander. I'm on it."

"Come on, let's get one more glass of wine before we call it a night."

Chapter 12

"What on God's earth happened to you?" Lenny asked, not sure what to make of the monster he was staring at.

"Jesse Buck happened to me." Darren replied, still talking with his horrific voice.

"That's nonsense!" Lenny fired back with authority. "I personally killed Jesse Buck and Rachael myself."

"Did you bring the morphine and the syringes?"

"They're in a bag in the trunk. The car is yours as well, just like you wanted, you just have to drop me off."

"Thank you, Lenny," Darren replied holding, out his bandaged hand to shake.

"Don't mention it," Lenny replied as he reached out to shake Darren's hand. Darren grabbed Lenny's right hand with his and then grabbed Lenny by the throat with his left, lifting him completely off the ground.

"You're an idiot, Lenny. If you had killed Jesse Buck when you were supposed to, I wouldn't be like this now. I wouldn't be a monster in a freak show!" Lenny was gasping for air and kicking his legs trying to break free from Darren's grip, but it was like having his throat in a vise, and there was no way he was able to escape.

"Every day I am overridden with intense pain. I get these impulses of adrenaline that I can't control!" Darren started to talk as loud as he could with his monstrous voice.

"ALL I FEEL IS PAIN! ALL I FEEL IS ANGER! ALL I FEEL IS ABSOLUTE RAGE!" Now shaking Lenny violently by the throat, an adrenaline surge came rushing through Darren's veins. "I FEEL LIKE I COULD TEAR YOUR HEAD RIGHT OFF YOUR SHOULDERS!"

Before Darren knew what he was doing, he did exactly that. While holding Lenny off the ground by the throat with only his left hand, he reached up with his right hand and nearly ripped Lenny's head completely off his shoulders with one swift motion. Darren dropped Lenny's lifeless body to the desert floor.

"You're next Buck." Darren said out loud to himself as he made his way to Lenny's Cadillac. "I promise you Jesse Buck, you and your floosy will die before I do!"

Chapter 13

The Sunday crowd finally went in their own directions. Rod and Meo took Georgia-Jean home for Pastor, so he could help clean up and talk with Jesse and Karma about what's happening now and what's coming up. The other couples, Doc and Sue, Hack and Barbara and Recon and Savannah all headed to their own trailers, which the group now referred to as "lily pads" for the evening.

"The Kaiser wants to know why we are not meeting at the Lasso," Pastor started right in, not wasting any time with pleasantries.

"Karma doesn't want to have *secret squirrel* meetings at the Lasso, that's why," Jesse told him, as if discussing the location was even an option. "You tell the Kaiser that Karma gets what Karma wants."

"Thank you, Buck," Karma said with a beaming glow.

"Where are we meeting then?"

"Atlanta." Karma replied with a smile.

"Atlanta?" Jesse and Pastor questioned together, looking at each other and then back at Karma.

"I thought you wanted to meet at your friend Allison's?" Jesse questioned.

"We are," Karma admitted with a smile. "Her place is in Atlanta."

"Do we *really* need to go to Atlanta?" Asked Pastor a little perturbed.

"What difference does it make?" Karma snapped. "We're not holding secret government agent GHOST meetings at *our* restaurant!"

"The Kaiser wants…"

"I don't care what the Kaiser wants!" Jesse interrupted. "I told Karma to set it up, and she set it up. Atlanta, it is. What's the next topic?"

"Darren Beaver."

"What about him?"

"There are suspicions that he's coming after you."

"Whose suspicions are these, exactly?" Jesse replied sharply. There was a moment of silence where no one said anything. Pastor and Jesse stared at each other; no words were spoken. Finally, Jesse continued verbalizing his thoughts.

"Let him. I don't fear that guy. Besides, he's not dumb enough to walk into an ambush and if he shows up here, that's exactly what he'll get."

"You killed his brother, his son and nearly killed him, Jesse. This guy is really pissed off."

"Let him be pissed off, Pastor!" Jesse replied while putting his arm around Karma and pulling her close. "What's the first rule about picking a fight with a Navy SEAL?"

"Don't."

"Exactly, don't; and he did! He and his brother both. If Darren had half a wit about him, he'd disappear to Mexico and never come back. The dust is settling here. Darren is certainly not a worry to any of us, so let's just focus on what we need to. My team and I will work with the Kaiser once or twice a year, but for the most part we're going to focus on us. Right now, that consists of the Lasso and taking care of each other. The next assignment or mission as you call it, is a distant third on our priority list."

"I hear you, Jesse."

"Is he missing something, Pastor?" Karma asked, just as curious as Jesse was.

"I don't think he's missing anything, Karma," Pastor answered in a very sincere way. "It's just that, as SEAL's, nothing ever seems to go the way it's planned."

"Maybe not in your life Pastor," Jesse asserted, "but I have absolute and total control of my plans and they are executed with precision and perfection."

"So, you planned to crash your car with Karma a few months ago?"

"Well, no."

"You meant for the Lasso to be blown up with Recon and Erin inside?"

"Okay, that was definitely not in the plan, no."

"Here's a good one," Pastor continued to poke. "You drove through Texas on your way back here, intentionally, you know, so you could pick up Savannah."

"Okay, so there may have been a few minor glitches in some of my plans." Pastor and Karma chuckled together while they watched Jesse squirm.

"The truth is Jesse, you don't have any more control over your life than I do mine or anyone else does theirs."

"It's too late for a sermon tonight, Pastor, and what does that have to do with the Kaiser?"

"You know I speak the truth."

"Your faith is strong Pastor; I will give you that," Jesse replied with caution. "I don't know, however, how much of the truth you choose to speak."

"Just because I'm not telling you everything doesn't mean I'm lying."

"Funny thing about the truth, Pastor. The truth is how you interpret what happened at the time it happened from your perspective. Try to relay that to someone else who has a difference of opinion and the truth may be lost forever."

"You're a minister, Jesse, search for the truth with your own heart."

Chapter 14

Three weeks later...

The Lost Lake property was finally cleaned up. All the debris from the fire, the damaged vehicles, the shot-up boat – everything had been discarded, and the property had been groomed and looked amazing. The entire group pitched in and took pride in where they all were living. The repairs that needed to be made to the shop had been taken care of and it was ready to store Jesse's toys once again. Peace and tranquility filled the air at Lost Lake and in the little town of Eureka.

Erin had things under control with the Lasso, and Pastor assured Jesse that he'd run the bar right while he and his team were gone. The time had come to meet with the Kaiser, but this time it was going to happen in Atlanta under the terms of Jesse and Karma.

"Tell me again," Recon started while walking through the Atlanta International Airport. "Why did we have to come down here for a meeting?"

"Because that's what Karma wanted," Hack answered from behind.

"Karma gets what Karma wants," Doc added.

"This is a team building exercise that Karma thought would be fun for all of us to do since we basically live our lives together," Jesse responded from the front of the group.

"Haven't we been team building for the last three weeks?"

"Recon!" Jesse snapped, "What's the problem?"

"No problem Commander, just making small talk."

"Make small talk about something else."

The group of seven, Jesse and Karma, Recon and Savannah, Hack and Barbara and Doc scurried the rest of the way through the airport in silence. When they reached the passenger pickup area, Kurtis was waiting there to greet them.

"Jesse!" Kurtis shouted with his big booming voice and a man hug. "Good to see you again!"

"Good to see you too, Kurtis!" Jesse replied with excitement. "Tell me Kurtis, how do you like the new car?"

"The limo is fantastic; I can't wait for you to see the inside!"

Kurtis was driving a brand new 2018 Cadillac super-stretch limousine, it's a sixteen passenger, completely custom vehicle. The car was Raven Black on the outside and wore a midnight blue and black leather trim interior, accented with carbon fiber on the inside. The limo boasted three HD LED flat panel TV's with a blue ray disk player. There was also a CD changer, accessory ports throughout, three bars, fiber optic star lights on the interior roof, two sunroofs and blue ambient lighting to die for. The limousine also had party lighting, including sound activated laser disco lights if the mood presented itself. All the sound came through a custom 28,000-watt 32 speaker stereo system, not including the dozen subwoofers. The new limo was a party on wheels.

"Well, I'd say your pimping now, aren't you buddy?"

"Jesse, I love the car, thank you so much!"

"Did you buy this car for your driver?" Savannah asked Jesse as quietly as she could, now inside of the vehicle.

"He sure did!" Kurtis yelled from the captain's chair way up front. "Why?"

"Savannah," Jesse replied, wondering if he should have to explain anything at all to the stunning redhead, "Kurtis is my driver. He is good to me. Just like all of you, I take care of him and I pay him well."

"How are the wife and kids, Kurtis?"

"They are doing great Jesse; they are at your Virginia estate while we're down here."

"That's perfect," Jesse replied with a smile. "I'm glad they are out there having fun. I have to tell you Kurtis, I'm having a custom swimming pool built up there soon. You're going to love it!"

"How far are we from Allison's?" Karma asked Kurtis who was now piloting the Caddy towards the meeting place.

"Just over an hour, Karma. Make yourselves at home. The bars are all fully stocked and there should be a bag of homemade venison jerky in the cooler underneath the seat. It's fresh and really tasty!"

"No alcohol before the meeting," Jesse commanded. "Everyone needs to be sober for the Kaiser."

Allison Lentz is the owner and head chef at Ally's Kitchen which is located in Atlanta, Georgia. Allison and Karma grew up together in Las Vegas until Allison moved to Atlanta with her parents when her father got transferred.

Somehow, miraculously, with the help of social media Karma and Allison were able to reconnect and the two women were excited to see each other after nearly twenty years. When the limo pulled up to Ally's place of business, she was outside waiting. Before it had come to a complete stop Karma was jumping out of the back and running to meet one of only a few friends she still had from her youth.

"Girl, you look so good!" Karma told Allison as the two women embraced in a hug.

"Me? You look fantastic, Rachael! Look at how fit and trim you are!"

"It's so good to see you!"

"It's been such a long time; I can't believe you're here!"

"Karma," Jesse said walking up to his wife. "How about some introductions?"

"Karma?" Who's Karma?" Allison asked with a look of question on her face.

"I go by Karma now. It's kind of a nickname that stuck." Karma admitted. "It's a long story."

"Somehow I'm sure it's fitting, and you'll have to give me the details one day," Allison told her while wondering what could have happened for her to earn such a nickname. "You'll always be Rachael to me."

"Thank you, Ally!"

"Rachael, who's the creepy weird guy that's been waiting for you inside?"

"The Kaiser is already here?" Jesse asked.

"That's really what he goes by?"

"Ally, this is my husband Jesse," Karma introduced while changing the subject. "Jesse, this is my BFF Allison. You can call her Ally!"

"Nicely done girl!" Allison whispered over to Karma with a wink.

"He's a good catch, Ally!" Karma whispered back.

The rest of the introductions were made and the group headed inside. Allison and Karma headed straight to another room to get in a few minutes of girl talk while the Kaiser briefed everyone else with what their next mission was going to be.

"As you know, Mr. Buck," the Kaiser started with his deep slow spoken voice, "Mr. Camper owned an island in the South Pacific."

"That information to date has only been rumored, not actually confirmed." Jesse acknowledged.

"Well, we need that rumor confirmed." The rest of the group listened intently while Jesse and the Kaiser dominated the conversation.

"What is the importance of his island?" Jesse asked, not really interested in this mission already.

"We need to know what, if anything, is going on there."

"Can't you point a satellite at it and take some real-time photos?"

"Mr. Buck, there are thousands of islands in the South Pacific. We can't run surveillance on thousands of islands with hopes of finding the one that belonged to Camper."

"How are we supposed to find an island that's more than likely deserted, if we don't know where to start looking?"

"That, Mr. Buck, is why we needed Camper alive. Since you killed him, it's your problem, not mine."

"Kaiser," Jesse spoke with an elevated tone in his voice. "There are twenty or thirty thousand islands covering over three million square miles of ocean in the South Pacific. Tell me you are not for real. This "mission" could easily take months or even years."

"We don't have months and years to get this done. You have 45 days from today to find it."

"Kaiser, you need to give…"

"I need to give you nothing," the Kaiser interrupted. "You're the one who killed him, Mr. Buck. You need to find his island and you have 45 days to do it."

"What'd we miss?" Karma shouted out when she re-entered the room with Allison.

"Nothing really, we were just wrapping up," Doc replied.

"Something fun for us to do I hope?"

"Yeah, if finding a needle in a haystack sounds like fun to you," Savannah answered.

"What about resources for this mission?" Jesse asked, very frustrated with how the Kaiser expects this to get done.

"Pastor has all of the details and resources you'll need for this mission, Mr. Buck."

"Is there anything else we should know about this assignment?" Hack questioned.

"I've given you all of the information that you need. Check with Pastor for the specifics." The Kaiser replied, standing up as he got ready to leave. "Pastor can fill you in with the rest."

"We came all the way to Atlanta for a five-minute meeting?" Hack asked thinking this whole thing was a waste of time.

"Negative," Jesse asserted. "We came down here for a team building exercise. It just happens that the meeting took place here as well."

"Oh, Mr. Kaiser," Allison said walking over to him, "you're not leaving, are you?

"My presence is generally not welcome at social settings, ma'am."

"Well tonight it is." Karma chimed in. "Your part of this team Kaiser. You're not going anywhere." Karma finished by throwing the Kaiser an apron to put on.

"I agree Kaiser, you're here with us tonight," Jesse added, doing his best to look the other way and include the man that he struggled to like. Even though he really didn't *want* the Kaiser to stay, he could see the benefit from making the effort. Sort of a "keep your friends close, keep your enemies closer" kind of approach, even though the Kaiser wasn't really the enemy.

"Let me grab Kurtis out of the car and we can all get started."

Before Jesse could get back inside with Kurtis, everyone had a glass of wine in their hand, including the Kaiser. There were meat and cheese trays set out for nibbling and socializing before the main event. The atmosphere was warm and casual, a very friendly and inviting environment.

Allison and Karma had picked out the menu for the night's dinner in advance. Now that everyone was inside and ready to go, Allison divided the group into teams of two and each team was given instructions on how to make their portion of the meal. Each team had a different suchef coaching them, while Allison overlooked the entire project.

Doc, Kurtis and the Kaiser, the only team of three, were matched up together to make the wild caught fish ceviche. Karma was teamed up with Hack to cook the beef tenderloin with chimichurri. Barbara and Recon shared cooking utensils to create saffron-paprika potatoes and roasted asparagus shallot which left Jesse and Savannah with desert - Rollo con dulce de leche.

Dinner and desert were absolutely fabulous. Everything was cooked to perfection, melted in your mouth and tasted amazing. Allison delivered a high-class experience that everyone, including the Kaiser enjoyed.

The Kaiser was the first to leave, ditching the others as soon as he ate. The rest of the group stayed and bonded over more wine and shared stories about the past and enlightened Allison with how they all came to be. When the evening finally did come to an end, the good nights were said and the group climbed back into the limo to head to a hotel for the rest of the night, followed by the trip back to Eureka in the morning. The trip was short but sweet and the time spent at Ally's Kitchen was well worth the it.

Kurtis headed south on Roswell Road when Jesse hollered up front to him.

"Kurtis, you know we have a 7:18am flight in the morning, right?

"I sure do Jesse and I'm sure…"
WHAM!!!

Out of nowhere a large black pickup slammed into the limo broadside, sending both the pickup and the limo clean off the road and down an embankment. The car rolled over several times before finally stopping at the bottom with the pickup coming to rest up against it. Two white cargo vans stopped at the scene and men dressed in black, all carrying semi-automatic weapons scurried down the hill and surrounded the limo.

"Jesse's mine." Darren Beaver instructed to the group. "You take the rest."

"Jesse!" Karma screamed out of sorts holding her bleeding head.

Before Jesse could get his bearings, the limo door was yanked open and he was hit in the head with the butt of a rifle, knocking him unconscious. Everybody else was shot with tranquilizer darts, no one was aware of what was happening to them. The element of surprise was successful. In seconds, the entire team of SEALS was immobilized.

"What do we do with the driver?" One man asked as he noticed Kurtis behind the wheel, unconscious.

"Kill him," another man answered.

"No bodies." Darren ordered. "Keep moving, we only have 30 more seconds! Take the driver with you."

Before any authorities showed up, the men in black, and their hostages were gone.

Chapter 15

"Hi, Sue," Pastor said, greeting the beauty as she took a seat at the bar in the Lasso. "You okay?" he asked, instinctively knowing that something wasn't right.

"No one has come home yet, Pastor. I'm a little worried."

"It's 4:30pm," Pastor replied while looking at his watch. "They should have been home hours ago. No one has called? No one has checked in?"

"No." Sue replied, with a stray tear falling from her eye. "I've left voice mails on Doc's and Jesse's phones."

"No one has gotten back to you?" Pastor asked again, with growing concern.

"No."

Pastor immediately grabbed his mobile phone and called Jesse. "Voicemail." He then proceeded to call Karma. "Voicemail again. This isn't right. Something has happened." Pastor told Sue with a worried look on his face. "I'll be right back; stay here."

Sue nodded her head as Pastor left the bar area to find Erin, who had been waiting tables. He finally located her back in the kitchen as she was picking up some food and pulled her aside.

"Erin, something's wrong."

"What is it, Pastor?" Erin asked, reading the emotion on his face.

"No one is accounted for."

"No one?"

"No one. I get nothing but voicemails with everyone's phone. Not even a ring, just straight to voicemail."

"That's a problem," Erin admitted.

"Call Desi. Figure it out and report back to me immediately."

"I'm on it," Erin confirmed. In seconds her apron was off, and she was out the door to get some answers. Pastor made his way back to Sue, who was still sitting at the bar.

"Sue," Pastor said to her as he approached her with a glass of water, "Where is Bourbon, is he with you?"

"No, he's back at the lake."

"Do you have any clothes with you?"

"Just what I have on. Why? What's going on Pastor? You're scaring me."

"I don't know what's going on, Sue. I'm not sure you should stay alone at the lake tonight, not until we get some answers."

The worry was oozing from Sue's pores. Pastor could tell that she was getting more and more frightened with every minute that passed. He needed to think of something. He needed to send her someplace where she wouldn't be alone.

"Do you know where Meo lives?

"Yeah," Sue answered, perking up a little bit. "Why?"

"I think she's off tonight," Pastor replied, speaking a little softer, trying to comfort her. "Why don't you go over to her apartment and pick her up. Tell her what's going on and the two of you go out to get Bourbon and some clothes together. I'll feel better knowing that you are not alone."

"Okay, do you think she'll mind?"

"Not at all. With Rod working doubles, she could probably use the company."

Pastor gave Sue a hug and sent her on her way.

"Why don't you and Meo come back here for dinner when you're done!" Pastor shouted as Sue approached the door. She stopped to turn and look back at Pastor, giving him a head nod and a waive. Without saying a word, she left.

When Sue arrived at Meo's apartment, she knocked on the front door. Hearing music coming from inside, she figured Meo couldn't hear her knocking, so she twisted the door handle to see if it was unlocked, and it was.

"Meo!" Sue shouted over the music as she let herself in. "Meo, it's Sue." Still there was no answer. "She's probably in the bathroom." Sue said to herself as she shut the door behind her.

"*Pow.*"

Before Sue could turn around, she was shot in the back of the head with a .22 caliber pistol. She instantly dropped to the floor, dead. Stepping over her lifeless body, the shooter locked the door handle behind him and fled the scene as if nothing were out of the ordinary.

Chapter 16

7:48pm.

Pastor looked at his watch and started to have concerns about Meo and Sue since they hadn't come back yet. He pulled out his mobile phone and started to call the list of missing persons, starting with Jesse.

"C'mon!" Pastor shouted out after receiving nothing but voicemails from everyone, *including* Meo and Sue this time. His next phone call was to Erin.

"Yes, Pastor." Erin answered with a completely business-like tone in her voice.

"Erin, where are you?"
"Pulling into the parking lot right now, coming to see you. Why?"

"I sent Sue over to get Meo a couple hours ago and they were going to come here for dinner. I haven't heard anything from either of them."

"You know how women are, Pastor." Erin told him as she came through the door. She disconnected the phone call to converse in person, not really concerned about the two of them.

"Knowing Meo, they're probably over at Café Jax chatting over a latte, talking gibberish like a couple of high schoolers."

"I'm getting their voicemails when I try to call."

"I'm not worried about them, Pastor. We have other things to talk about." Erin told him nodding her head in the direction she wanted him to follow so they could talk privately. Just as Pastor was taking a seat at a corner table with Erin, his phone rang.

"See," Erin said nonchalantly, "that's probably Meo now."

"Actually, it's Fire Marshall Ren," Pastor replied with eyes locked on Erin.

"Pastor, Ren, here."

"Go ahead Ren, what's up? You need some praying done?"

"I don't Pastor, but someone might. We just got a call for... count them, five separate fires burning at Lost Lake. We're on our way there now, thought you might want to know."

"Lost Lake?" Pastor questioned. "Are you sure?"

"Yeah, I'm sure Pastor, that's where we're headed."

"That's Jesse Buck's place!"

"The restaurant, guy?"

"Yeah, that's the guy, Ren. I'm on my way!"

"Pastor, what's going on?" Erin asked with a concerned look on her face.

"Fires at Jesse's place, I've got to go, Erin!"

"Pastor! I need to talk to you about Jesse!"

"Erin!" Pastor shouted back to her as he was running toward the door. "Stay here and CALL SHERIFF RODNEY!"

By the time Pastor arrived at Lost Lake, the damage was done. There was nothing but five piles of warm ashes, all the trailers had burned to the ground. The garage was destroyed. This time, there was nothing left, nothing. Pastor got out of his pickup and made his way over to Fire Marshall Ren.

83

"Thanks for coming out so fast, Pastor," Ren said greeting Pastor with a handshake.

"You bet, Ren. What have we got here?"

"Arson, Pastor." Ren confirmed. "The good news is it wasn't kitchen flour this time."

If that's the good news, what's the bad news? Pastor wondered.

"The bad news is," Ren continued, "we don't have a single clue as to who might have done this. There is no evidence to be had here."

"Where's the dog?" Pastor asked.

"What dog?"

"Where's Bourbon?"

"Bourbon?" Ren asked with confusion.

"The dog's name is Bourbon! Where is Bourbon? Where is the dog?"

"Pastor, no dog survived any of these fires," Ren explained with as much compassion as he could. "Trailers burn hot and fast. Once the propane tanks on the front of them go, well. You can see what happens. I'm sorry Pastor, if there was a dog here, he died in one of these fires."

Ring… ring… ring… was the sound coming from Pastor's pocket, from his mobile phone.

"It's Erin, Ren. I need to take this call," Pastor told him, answering the phone.

"Go ahead Erin, you okay?"

"Yes, I just thought you should know that I've called Sheriff Rodney three times and all I get is his voicemail."

"Are you for real?"

"I'm not messing with you Pastor, of course I'm for real. Call him yourself."

"All right, Erin. I'm on my way back to The Lasso now. Please stay there; we'll talk when I get back."

"I'll be here."

"Ren, is there anything that you need me here for? I need to get back to the restaurant."

"Not at all, Pastor. We've got this under control; the fires are out."

"Thanks Ren, and call me if you find anything!"

Chapter 17

Cough, cough. Jesse coughed as he blinked his eyes. *Where am I?* he thought to himself as he tried to get his bearings. With hands and feet bound, apparently in the back of what looked like a cargo van, he determined that he was completely incapable of breaking free of his bindings. Whoever had him tied up, tied him up well.

"I see you're awake now." Darren Beaver said to Jesse, through the cage wall in the front of the cargo van. "Don't worry, Mr. Buck," Darren assured him with a sinister attitude, "I promise you; your wife's death was quicker than yours is gonna be."

"Do I know you?" Jesse asked, not able to recognize Darren's appearance or his voice.

"If you don't know who I am now, you'll soon remember," Darren told him right before he shot Jesse with another tranquilizer dart. "You will soon remember! Bwhahahaha!"

Chapter 18

By the time Pastor got back to the Lasso, Desi was there, talking with Erin at a secluded table near the piano, in the back. Walking right up, Pastor wasted no time with pleasantries. He needed any and all details, nothing more.

"Desi, Erin." Pastor commanded with authority. "What have you got?"

"We have a crashed limo in Atlanta with no bodies inside." Desi started out. "No driver, no passengers."

"Don't tell me what you don't have Desi; tell me what you do have," Pastor ordered, not impressed with the information thus far.

"I'll tell you what I do have, Pastor. I have two dead females in Meo and Rod's apartment, exact time of death currently unknown but pretty recent, only a few hours dead." Pastor and Erin were shocked with the news, not sure how to react yet.

"Do we know who the victims are?" With a somber heart, Desi dropped her head and answered the question. "I found Meo and Sue dead an hour ago; they are still there. I called Sheriff Rodney and got his voicemail; I didn't leave a message."

"How?" Pastor asked with grief in his voice.

"Gunshot wounds, both of them, to the back of the head. Meo was apparently taking a shower when she was killed, which is where her body still lays, and Sue's body is lying by the door.

"Did you call the hospital? Did you try to save them?"

"Pastor, they were shot dead!" Desi reiterated sternly. "There was no way to save either of them. Besides, I'm an informant. My job is to observe and report, not to get involved, not to blow my cover, not to reveal my true identity. Here's another fun fact, Pastor," Desi continued. "This is a one-horse town, and right now, no one knows where that horse is."

"I know what your job is, Desi. I'm the one that brought you in," Pastor mentioned, just as a reminder. "Erin, what have you got?" Pastor asked, hoping her information was better than Desi's.

"I've got nothing."

"What do you mean you have nothing?"

"Pastor, I've got nothing."

"Erin! We have a sheriff that no one can get a hold of, two dead friends and five piles of ash at Lost Lake. Having nothing is not helping this situation right now! Not to mention, a missing SEAL team!"

"Pastor, I'm running the show here. I can't close the Lasso to go on an informational scavenger hunt. That breaks protocol," Erin reiterated to him. "Like Aunt Desi, I am an informant…"

"I know who you are and what your job is, Erin," Pastor interrupted with frustration. "You can't inform me of anything if you don't know what's going on, can you?" Pastor shouted.

"There is no reason to shout at either of us, Pastor. Seek a solution," Desi replied firmly. "Don't be part of the problem."

"Ladies," Pastor addressed Desi and Erin very calmly, "we can't lose control of this situation. There is way too much at stake here. Who do we know, or at least suspect is involved?"

"There are too many unknowns here to make any sound decisions," Desi replied. We suspect that Darren is hunting down Jesse, and if he's hunting down Jesse, what happens to the rest of the group?"

"They're probably eliminated, taken out of the equation just for the inconvenience Jesse has caused."

"All we know for sure," Erin reiterated "is that we can't find Sheriff Rodney."

"Yeah, how do we know Rodney isn't dead somewhere?"

"How do we know Rodney isn't part of the problem?" Desi asked.

"Rodney isn't going to kill his wife. I just don't see that happening," Pastor replied. "If Darren Beaver is involved, and we suspect he is, he's going to bury bodies on the Christmas tree farm." Pastor said getting up from his chair. "Where are you going?" Erin asked. "We have no facts."

"To get my rifle," Pastor replied with a hard look on his face. "Erin, you run the Lasso. Desi, you call the hospital, have them send an ambulance over to Meo's. We can't leave the bodies in her apartment. Then your next move is to find Sheriff Rodney."

Chapter 19

This is not happening! Pastor thought to himself as he hurried to get his rifle. His rifle is a Weatherby, .338 Winchester magnum. It boasts a Leopold scope for precision accuracy at long distances. The deadly combination can reach out over 2000 yards, making it one of the deadliest bolt action rifles on the planet.

In Pastor's previous life, as a Navy SEAL, he was *the* expert marksman. *He* holds the unofficial world-record for the longest kill shot with his beloved .338. Forget the hype of what you hear today; Pastor is arguably the world's finest sniper and certainly the best there ever was with a .338-win mag.

What makes Pastor the marksman that he is, isn't only the skill of firing the weapon, it's the skill of hand loading every single round of ammo that he fires through it. Precision measurements, premium lead, brass and powder, nothing is compromised, ever. There is a whole lot more to precision shooting than just feeding a bullet into the firing chamber and squeezing off a round. You must take into consideration wind speed, gravitational pull, distance, velocity and so much more. Precision shooting is as much an art as it is a learned skill.

Pastor loaded his rifle and grabbed a box of ammunition containing 20 rounds of precision loaded bullets along with his day/night vision binoculars. Not knowing what to expect, he headed out to the Beavers' property. While he was praying for the best, Pastor was certainly a little concerned about the worst.

An hour later, he had positioned himself on a ridge that overlooked the vast majority of the Beaver Pines Christmas Tree Farm, watching, waiting for Darren to show up, knowing in his heart that he would. Pastor just hoped that Jesse and the others were still alive.

Jerking awake, out of a sound sleep in the crisp morning Montana air, Pastor was fearful that he might have missed something. He checked his phone for messages. There were none, no word from Desi or Erin. Pastor then grabbed his binoculars and started to scan the area. He panned from left to right, carefully scanning, looking for something, looking for anything.

After several long moments of finding nothing, he stopped. Another hour passed. The sun was just peeking up over the horizon when Pastor noticed a dust trail in the distance, at the far edge of the Christmas tree farm. Not being able to see much detail from his current location, Pastor decided to carefully relocate a couple of hundred yards to the left of where he was.

"Get him out," Darren ordered the two other men with him. "Tie him to the cross securely before you wake him up."

Darren's bandages were dirty and unchanged. They were stained from where blood and puss had been seeping through them. Other places have tried to crust over where they were not covered with clothes. Not really a scab, just a hard crust. Infection was starting to grow fungus beneath them. Black cowboy boots, dirty jeans and a sleeveless sweatshirt were all that covered Darren's bandages.

He was a mummy, wearing clothes. His head was still wrapped up with only cut outs for his eyes, nose and mouth. Darren sat in the front seat of the cargo van and injected himself with a heavy dose of morphine, while the two thugs removed Jesse from the back.

As Darren Beaver exited the cargo van, he could see Jesse bound to the cross with a heavy coarse rope. The rope was wrapped around each wrist and just above both ankles at the bottom.

"Tear his clothes off!" Darren instructed. "Strip him down to his underwear."

The two men did as they were instructed. A few minutes later, Jesse lay on the ground, bound to a cross made of railroad tie-like timbers, wearing nothing but a pair of multi-colored boxer briefs.

"Wake him up," Darren commanded.

The two thugs poured water cold water on Jesse's face. Slowly, Jesse came out of his trance and started to cough and choke.

"How nice of you to join us today, Mr. Buck." Darren spoke sarcastically, with his still charred monster-like voice. "You have caused me and my family a lot of grief, agony and pain, so today I am going to return the blessing."

"Do I know you?" Jesse spoke out with a groggy voice, unable to get a clear look at Darren with the morning sun in the background.

"I'm the guy your buddies hog tied and left for dead when you blew up my building," Darren said, kicking Jesse in the knees.

"Darren!"

"You remember me now, don't you!"

"You're the guy who tried to kill my wife and I." Jesse replied, just to agitate the man. "You look good."

"How do you like being tied to that cross, Jesse?"

"It feels nice," Jesse answered, not giving into the situation. "It makes me feel like I am one with Christ."

"I'm glad to hear that, Jesse. Knowing you are so close to Christ, today you shall die a Christ-like death."

"Today's not my day to die, Darren," Jesse replied in normal conversation.

"Get the hammer and the nails!" Darren ordered to the thugs. "The first thing I am going to do to you today Jesse, is inflict as much pain on you as you have on me," Darren explained. "I have 6" wrought steel nails for you today, Jesse. They have a large head on them so you can't pull out of them. Four nails for you today. One for each of your hands and one for each ankle."

Jesse started to panic and tried to free himself, but there was no use. He was bound tight, and whatever was about to happen, was not going to be good.

"You know, Darren, maybe we can work something out here."

"Get ready to nail his hands!" Darren ordered. The two thugs moved to either side of Jesse and knelt down beside Jesse's hands. Jesse clenched his fists tight to try to prevent the nailing of his hands, but it was no use. The thugs easily pressed the wrought steel nails firmly through Jesse's fingers to the palms of his hands and waited for Darren's command.

"Nail him!" Darren ordered.

"AAHHH!!" Jesse let out a bellowing scream as the wrought steel nails, which were more like stakes were driven through his palms and into the cross. Before giving Jesse a chance to recover Darren gave the next command.

"Nail his ankles as well! Nail them hard to the side of the cross."

Immediately, the thugs moved down to Jesse's feet and drove a nail through each one of Jesse's ankles. Jesse screamed in pain as the thugs followed their instructions.

"How does that feel, Jesse?" Darren asked with sarcasm, knowing the pain must have been tremendous. Jesse just lay on the cross gasping for air, unable to answer, already covered with his own sweat.

"Stand him up," Darren ordered the two thugs.

The men grabbed each side of the cross and lifted it into the air. Taking just a few steps, they set the base into a pre-dug hole and filled in the dirt around it. Jesse screamed again now that gravity was pulling his weight against the rope and the nails through his body.

Pow, pow! rippled through the morning air.

"I don't need you two clowns anymore." Darren said out loud to the two, now dead, thugs. "I'll bury you idiots when I'm done torturing Mr. Buck."

The two men were guys that came off a list of "expendables" that Camper had. Men that no one would miss, and they were easily persuaded to do "dirty work" when you needed it done. They were thugs.

"Gun shots. That's not a good sign," Pastor said to himself, hearing the gun fire in the distance and still unable to get a good view of anything from where he was.

Darren walked over to the back of the cargo van and traded his pistol for a leather whip. Without warning he cracked it right across Jesse's back, sending him screaming in pain once again.

"What is going on down there?" Pastor asked himself, unable to get a good view of anything. "I have got to get closer!"

"How does that feel Jesse?"

Crack! Snapped the whip across Jesse's back again, in a different location. "This feels really nice to me," Darren told him. "This just might go on for hours!"

Gasping for air through his pain, Jesse managed to speak a few words. "It doesn't matter... what you do to me today. Jesus Christ... is my Lord and Savior. He has my back."

Crack! snapped the whip across Jesse's back, tearing his flesh open.

"Wrong Jesse!" Darren spoke as he cracked the whip on Jesse again. "I have your back!"

Crack!

"AAHHHH!!" Jesse screamed through the pain. "Stop!" Jesse shouted, not wanting any more. "Stop Darren, stop!"

"Okay, Jesse." Darren answered with a compassionate tone in what voice he had, tossing the whip onto the ground as he walked around the cross to face Jesse. "No more whip today."

Without warning, Darren wound up and landed a rib-crushing punch on the left-hand side of Jesse's body, knocking the air right out of him. Jesse hung on the cross, unable to breath, gasping, trying to catch his breath.

"Is that better, Jesse? That's for killing my son." Gasping for air, Jesse managed to get a few words out. "Easy... on the ribs..., I just... got those healed."

Darren landed a left hook on the right side of Jesse's body, breaking the two lower ribs. "That's for killing my brother, Jack."

"What... makes... you think," Jesse started, barely able to breathe, let alone talk, "...that I... killed... your brother?"

"Because I told him you did, Jesse," Sheriff Rodney calmly answered, coming up from behind.

"Rodney..." Jesse barely got out, "help me!"

"AAHHH!" Jesse screamed out as Darren landed another right hook onto Jesse's rib cage, breaking two more ribs.

"I can't help you, Jesse." Rodney calmly replied. "See, a brother's love is far greater than anything, and you have harmed my brothers."

"What? What... huh... what... are you... talking about?" Jesse barely got out again. "Your last... name is Sampson!"

"I was adopted, Jesse. Darren and I have the same birthday which makes us twins, from my perspective."

"AAHHH!" Jesse belted out as Darren crushed another punch into Jesse left side, breaking even more of his ribs.

"The Beavers took us in when we were just young boys, and we always swore to have each other's backs over anything. You, Jesse, are playing in *our* sandbox today and after we torture you and kill you, while your attached to that cross, we're going to bury you in it."

"It's... not... my... day... to... die..." Jesse barely spoke out between gasps for air.

"HUH!" Jesse let out as Darren punched Jesse right in the jaw, knocking him senseless.

96

"Jesse, we thought at first you were a great guy and the perfect distraction for the rest of the town, until you started dating that floozy, Rachael. By the way, who only knows what experience she and your SEAL team are having right now, Jesse. Maybe you should pray for them," Sheriff Rodney told him sarcastically. "Oh, wait. It's too late for that, Jesse. They're already dead by now. We promised each other to kill you last."

Punch, punch, crack! Darren landed punches on both sides of Jesse's rib cage and then landed a left hook on his face. Jesse could barely breath, the pain was unbelievable. He could barely hold onto his consciousness.

"See Jesse," Sheriff Rodney continued, with as much attitude as he could drum up, "There isn't much of a retirement for a small-town sheriff, but there is in our tree farm. We get paid ten thousand dollars for every single body that I let get buried here. Ten thousand dollars each!" Rodney said with a smile. "Hell, the best part is we get paid more to plant them than we do to cut them down. The instant Darren and I heard about Jack connecting with Camper, it was like Christmas came early!"

"I... pray... for... you... Rodney" Jesse barely got out over the pain and his gasping for air.

"What was that, buddy?" Rodney asked while picking up the whip from the ground.

"I told him no more whip today," Darren mentioned with what smile he could.

"You lied!" Rodney answered angrily while he cracked the whip across Jesse's chest.

AAHHH!!

"That's what you get for not telling your wife to mind her own business."

Crack! Again, the whip snapped across Jesse's chest, this time against his broken ribs, tearing his flesh open. Jesse couldn't scream because he couldn't catch his breath from the intense pain.

"I had to kill Meo yesterday because she was medaling where she shouldn't have been, all because your wife was running her mouth," Rodney admitted while he continued to whip Jesse. "I loved my wife, Jesse!"

Crack! Snapped the whip across Jesse's chest again.

"Then her friend, Sue, I believe her name was, showed up unexpectedly, so I had to kill her too!"

Crack! Sheriff Rodney cracked the whip across Jesse's chest again, even harder, tearing off more flesh before he continued his story.

"I have a confession to make, Jesse," Sheriff Rodney told him as he whipped Jesse across the back again and again.

"Tim Johnson didn't commit suicide, Jesse. I hung him! I hung him for being an inconvenience. I should tell you, that wasn't as much fun as this is!"

Crack! Sheriff Rodney whipped Jesse on his side, tearing the skin and exposing a broken rib. Jesse was barely conscious at this point and nearly numb from the overload of pain he was feeling. Shock was taking over, Jesse started to realize he was going to be dead soon.

"Want to hear some more Jesse?" Sheriff Rodney asked, looking at his watch. "If I wait just a few more minutes to kill you, your wife will be waiting for you in heaven by the time you get there!"

Suddenly, Darren Beaver dropped to the earth's floor. A "*Ka-pow*" rippled through the morning air from a distance, indicating a shot from a very high-powered rifle. Sheriff Rodney looked around, seeing Darren lifeless, lying in the dirt. He was suddenly fearful of who might be watching and felt an urgent need to finish the job and leave. Dropping the whip Sheriff Rodney reached for his sidearm.

"Well, Jesse," Sheriff Rodney told him while pointing his gun inches from his face. "I can't let you..."

Jesse heard Sheriff Rodney's body hit the ground, followed by another "*Ka-pow*" coming from somewhere in the distance. Unable to catch his breath, Jesse passed out.

Chapter 20

Three days later…

Jesse opened his eyes to find Pastor, Desi, and Erin sitting in his hospital room.

"How are you feeling, Jesse?" Pastor asked with a warm smile on his face.

"I don't know how or even what to feel right now, Pastor." Jesse replied, feeling there was more to this situation than he was aware of. "I guess, by the looks on everyone's faces, the news I'm about to hear is not good."

"Jesse," Pastor started to reply, "do you remember when I told you everything happens for a reason?"

"Of course, I do, and you know I believe that."

"The Lasso," Pastor started to tell him, "has been completely destroyed, again, Jesse. It was burned to the ground in the middle of the night, right before the morning they tortured you." Jesse just lay in the hospital bed and listened to the words falling from Pastors lips. His heart sunk as he knew the Lasso being destroyed again was just the tip of the iceberg as far as the avalanche of bad news about to burn his ears this morning.

"The trailers at Lost Lake, all of them, have been burned to ash and there is nothing left of your garage. It's been burned up as well. No one knows where Bourbon is, we suspect he died in one of the trailer fires. I'm sorry, Jesse."

"Does anyone have any good news?" Jesse asked, not looking up from his stare.

"Maybe we should get through the bad news first," Desi told him. When Jesse heard this come from Desi, he looked up. Fearful with what was about to be said, tears started to fall from Jesse's eyes.

"Please don't tell me Karma's dead."

"There were packages of mutilated bodies left at the Lost Lake property two days ago. One package for everyone's body, including your driver, Kurtis." Erin told him, also with tears falling from her eyes. "The bodies were so bad they had name tags on them, that's the only way we knew who they were, Jesse." Erin started to cry uncontrollably, unable to hold back her emotion.

"We buried the bodies yesterday, Jesse, along with Sue and Meo," Pastor continued. "Everyone is dead, Jesse. Everything is gone."

Jesse pulled his hands up over his eyes and wept. Desi, Erin and Pastor all surrounded Jesse and cried together over the loss of their beloved friends.

"I have to see this for myself." Jesse told the group, pushing them away and wiping his eyes. "I need to go out there."

Jesse threw the blanket off himself and gave his hand to Pastor to help turn him sideways.

"Should we tell him the good news now?" Erin asked cautiously.

"What news do you have that could possibly be good news at this point in time?" Jesse asked.

"Erin and I picked up your truck," Desi started to reply. "It has your backup bag of clothes, your laptop and a few weapons, still neatly tucked away inside."

"How did you know where to find my truck?" Jesse asked with great question, wondering now if he could trust them. "I didn't leave it at the airport, no one knew where it was but me."

"Jesse," Pastor said calmly, intercepting the conversation, "Desi and Erin aren't really who you think they are."

"Then who are they?!" Jesse asked loud and offensively.

"They're our informants, Jesse."

"What? You're both GHOSTS?" Jesse questioned in disbelief.

Desi and Erin nodded their heads, without saying a word. Jesse was stunned at the discovery; he had absolutely no idea.

"They are both highly trained and highly skilled, just like your SEAL team, just like all the other GHOSTS are," Pastor finished.

"Does either one of you have anything interesting to say? Any news at all?" Jesse asked them, still in disbelief. "What do you know that I don't at this point?"

"Karma was shot by Jack Beaver, not Dennis Rybka." Erin told him. "Sheriff Rodney was in on it as well, he's the one that killed Meo and Sue," Desi added.

"I know he killed them. He told me while he was whipping me on the cross," Jesse replied. "Ladies, please let me be," Jesse said to them while looking down at the floor. Without saying a word, Desi and Erin left Jesse and Pastor alone in the room. When the door closed, Jesse spoke freely.

"Pastor, I need you to help me get dressed and take me to Lost Lake. I need to see the graves."

"Jesse, you're not going to be able to walk!"

"Pastor, I need to go. I need you to help me."

"Jesse," Pastor replied with a heart full of compassion. "You have holes in both of your hands and both of your ankles. You have over two hundred stitches and eight broken ribs. Your hands are bandaged up, you're bruised from head to toe. You can barely see out of your left eye. Maybe it would be better if you just stay here and rest for a few more days."

"I'm going with you or without you Pastor, but with you will be much easier on me."

"Jesse, this is a bad idea."

"DON'T TALK TO ME ABOUT BAD IDEAS RIGHT NOW!" Jesse shouted explosively. "DON'T TALK AT ALL! SHUT UP! DON'T TALK, JUST HELP!"

"Take it easy, Jesse…"

"SCREW EASY! TAKE EASY AND CHOKE ON IT! GET AWAY FROM ME!! I CAN DO THIS WITHOUT YOU!!!"

"No, Jesse. No, you can't."

Chapter 21

Against his better judgment, Pastor helped Jesse get dressed in the clothes from his pickup and drove him out to Lost Lake.

"You know, Jesse, Erin is the one who saved your life the other day."

"Erin? How is that?"

"She's the one who got the second shot off. Erin is the one who shot Rodney, before he shot you."

"How can that be?" Jesse asked, not knowing Erin even knew how to use a firearm.

"Erin used the rifle out of your pickup to cover Desi as she got a closer look. She was watching through the scope when she saw Darren hit the ground and heard the first gun shot. Rodney was smart enough to move and when he did, he stepped out of my sight. However, in doing so he stepped right into Erin's. As soon as Rodney pulled his gun on you, she took him out. I didn't have a clean shot on him. Neither did Desi. She instinctively took it."

"I'm glad she didn't miss," Jesse replied, still stunned with the new information.

"She didn't miss from over 1400 yards, Jesse."

"That's an impressive shot."

"Yes, it was."

When Pastor drove Jesse by The Lasso, there were no words spoken. There was nothing but a pile of black. For the second time now, his dream had been burned to the ground. The rest of the drive was silent. Jesse just stared out the window of the pickup and watched the scenery go by while Pastor drove.

When they reached Lost Lake, Jesse's heart sank to a new low as he looked around at the separate piles of ash and debris that used to be called "lily pads" for his family. A destroyed shop. A broken dream. A shattered heart. Jesse had never felt such sorrow in his life. His heart had never hurt this bad, ever.

"Help me out, Pastor. Take me over to the grave sites."

Without saying a word, Pastor did what he was asked to do. He helped Jesse out of the truck and over to the nine crosses that lay facing the lake, on the same knoll where Louie was buried.

"We buried Rachel next to Louie. We figured you would have wanted that. There is a space next to her, for you, when that day comes. Recon is next, then Savannah, Hack and Barbara, Doc and on the end are Sue and Meo."

"Go home, Pastor."

"But, Jesse…"

"GO HOME!" Jesse shouted. "LEAVE, NOW!"

Pastor left without questioning his friend. When he was gone, Jesse broke down.

"RACHAEL!!!!" Jesse screamed at the top of his lungs, and broken body, at the lake. Her name echoed across the water and into the distance.

"THIS WAS NOT SUPPOSED TO HAPPEN!!!" Jesse was exhausted from yelling and had to catch his breath for a moment. "What do I do now, God?" Jesse spoke calmly for a moment. "WHAT DO I DO NOW? "I NEED A SIGN!!! GIVE ME A SIGN, GOD!!! I DON'T KNOW

WHAT TO DO!" Jesse cried uncontrollable. "I don't know what to do."

Out of air and in great pain from yelling with broken ribs, Jesse collapsed to the ground, right on top of his beloved wife's grave and continued to weep uncontrollably. "Take me now, God," Jesse spoke out loud. "I don't want to live anymore. Please take me." Jesse cried himself to sleep.

The next morning Jesse was still lying on his beloved wife's grave when he could feel something sniffing him. The first thought that went through his head was that he was being sniffed by a bear, so he lay perfectly still until he felt the *lick, lick, lick.* The uncontrollable licking from Bourbon's tongue was washing the dirt off Jesse's face."

"Bourbon!" Jesse shouted as tears of joy instantly free fell from his eyes. "It's so good to see you puppy!" Jesse grabbed the dog and petted him all over. Bourbon's red and white fur was tarnished with dirt and smoke from the fire that he somehow escaped. His paws had faint spots of blood on them, more than likely from glass as he jumped out of a window of one of the burning trailers. Bourbon the pup was alive and well, a true blessing.

"Bourbon," Jesse told the pup between hugs. "You definitely need a bath!" As Jesse sat up, Bourbon made his way onto Jesse's lap and continued to try and lick his face. "Thank you, God," Jesse said while looking up to the sky. "Thank you, God. Thank you, God. Thank you, God."

Just then, Jesse was startled when he saw Pastor and the Kaiser standing just a few feet away. He was so engulfed with giving Bourbon some much needed love that he didn't realize their arrival until that moment.

"Based on everything that has happened Jesse, I have relieved you of your duties as a GHOST," the Kaiser said to him, with his head hung low. "You can have your life back."

"What life is that, Kaiser? My life as I knew it, has been destroyed." Jesse replied, struggling to stand. "Whatever life you are giving back to me, Kaiser, you can keep."

"Jesse…."

"I don't really feel like talking with you right now, Kaiser," Jesse told the man. "I'm going to give my dog a bath and then we're going to eat some breakfast together. You found your way onto my land, now you can find your way off it." Jesse continued, not looking at the Kaiser at all. "Pastor, let's go." Jesse commanded while he limped over towards his truck. "Actually, let's have breakfast first."

Chapter 22

After breakfast was over, Pastor dropped Jesse and Bourbon off at *The Buck Stops Here*, a bed and breakfast that originally started out as a massive 17,000 square foot custom mansion for an unknown celebrity who filed bankruptcy right after the construction was completed.

Robert and Peggy Hodgkins bought the house for pennies on the dollar and turned it into a bed and breakfast some number of years ago. It's a spectacular place with views from every window. It over looks an unnamed mountain lake that has a waterfall pouring into it from a river of snowmelt during the warmer months. The Hodgkins' had befriended Jesse and always told him if there was ever anything, he needed to just let them know. Today, Jesse needed them to waive their "no pets policy" and with the current set of circumstances, they were glad to accommodate his needs.

"First things first pup," Jesse said to Bourbon as he started to fill a tub of warm water for Bourbon's bath.

"Let's get this collar off you." Jesse continued as he unhooked the collar and tossed it on the floor. "In you go buddy." Bourbon squirmed a little as Jesse struggled to lift the pup with bandage covered hands and lowered him into the tub of warm water. "This will make you feel a lot better, boy." Jesse assured the Aussie as he poured shampoo all over the dog and proceeded to lather him up.

"I'll get your white fur white again and your red fur red. Then I'll get you all fluffed up." Through the throbbing pain from his injuries, Jesse continued to talk with the Aussie as if in a normal conversation with any human.

"You know, Bourbon, it's just you and me now. Mama's not coming home." When Jesse heard what he'd just said he broke down and cried, still washing the dog.

Bark! Bourbon almost shouted, bringing Jesse back to reality. "I don't know what we're going to do, Bourbon." Jesse said, continuing the conversation that was part dog talk and part think out loud. "It doesn't look like Eureka likes us very much. Maybe we should go back east. I have a place back there that you would like, lots of room to run and lots of critters for you to chase."

By now Bourbon was clean and just needed to be dried off. Jesse lifted the wet pup above the water and let him drip dry for a moment. Setting him down on a towel that was on the floor, he reached for a second towel and continued to remove the water from the pup's fur.

"You're gonna need this," Jesse said, reaching for Bourbon's collar. "What's this?" Jesse noticed something tucked into the fold of Bourbon's black collar and proceeded to pull it out. "No way!" Jesse said in disbelief.

"Thank you, Hack!" Jesse said out loud as he pulled the micro SD card out from Bourbon's collar. "Thank you, Hack! Thank you, Hack!! Thank you, Hack!!!" Jesse kept yelling excitedly. "Let's see what we've got on this thing."

Barely being able to hobble with a cane, Jesse hurried to grab his laptop out of his pickup and raced back inside, limping frantically all the way. As soon as the laptop fired up, Jesse inserted the disk and started perusing through files. "What'd you have going on, Camper?"

For the rest of the afternoon and evening Jesse reviewed every file on the disk, trying to break the code that had Hack and Barbara stumped. It wasn't until 5:27am the next day when he finally figured it out. Jesse finally solved the mystery to the code.

"I've got it." Jesse thought out loud to himself. "I think I just found your island, Camper." Jesse continued digging and double checking, knowing he was on the right track. There were random names and numbers that Barbara had found. There was an algorithm in a previous file identifying two unknowns. "S's" and "W's." Jesse couldn't figure out how "S" and "W" referred to anything at first. As it turned out, the "S" was for first names and the "W" was for last names.

When the names were broken down by these numbers and put into a numerical sequence, they looked to be too large to do anything with. Jesse then took these numbers and divided them by Pi, which Hack and Barbara found on the disk some time ago and weren't sure as to why it was there. When doing this, Jesse ended up with 46 and135. 46° South and 135° West.

"This has got to be it, Bourbon!" Jesse pulled up Google Earth on his laptop computer and plugged in the coordinates.

Sure enough, Google Earth pinpointed a small cluster of islands in the south pacific, just about halfway between New Zealand and Argentina with the largest one being the obvious location he was looking for. There was, however, only one way to know for sure.

"Bourbon!" Jesse shouted excitedly at the pup lying next to him on the floor. "It looks like we're going for a boat ride!"

Chapter 23

"Pastor," Jesse spoke into the phone with assertion, "I need to see you and the Kaiser immediately."

"I'm glad to hear that, Jesse," Pastor responded with a confident voice. "We're actually on our way to come see you."

"When will you be here?"

"We're walking in the door right now."

Before Jesse could hang up the phone in the reception area of *The Buck Stops Here*, Pastor and the Kaiser were coming through the door. Acknowledgements were made and they headed up to Jesse's room so they could talk in private. The Kaiser, being the man that he was, jumped into conversation first.

"Mr. Buck, I just wanted to let you know that my offer still stands. With everything that you have been through, just say the word and you can have your old life back."

"The problem Kaiser," Jesse snapped back with a bit of attitude, still not happy to see the man, "is I have no old life to go back to. The most important people to me, my wife and my SEAL team have all been killed." The Kaiser looked sheepishly at the floor while he listened to Jesse lay it on the line.

"You gave me a mission, that mission was to find Camper's island. I will complete the mission you have assigned me."

"Mr. Buck, while I am pleased to know you are a man of integrity, I have my doubts that you will be able to focus on the tasks at hand with all of the losses you have experienced, and the physical pain I know you are constantly in."

"Since there is no *Lasso* anymore, you can afford to send Pastor with me," Jesse responded pointing to Pastor. "He can personally monitor my actions and if there is ever any doubt about my ability, intention or motives, you can give him the reins. He can call the shots."

"I have no problem with that," Pastor immediately added, not letting the Kaiser respond first. "I trust you, Jesse."

The Kaiser eyeballed Jesse for a moment. He could tell that Jesse was serious. He then looked over at Pastor and saw the commitment in his eyes. After a moment of silence, the Kaiser finally spoke.

"Who's going to preach in church with Pastor gone?"

"Why don't you do it?" Pastor replied. "You've covered for me before."

"You know I don't really care to preach," the Kaiser offered.

"You figure out whatever it is that you need to figure out, Kaiser," Pastor said stepping into the Kaiser's personal space. "I'll be completing the mission with Jesse."

Deafening silence filled the room as the three men stood frozen like statues.

"Pastor." Jesse asserted with his eyes still locked on the Kaiser. "You and I need to work out some details over lunch today. We'll be leaving tomorrow."

"Where are we eating lunch?"

"Valley Pizza."

The Kaiser was reluctant to let Jesse move forward in his condition, but with no other options on the table, decided to let him and Pastor do what they needed to do. As soon as Jesse and Pastor arrived at Valley Pizza, they secured a corner table, away from what little crowd there was, and the conversation began.

"Talk to me Jesse, what are you thinking?"

"Do we have access to Camper's yacht?"

"If we want it, we can just go take it." Pastor replied to Jesse. "It's been seized; it's ours to use as we see fit as long as it's for official government business."

"Who do we have available? Who can join us?"

"It's just you and me, pal."

"What about Desi and Erin?"

"They're informants, we can't…"

"You told me Erin was a good shot," Jesse interrupted. "We might be able to use her or use them both. You yourself just told me not long ago that they are both highly trained, right? Highly skilled?"

"Jesse, all we're supposed to do is find the island."

"I found the island, Pastor. We're going to go see what's happening on it."

"We can't involve Desi and Erin in that!"

"Why the hell not?"

"They absolutely cannot, under any circumstances blow their cover, Jesse. Remember the knife to Erin's throat?"

"How could I forget?"

"Erin could have dropped Beaver in a heartbeat, but she can't blow her cover! The women are out, absolutely, no way, forget about it, out!"

"Ask them. Ask them both. Get Georgia-Jean involved. We may need a nurse on the ship. After we eat, we'll get Bourbon and head back to Lost Lake for supplies."

114

"Jesse, have you lost your mind?"

"I've lost everything *but* my mind, Tom. Everyone I held close and loved is dead. I need to do this for them. I need to do this for Karma."

"I told you to never call me by my real name again, Jesse. That guy is dead."

"Pastor, you're either with me or you're not. What's it gonna be?"

"Damn it, Jesse. You're going to get us killed!"

"I've got nothing else to lose."

"Doing this isn't gonna bring Karma back, Jesse."

"Nope. But it's sure gonna make me feel one hell of a lot better."

Chapter 24

Immediately following lunch, Pastor drove Jesse and Bourbon out to the Lost Lake property. Upon arrival, Bourbon was quick to jump out of the pickup and check things out. He was cautious not to wander too far for he couldn't figure out why Jesse was alone and where everyone else was. Jesse and Pastor walked over to the shop and Jesse stood on the floor where the black Trans Am once sat. After pressing the button on the key fob, the floor started to drop down, this time all the way down to the third floor.

"This ride safe?" Pastor asked Jesse, for he had never experienced anything quite like this. Jesse raised an eyebrow to Pastor as a smile appeared on his face.

"Oh yeah," Jesse finally said. "It's safe for us."

Once the elevator stopped, Jesse instructed Pastor to stand still while he hobbled over and turned on the lights.

Thud, thud, thud, thud, thud, was heard in the distance as the overhead lights came on across the room, illuminating the bottom level of the garage from one side to the other.

"Jesus, Mary and Joseph!" Pastor said in disbelief. "I guess you're ready for just about anything, aren't you?"

The lower level was filled with military grade weaponry. Ak-47's lined the walls. Hundreds of thousands of rounds of ammunition were neatly stacked on steel shelves set up in perfect rows. There were boxes of grenades, rocket launchers, combat vests, self-inflating rafts, night vision goggles – anything and everything anyone would ever need or want if they ever had to go into combat.

"What's that?" Pastor asked pointing to the H1 Hummer in the corner.

"That, my friend, is an armored Hummer. It's capable of withstanding direct fire from a .50 caliber machine gun or any land mine it chooses to drive over. It's the real deal."

"Where did you get all of this, Jesse?"

"The short answer is the United States Navy," Jesse replied, heading over to some shelves to get a couple of duffle bags.

"Ultimately, all of this came from taxpayer dollars. You know the drill, use it up so we can get some new. Instead of using it up, I stockpiled it."

"Very clever, Jesse, very clever."

"Start filling your bag Pastor," Jesse instructed as he tossed a duffle bag over to him.

"With what?"

"Whatever you think we're going to need. Some of everything."

"Jesse, what are you expecting to find on a deserted island?"

"It's not about what we find, Pastor. It's about what finds us." Jesse answered without making eye contact, focused on filling his bag.

For the next hour Pastor and Jesse loaded up duffle bags with knives, vests, ammo, guns, grenades, night vision goggles, rope, cutting wire – all the ingredients that a seasoned Navy SEAL needed for a mission that had no deliverables. Once Jesse double checked the contents of each duffle bag, Pastor would run it up to the bed of the pickup. Four duffle bags, one inflatable raft and one 30 HP Evinrude tiller engine later, Jesse was ready to leave.

"BOURBON!" Jesse shouted, hoping the Aussie wasn't far.

"What's next, Jesse?"

"As soon as you're packed and ready to go, we're heading to Santa Monica."

"What about Georgia-Jean, Desi and Erin?"

"You drive, I'll start making phone calls."

"Jesse, we can't just…"

"Can't is not in my vocabulary right now, Pastor," Jesse asserted, not wanting to deal with any excuses. "Just drive."

As soon as Bourbon jumped in the truck Pastor and Jesse headed to Pastor's house while Jesse made the phone calls. A few minutes later Jesse hung up his phone in disbelief.

"What's the matter, Jesse?"

"Nothing but voice mail," Jesse said to Pastor, "for all three of them."

"Well, you did what you could. You left them all messages."

"Yeah, but we're leaving in a few hours."

"Jesse, we can handle this."

"We have a couple of days for them to get back to us. We're making a slight detour through Texas."

"How is Texas on the way to Santa Monica?" Pastor asked, wondering if Jesse was out of his mind.

"It's not," Jesse said with an evil grin. "Let's just say I have a score to even."

Chapter 25

A day and a half later, Pastor and Jesse rolled up to the biker bar Dissenters. It was 4:17 in the morning and there wasn't a soul in site, not a bike in the parking lot, not a person on the premises.

"Why are we here, Jesse?"

"Give me a hand, Pastor," Jesse instructed as he got out of the pickup and hobbled to the back. Handing Pastor a loaded rocket launcher named *The Gladiator*, Jesse told him to "take aim."

"Jesse, are you crazy?" Pastor asked while Jesse got a second *Gladiator* from the bed of his pickup.

"This is where Savannah jumped on the back of my bike," Jesse replied, taking aim on the building just a few hundred yards away. "This is for her!"

Jesse squeezed the trigger and sent a rocket right into the front doors of the bar. The explosion left Jesse smiling.

"Well then," Pastor replied taking aim himself, "why didn't you just say so?"

Rocket after rocket was fired into the bar, leaving nothing left but a pile of burning debris. Complete annihilation was the objective and the objective had been achieved. The last rocket launched was sent directly into the fuel pumps, sending a grand finale type of explosion into the early morning sky. Jesse and Pastor repacked the rocket launchers, jumped in the pickup and headed west. No one was the wiser. Not a single living soul witnessed what had happened other than the two of them.

"That was actually a lot more fun than I thought it was going to be," Pastor admitted with a big smile on his face.

"Yes, it was, Pastor," Jesse agreed. "It most certainly was."

Conversation was non-existent while the gratification of getting one in for Savannah flowed through their veins. After about an hour, Pastor broke the silence.

"What was it like?"

"What was what like?" Jesse asked for clarification.

"You know, being crucified. What was it like?"

"You had to ask that question, didn't you?"

"C'mon, Jesse. Did you think I wouldn't?"

"I was hardly crucified."

"You were nailed to a cross, weren't you?"

"I was abused a bit, yes." Jesse answered while looking at the bandages wrapped around the holes through his hands; "but there was no crown of thorns smashed onto my head. There was no stake in my side. I didn't have to carry my cross. I wasn't left for dead. I was saved. I was taken down. I got off easy. I didn't go through anything even *remotely* close to what Christ went through. Any man of the cloth should be able to recognize that."

"I would hardly call what you *did* go through getting off easy," Pastor offered, looking over at Jesse. "How many broken ribs do you have? How many stitches?"

"Well, Pastor," Jesse told him looking straight ahead, "knowing what I know now, you should have left me up there to die. Burying Rachael, for the second time, hurts far more and much deeper than any of these wounds to my flesh."

"I know Jesse. I know you're hurting. I can also feel your pain, Karma was an amazing woman and she'll be missed by many. Is that why you're going to find this island? To settle a score?"

"What score is there to settle on a deserted island? I'm going there to take it over, Pastor. Bourbon and I aren't coming home."

"You know I can't leave you out there, Jesse."

"You know you can't stop me from staying there either."

Chapter 26

After nearly seven hours of quiet driving time, Jesse finally broke the silence with questions about what's happening next.

"Do you have a plan as to *how* we're going to leave on Camper's yacht?"

"Yeah," Pastor replied as if it were nothing. "We're going to board it and leave."

"Just like that, board it and leave."

"Yeah."

"Doesn't that plan seem a little *overly simplistic*?" Jesse questioned, knowing from past experience *nothing* is ever that easy.

"You have lost your faith, Jesse."

"Faith has nothing to do with it, Pastor. We can't just walk onto a two hundred-million-dollar yacht and tell the captain it's time to go with no advanced warning, especially when it doesn't belong to either one of us!"

"On the contrary my friend," Pastor replied with a devilish grin spreading across his face, "it *does* belong to us, now."

"I'll believe it when I see it." Jesse replied as he leaned his seat back and closed his eyes. "Wake me up when we get to Santa Monica."

I-40 West to I-10 West, Pastor drove while Jesse got some much-needed rest for his healing body. I-10 ends just a few miles north of the Santa Monica Yacht Club. A quick jaunt down historic CA-1 and they were there.

"Wake up!" Pastor snapped at Jesse as they were pulling into the yacht club. "Put your game face on, it's go time."

"I'm awake," Jesse replied sitting up in his seat. "How could I sleep with you jerking the pickup all over the road? I hope you're not driving Camper's ship!"

"Very funny, Jesse," Pastor fired right back not seeing the humor in Jesse's comment, "and it's a yacht, not a ship."

"Technicality."

"Not really. A ship is a commercial vessel while a yacht is a personally owned boat typically used for pleasure."

"Pastor, really?" Jesse asked in disbelief. "Did you really just go there?"

"Well, it's really not a technicality at all."

"Wow."

Pastor pulled up to what seemed to be a valet asking, "Excuse me sir, can you please tell me where I can park while I get checked in?"

"Certainly, I can sir, but before I do that, are you by any chance with the "Buck Party?"

"Why, yes," Pastor responded slowly, not sure what to make of the question. "How did you know?"

"Your yacht broker, Ms. Desi Whittaker, is already here and waiting for you. My instructions are to bring your bags to the yacht for an immediate departure. If you don't mind, sir." The valet then opened the passenger's side door for Jesse to get out. "We can take it from here."

Jesse and Pastor just looked at each other and hesitated to get out. Finally, Jesse decided to go for it and, as he turned to get out of the truck, he saw a familiar face walking up the dock from the water.

"The bags are in the bed of the pickup", Jesse told the valet. "Be careful with them, they're heavy – and don't forget the engine for my inflatable raft."

"I'll help the valets with the bags, Jesse." Seeing Desi approaching the truck, Pastor continued, "you go on ahead with Ms. Raines."

"Bourbon, come!" Jesse commanded, leaving the door open for the Aussie to follow. "It's time for you to try out your sea legs!"

"Hello, Ms. Whittaker," Jesse said, reaching out to shake hands with Desi as she walked up to him. "It's always a pleasant surprise to see you!"

"We got your messages, Mr. Buck. I'm here with my assistant Erin, per your request. We're going to give you a full demonstration of the yacht. If you'll follow me, I'll show you the way."

Desi was acting very professional, completely dialed into her perfect lie. Jesse was dying to hear how she pulled this off but knew he would have to wait for the details, and for how long was completely unknown. He followed Desi down the dock and over to the right where the 341' Dorries yacht sat tied to the pier. It was a beautiful vessel. The yacht was named *Castle X* just like the casino. It was white with black and grey hull graphics that had hot pink highlights in them. Very elegantly done. When Jesse reached the back of the vessel to board, he was greeted by another familiar face.

"Mr. Buck, my name is Erin. I'm the one you talked with on the phone." Jesse greeted Erin as he should. Erin was wearing a white captain's outfit, complete with hat. She looked absolutely stunning in it. Jesse couldn't help but to notice how sexy a woman Erin really was. Why she remained single was beyond his understanding.

"Are you also piloting this thing?" Jesse asked with a smile.

"Oh, no, Mr. Buck," Erin replied with a wink. "Just fun attire for our adventure. I'll be introducing you to the captain after we get into international waters. My job right now is to make sure you have everything you need, and if I had to guess, you look like you need a drink, am I right?"

"A drink would be perfect, Erin. Thank you."

"You look like a Scotch man, am I right again?"

"Indeed, you are," Jesse answered, playing along with the charade. "I am a Scotch man. Johnnie Walker Blue, on the rocks if you have it, and a bowl of water for the pup if you don't mind."

The yacht boasted a 52' beam and had decks made of wood that shone like nothing Jesse had ever seen. They looked like they had never been walked on. Before Erin returned with Jesse's Scotch and a bowl of water for Bourbon, Pastor and the valets were walking up behind with all their gear.

"I'll show you gentlemen where to put that stuff, if you'll just follow me," Desi instructed as she walked away.

"Here you go, gentlemen," Erin said to Jesse and Pastor as she handed each one of them a Scotch. "If you follow me, I'll give you a brief tour now and a more extensive tour when we are on our way."

"A little early for Scotch, isn't it?" Pastor questioned as he followed behind.

"Not today." Jesse answered back with a smile, clinking his glass against Pastors.

"Mr. Buck," Erin said to Jesse, "I see your limping a little bit, with both feet, is there something I can get for you to help you walk? Something more than that cane?"

"No, ma'am. Just walk slow."

"Were you in an accident or something?"

"Let's just call it a religious experience," Jesse fired back, knowing she already knew the truth, and wondered why she was asking.

"Oh, okay."

The yacht was amazing. It boasted two different helicopter pads, one in the front and one in the rear. The top four floors, or decks as they are known in the yachting world, all had open air afts that could be closed with glass doors when so desired. There was a massive in-deck pool, massage room, sauna, gym, steam rooms and more. There was even a 30-person theater. The interior was finished with the finest of coverings. Crystal chandeliers, LED lighting, marble accents, Italian leather – it was truly a floating palace.

Jesse's state room was magnificent, it was a full beam suite, as wide as the boat, with windows on both sides. At over twenty-two hundred square feet, it was far nicer than the apartment he lived in just a couple of years prior. A goose down comforter and Egyptian cotton sheets covered the oversized king bed in the center of the room. The bath was open and invited the most playful couples with a walk-through shower and huge jacuzzi tub. The private suite also included a separate hot tub for those romantic evenings for two. There was a separate relaxing area and dining area as well. If the mood presented itself, you could watch the curved eighty-inch LED television from just about anywhere in the room.

"Karma would've absolutely loved this," Jesse said to Bourbon as he kneeled to give him a scratch behind the ears. "Wouldn't she, pup?"
"Ruff" was the sound made as if Bourbon were in conversation with Jesse. "I know boy, I miss her, too."

By the time Jesse had a shower and put on some fresh clothes, the yacht was headed out to sea. He made his way back up to the main deck with Bourbon close behind. When he got to the lounge where everyone was gathering, he was greeted by one more familiar face.

"I was wondering where you'd run off to!" Georgia-Jean said, greeting Jesse with a hug.

"I didn't know you were here with us. Where were you hiding?"

"I was down in my state room, freshening up. You didn't think I would miss this, did you, Jesse? Desi tells me you're thinking about buying this!"

"Did she now?" Jesse replied to Georgia while shooting Desi a look. "This is a little out of my budget."

"Jesse," Desi interrupted, "I would like to introduce you to the crew." Desi stepped aside while thirty-five of the most incredibly gorgeous women lined up and introduced themselves. They were all between 5'2" and 5'5" in height. Every one of them had on white polos and black shorts. The ladies all had beautiful bodies and perfect skin. Blondes, brunettes and redheads stared at Jesse, waiting to introduce themselves. All of them had at least shoulder length hair and perfect smiles, almost like they had been handpicked, or possibly forced, to do the job.

They were respectful and delightful and ready to serve their guests. *How does one hire such a staff?* Jesse wondered to himself. *Something is definitely odd here.* After the introductions were over, the all-female crew vanished back to their assigned tasks.

"That's a lot of crew for just us," Jesse said to Desi as he watched the ladies scatter.

"It's a full demonstration, including full crew," Desi reiterated. "Now that we're underway, why don't you let me take you two gentlemen to the control room, so you can meet the captain."

This ought to be interesting, Jesse thought to himself as he and Pastor followed Desi with Bourbon close behind.

"I'll hang back here and take in the sun," Georgia-Jean insisted. "Those gadgets up there don't mean anything to me."

As Desi led Jesse and Pastor to the control room, they walked silently. Jesse cautiously reached behind him and jacked a round into the firing chamber of a black Colt .45 and tucked it neatly back into his pants without anyone noticing. Not knowing where this was going and feeling that it could get out of control quickly, he wanted to be prepared, just in case. As the trio entered the control room, the captain was finishing a conversation on the UHF radio. This is what they heard.

"Copy that sir, I will await your command."

Chapter 27

"Captain," spoke Lieutenant Commander Zier, of the Coast Guard Cutter *Diligence*, "I have them on radar, sir. They are approximately thirty-seven miles out, ten degrees north northwest just off our starboard bow, Sir.

"Copy that, Lieutenant," replied Captain Onu. "Full speed ahead and remember, we will address this as a routine boarding and inspection. We don't want to alert the pirates to anything suspicious. This could be nothing more than some joyriders pulling a prank; however, it could be something else. Since this seems to be a non-hostile takeover, we want to keep it that way if at all possible. That being said, you'd better notify the Navy and see if they can send us backup. Anything they have will be just fine. Camper is our largest private donator and if his captain needs our help, then we're damn sure going to help him."

"Yes sir, Captain. I'm on it."

Lieutenant Commander Zier immediately contacted Naval support to see if there was anything in the area that might be available. After just a few short minutes, he had the confirmation he was looking for.

"Captain Onu, sir."

"Yes, Lieutenant, what is it?"

"The North Island NAS informed me of a small fleet of ships that left the port of San Diego this morning, sir. They are sending us a DDX-A1 Class destroyer, *Cyclone*, sir."

"Well done, Lieutenant. We'll sink 'em if we have to."

Chapter 28

"Jesse, Pastor, this is Captain McQue," Desi introduced. The gentlemen all shook hands, but everyone could sense an uneasy tension in the air. Desi did her best to act as if nothing was out of the norm, but even she was a little off.

"Who's going to pilot this yacht?" Captain McQue asked, trying to size up the pair of men that stared him in the eye.

"I'm Mr. Buck's Captain," Pastor answered immediately. "Navy, retired, sir. I'm the guy in charge of the boat."

"Wrong, Mr. Pastor, is it?" Captain McQue fired back immediately. "I'm in charge here. You are nothing." The words spoken were cold and hard. The message was loud and clear. Trouble was on the horizon.

"I mean no offense, Captain," Pastor continued. "I was simply…"

"That's enough" Captain McQue ordered, holding up his hand, instructing Pastor to silence his words. "It doesn't matter what you were about to say. Your words mean nothing to me. I only take orders from one man and neither of you is him. Let's get on with this demonstration so I can rid my control room of you two wannabes."

Just as Captain McQue turned his focus to the instrument cluster on the dash, the coast guard was heard over the radio.

"Castle X yacht, this is the United States Coast Guard. Do you copy? Repeat, Castle X yacht, this is the United States Coast Guard. Do you copy?"

"You clowns are done!" Captain McQue said as he reached for the radio handle.

"Coast Guard, this is Castle X yacht. We copy."

"You are instructed to stop immediately. We are boarding your vessel."

Jesse and Pastor locked eyes. Pastor shook his head no, just enough for Jesse to take heed and not do anything.

"Glad to see you Coast Guard," Captain McQue started while he pulled the throttles back into the neutral position. "Please tie up and board as you will."

"What's this all about?" Desi asked, now ready for anything.

"You're a fake," Captain McQue announced. "You're all fakes. I don't know what you want, or what you think you can do, but no one…"

"I won't tolerate any of this…" Desi shouted at the Captain as she started to walk away.

"Freeze, woman! Now!" Captain McQue demanded as he pulled a gun on Desi. With lightning fast reflexes Jesse drew his pistol and held it inches from Captain McQue's face.

"Drop it now or I'll burn you down."
Desi stood there with eyes locked on Captain McQue, not flinching a bit, watching his every breath of air.

"I'm telling you," Jesse said again, "Put it down or you're fish food."

Captain McQue took his eyes off Desi for just a split second, giving her all the time, she needed. With the reflexes of a professional athlete, she grabbed the Captains pistol, twisted it out of his hand and had it pointed at his face saying, "Tell us again who's in control of this boat?" Pastor just stood their smiling, knowing the yacht was about to be theirs.

"Your pistols don't scare me. You don't scare me. As soon as the Coast Guard gets here, you all are done."

"Is that a fact?" Pastor asked, still smiling.

"Yeah, that's a fact."

"Step aside." Jesse said as he waived his black Colt .45 in the direction he wanted the Captain to move, giving Pastor the necessary room he needed to reach the controls. As if it were second nature, Pastor took to the helm and throttled up the engines. The Castle X yacht was once again on its way.

"Captain Onu, they're accelerating, sir." Lieutenant Commander Zier announced to his Captain, who was now reaching for the radio handle.

"Castle X yacht, this is Captain Onu of the United States Coast Guard. You are instructed to stop immediately, or you will be fired upon. Do you copy?"

"Sir," Lieutenant Commander Zier stated, "They are out of our gun range, sir."

"Check your Radar, Lieutenant. The Navy's here."

"Castle X," the Captain repeated, "This is Captain Onu of the United States Coast Guard. If you don't stop immediately, we will sink your vessel. Do you copy!"

"They're not in gun range," Pastor said over his shoulder, ignoring the Coast Guard. I'm not worried about that guy.

"There is still no response, Sir," Lieutenant Commander Zier announced.

"See if the Navy can reach them."

Lieutenant Commander Zier contacted the Navy destroyer and asked if they could try to reach the Castle X yacht before aggressive measures were taken. On a mission, the Captain of the destroyer grabbed the handle to the UHF radio and attempted contact.

"Castle X Yacht. This is the United States Navy. Stop your vessel immediately or you will be fired upon. Do you copy?"

"You hear that?" Captain McQue said with attitude. "They'll sink us if you don't stop. I suggest you listen." Pastor grabbed the handle to the UHF radio and waited for a second message.

"Castle X motor yacht. This is the United Stated Navy destroyer *Cyclone*. This is your last warning. Stop your vessel at once or you will be fired upon."

"US Navy destroyer, please allow me to identify. Repeat. Navy destroyer *Cyclone*, I am requesting to speak with your captain for the purpose of federal identification. Please allow me to identify," Pastor said, wearing a mischievous grin across his face.

"Jesse, Desi, make sure that guy doesn't move," Pastor instructed while waiting for a response. Jesse and Desi stood there, both with pistols on their target.

"He's not going anywhere, Pastor," Desi assured. "Castle X yacht, this is Navy Captain Thomas. Identify yourself immediately."

"Captain Thomas, federal identifier is as follows. Golf-hotel-tango-zero-four-niner-four. Repeat – golf-hotel-tango-zero-four-niner-four; do you copy?"

"This is Captain Ted Thomas with the United States Navy. Pastor, old friend, you seem to have the Coast Guard's tail feathers ruffled. What's going on over there?" Jesse and Desi couldn't believe their ears. They listened carefully, while they kept Captain McQue at gunpoint.

"Good to see you Ted," Pastor replied with a smile. "The U.S. Government has seized the Castle X yacht. We're on official government business."

"That's crap and you know it!" shouted Captain McQue. "Why wasn't I notified! You're a liar!"

"Shut your pie hole!" Jesse commanded, "or your next word will be your last, got it?"

"Captain Onu, are you hearing this, sir?"

"Quiet Lieutenant, listen."

"Can you confirm this, Pastor?" asked Captain Thomas.

"It can be confirmed on the red line, Ted. We'll stand by while you check it out."

The "red line" is a top secret, highly confidential emergency line that is only for GHOST operation confirmation. In short, it's the private mobile number to the Kaiser. Only the Kaiser himself, can confirm or deny GHOST operations and only captains in the Navy and a few other select high-end officials have the ability to request confirmation. The silence in the control room was deafening. Beads of sweat were dripping off Captain McQue's forehead while the foursome waited for federal confirmation.

"Coast Guard cutter *Diligence*, this is U.S. Navy Captain Ted Thomas, your presence here is no longer needed. Thank you," was the message heard over the radio.

"That's crap!" shouted Captain McQue.

Smack! Worth every bit of pain he felt, Jesse landed a hard right hand hook across Captain McQue's face, nearly knocking him off his feet.

"Your next word *will* be your last. Any questions?" Captain McQue shook his head and raised his hands, not wanting any more trouble.

"Pastor, this is Captain Thomas. Where is the captain of the yacht?"

"Talk." Pastor instructed as he held up the handle to the radio.

"Captain Thomas, this is Captain McQue. These pirates have kidnapped me! Please help me! They're animals and I fear for my life!" Jesse, Pastor and Desi all chuckled at the comment that Captain McQue made, listening to him squeal like a little girl.

"Captain McQue, this is Captain Thomas. Your vessel has been commandeered by the United States Government. You are now under the direct command of Captain Pastor Raines. Failure to obey his command will be a direct violation of federal law and you will be prosecuted to the fullest extent of the law. Do you have any questions, sir?"

"How can this be?" Captain McQue questioned. "What is my command? He has given me no instructions!"

"You're taking us to Castle Island," Jesse answered.

"That'll never happen. I'll die first and you can't find the island without me."

"Thank you, Captain Thomas," Pastor confirmed into the handset. "We've got this from here."

"Call me if you need me, Pastor."

"Will do, Ted."

"So, jackass," Desi said with a smile. "Do you need to hear those instructions again?"

"Screw you, bitch!"

Smack! Jesse landed a second hard right-hand hook onto Captain McQue's face.

"Don't disrespect the lady."

"You want the island?" Captain McQue asked, shaking off the punch and collecting his thoughts. "Find it yourself!"

Pow!

Captain McQue pulled out of his pocket a single shot revolver, put it to his head and squeezed the trigger before anyone could stop him. His lifeless body fell to the floor, the room filled with silence.

"Oh!" Desi shouted as she looked away.

"Sorry, Pastor. I didn't see that one coming."

"Neither did I, Jesse. Take Desi downstairs. She doesn't need to see this," Pastor ordered. Jesse put his arm around Desi and walked with her down to the lounge, where Georgia Jean was still basking in the fresh ocean air.

"You okay?"

"I will be," Desi replied as she headed straight for the bar to make a drink.

"Get some fresh air down here while Pastor and I take care of the mess upstairs."

Jesse headed back to the control room where Pastor was piloting the vessel, like a pro.

136

"What do we do with this joker?"

"Pitch him overboard; we don't need him."

"You know what you're doing up here, Pastor? You know how to opperate this thing?"

"I haven't always been a minister, Jesse, remember?"

"Yeah, I know. You've mentioned that a few times now," Jesse responded, still looking at the body lying in the floor. "You know where we're going?"

"I thought you had that all figured out?"

"I have the coordinates in my laptop."

"I'll pitch the body; you get the coordinates and we'll be on our way."

"Yeah" Jesse thought to himself. *"Just like that, we'll be on our way..."*

Chapter 29

With the ladies, Desi, Erin and Georgia-Jean taking in the sun, Jesse showed Pastor the coordinates he found and explained how he found them.

"Your guess is as good as mine."

"It's not a guess, Pastor. This is where the island is.

"The Kaiser is going to be…"

"I don't care about the Kaiser," Jesse interrupted. "I don't work for him anymore."

"You'll never *not* work for him, Jesse. You're a GHOST now."

"Once you drop me and Bourbon off on that island, I'll be retired."

"You know it doesn't work that way, Jesse."

"It will for me," Jesse commanded while turning to walk away. "I'll be in my stateroom. Don't worry about me for dinner; I'll just catch up with everyone tomorrow." With nothing more said, Jesse was gone.

Pastor could see the weight on Jesse's heart with the loss of Karma and his SEAL team. He feared that Jesse didn't want to go on living, that Jesse might even try to take his own life. With nothing to live for, and no one to stop him, who's to say he wouldn't.

Jesse ate alone in his room. He ordered filet mignon and lobster from the galley. It came with garlic sautéed asparagus and a baked potato with all the trimmings. The meal was also accompanied by a bottle of sauvignon blanc which added the perfect touch to his meal in solitude.

Jesse and Bourbon made short order of the meal, with Bourbon eating most of it. After dinner Jesse sat on the love seat facing the window, watching the sun go down while drinking what was left of the bottle of wine – straight from the bottle.

"I miss you, Rachael." Jesse said softly, while a tear ran down his cheek. "I miss you so much! It wasn't supposed to happen this way," he continued with tears now falling from both eyes. Bourbon jumped up on the love seat with Jesse and made his presence known.

"You miss Karma, too, don't you, boy. I know you do, pup. It's just us. She's not coming back, Bourbon." Jesse said to the Aussie pup while giving him a pet. "She's not coming back," Jesse sobbed.

After an hour or so Jesse made his way over to the bed, removing his clothes on the way. As he pulled back the covers and climbed in, Bourbon was right by his side, feeling the same pain that his owner was with the loss of Karma, and for Bourbon, the loss of Savannah as well. Completely confused, Bourbon closed his eyes after laying his head on Jesse's pillow and the two of them were fast asleep.

"Knock, knock, Mr. Buck," was heard on the door. "Are you in there?" Jesse heard the door to his state room open, and he jolted awake.

"It's Issy and Lexi, Mr. Buck. We're here for you."

The voices were sweet, and their perfume was fragrant. As Jesse opened his eyes to lights that were turned on dimly, he focused on two of the most incredible looking women he had ever seen. Both of them had long blonde hair and bodies made for sin.

"We heard you were a little lonely down here, so we decided to come cheer you up," one of the girls said as they walked closer.

"I'm Lexi and this is Issy," the one girl said pointing to the other. "We're here to service you and make your time on board a little more enjoyable." Just like that, the two women removed their summer dresses to reveal themselves to Jesse, completely naked.

"We'll love you as much as we love each other," Issy said as she walked around to Jesse's right.

"There isn't anything we won't do with you or for you, Mr. Buck," Lexi assured him while she crawled onto the bed to Jesse's left and gave him a pet.

"Ladies, I'm not in the mood. Please see yourselves out," Jesse ordered as the two women continued to get *close* to Jesse.

"Ladies, leave now! I am not interested!!" Jesse commanded with authority.

Instantly, the pair of divas did an about face and scurried toward the door, picking up their dresses and putting them on while they ran out of the room. When they were gone Jesse laid his head back down on the pillow and closed his eyes.

"Women," Jesse spoke to Bourbon. "Some guard dog you are." Jesse continued after a pause as he gave the Aussie a pet. "You could have barked or something. Growled at least."

As Erin made her way to Jesse's state room, she encountered the two women walking up the hall. "Don't waste your time," Lexi said while looking Erin up and down. "If he didn't want us, he certainly won't want you," Issy added as the two walked by giggling.

"Bitches," Erin said to them as they continued up the corridor.

"Don't worry, Lexi," Issy told her while reaching down to hold her hand. "You can still have sex with me tonight!" The two women kissed each other on the lips and continued on their way, never stopping or giving Erin a second thought.

Just a moment later, Jesse heard the door to his state room open again and without even opening his eyes, shouted "I SAID GET OUT!"

"Jesse, it's me, Erin, not one of your toys."

"I'm not in the mood, Erin, and they were certainly *not* my toys."

Erin closed the door behind her and quietly walked over to Jesse lying in the bed. Completely dressed, she lay down next to Jesse, of course with Bourbon in between them. Lying on her side, with her hands up underneath her pillow, she started to talk.

"I'm worried about you, Jesse," she whispered softly.

"Well, don't," Jesse answered abruptly. "And get off my bed. I don't want you here right now."

"Well, tough," Erin fired right back, aggressively. "I'm not leaving."

"Why are you here?" Jesse demanded with a stern tone. "Don't bother taking your clothes off."

"I'm not here to bed you down, Mr. Buck. I'm here because I care. I'm here because I know your hurting. Karma was as much my friend as she was your wife!"

"I don't want you to care about me, Erin. I want you to leave. Please go."

Erin just lay there, gently petting Bourbon, while tears of pain fell from her eyes. Truth be known, she *was* in love with Jesse. Erin was deeply in love with a man that she knew she could never have. A secret that she'll admit to no one, and an emotion that she'll never be able to experience. Erin knew that Jesse's heart was shattered and he would mourn the loss of Karma until the end of time. Erin felt the same pain that Jesse was feeling. The only difference was that the heartache she was feeling was for someone that was still alive.

Morning came and the sun was shining bright through the windows in Jesse's state room. Bourbon wasted no time waking Jesse with morning kisses, and when Jesse finally got his bearings, he was distracted with the sound of running water coming from the bathroom. Cautiously, Jesse got out of bed, of course wearing nothing, and tip-toed toward the bathroom where the noise was coming from. As he peeked around, he saw heavy amounts of steam and came to the conclusion that it was Erin in the shower, but he needed a visual for confirmation.

Jesse snuck around the corner of the walk-through shower to find Erin washing herself, lathering up her body from head to toe with soap, watching her hands roam her flawless skin. Her body was amazing. Her long blond hair was thick, and her proportions were perfect. Erin had a toned body, with a flat tummy. Her legs were some of the sexiest he had ever seen, and her breasts were perfectly shaped and sized.

Jesse looked over the naked beauty cautiously, while secretly he wanted to join her in the shower. His urges of lust made him want to walk up behind her and gently pin her to the wall, just to have his way with her, to take her from behind, to take control of her and turn her on before she could resist. The two of them would experience that intense sexual moment together that would leave them both breathless.

The twitch in his manhood begged him to enter, but his shattered heart wouldn't allow it. His love and devotion to another woman would keep him honest, long after the grave had separated them. Jesse backed away quietly and tiptoed back to the main area where he promptly got dressed and left the room, taking Bourbon with him.

Chapter 30

"Pastor," Jesse spoke abruptly while entering the control room of the yacht. "Don't you ever sleep?"

"About as much as you do," Pastor replied, while turning and greeting Jesse with a man hug. "Where's the pup?"

"Bourbon? He made a few new friends on the way up here and won't be joining us for the morning meeting." Jesse replied chuckling.

"What morning meeting?" Pastor questioned with a look of surprise on his face.

"The one we're about to have right now," Jesse answered sternly. "As soon as Desi…"

"I'm here," Desi interrupted, walking into the room. "Erin will be here momentarily."

"What's this all about, Jesse?"

"We need some answers, Pastor. I want all the staff rounded up and questioned. Where are they from, how much are they paid – everything."

"Why does any of that really matter?" Desi asked.

"I think these women are conditioned," Jesse replied while staring at Pastor.

"How do you condition an entire staff without defiance?" Pastor questioned.

"I don't get that vibe," Desi added, "However, I follow your logic. If they have everything they need on the yacht, and they are afraid to leave for whatever reason, why would they?"

"Coffees for everyone," Erin said, entering the room carrying a small tray of coffees. "What'd I miss?"

"Jesse is trying to figure out the staff and their reason for being here," Pastor replied, reaching for one of the coffees.

"I think they are conditioned," Erin spoke out, looking at everyone in the room.

"So do I." Jesse reiterated. "Erin, let's do this. Why don't you round up all the staff and have them meet us on the main deck, in the lounge area where introductions were made? Have them meet us in thirty minutes and I'll take it from there."

"Jesse," Pastor proceeded with caution, "we can't just go around stirring the pot. We don't know what the staff is capable of."

"Erin, "Jesse replied with a sigh, "assure them that no one's in trouble, no one's fired. We are just having an all hands meeting."

"I'll help round everyone up," Desi said as she followed Erin through the door.

"Jesse, do you know what you're doing?"

"The women on this boat know more than we think they do, Pastor. It's time we got some questions answered – which reminds me. Did you ever find the captains log?"

"I haven't looked for it."

"Why don't you work on that while I go talk with the staff?"

"Yeah," Pastor replied while he followed Jesse out of the control room. "The boat's on autopilot. I'll look for the captain's log after the meeting."

By the time Jesse and Pastor made their way down to the lounge, the entire staff was already there, and many of them were taking turns feeding Bourbon pieces of bacon from the breakfast buffet that had been set out.

"Ladies, ladies," Desi spoke with a soft kind of authority. "Mr. Buck is here; can we please give him our attention?"

The all-female crew seemed unsure of what was about to happen. Many of them looked frightened and a few looked downright scared. Jesse picked up on this immediately and wasted no time setting the stage and getting right to the point.

"Ladies," Jesse announced with a calm friendly voice. "It's okay to relax. Take a deep breath and let your shoulders down, it's okay."

There was a huge weight lifted out of the room immediately. Girls sighed and chuckled, mumbling amongst themselves as relief filled the air.

"It's important to let you know" Jesse continued, "That your captain, what was his name?" Jesse asked aside, looking over at Pastor.

"Captain McQue," Desi whispered before Pastor could answer.

"Captain McQue" Jesse continued, "has been relieved of his duties."

"I heard he was dead!" an unknown voice immediately shouted as the other women confirmed with whispers and muttering. Jesse, Pastor, Desi and Erin all looked at each other carefully, wondering if they should confirm this.

"That is correct," Erin said, taking the conversation over. "He took his own life." The female crew immediately clapped and cheered wildly as this news to their ears was fantastic! The leaders of the boat looked at each other in awe. They were shocked to see this kind of reaction from the crew and chuckled until, suddenly, the room became quiet again.

"Mr. Buck?" asked a stunning brunette woman stepping up from the back of the group. "What does that mean for us, exactly?"

The light came on. Jesse and Erin locked eyes as their suspicion had just been confirmed. These women *have* been conditioned. Jesse struggled for the right words as he thought cautiously and quickly to find them.

"Whatever life you have been living," Desi blurted out, trying to keep things moving forward in a comfortable fashion, "has been changed."

"We are not affiliated with the captain or his business." Pastor spoke out, trying to help without saying too much.

"What about Mr. Camper?" an unknown voice shouted from the group.

"Camper is dead." Jesse fired back immediately. There was panic amongst the ladies. Fear filled their eyes as the whispering began.

"How do we know that?" the brunette-haired woman spoke out.

"What is your name?" Erin asked the woman.

"My name is Marcy. I have been here the longest. I speak for the group." The women surrounding Marcy whispered "yes" and encouraged her to represent all of them.

"Marcy," Jesse asked softly, "Do you have a last name?"

"Answer the question," Marcy demanded with a stern voice.

"I shot and killed Camper myself," Jesse answered with authority, not needing to explain his late wife at this point, "and then I blew up his casino. Ladies, Camper is dead."

The women went wild, cheering and hugging each other. Tears of joy filled the room as the news they just heard was good cause for celebration.

"QUIET!!" Marcy demanded, and instantly the celebration was over. "Camper is dead you tell us. What about the other guy?"

"What other guy?" Desi asked stepping in, thinking this was just a decoy in the conversation to test the waters, to feel out the situation.

"The other guy!" Marcy shouted. "What about the other guy?"

"There is no other guy," Erin answered her.

"Pastor," Jesse ordered, "get the Kaiser on the SAT phone and ask him about a partner of Campers. DO IT NOW! Marcy, I need you and Erin to have a conversation in private, immediately. Marcy, we need to know everything you know. Ladies," Jesse said pointing to everyone else in the lounge, "you are on a break. Take some time to catch your breath and meet us back here in one hour."

"What would you like us to do?" Georgia-Jean asked, holding Bourbon on her lap.

"Go make some new friends," Jesse said with a hand wave.

Chapter 31

Marcy led Erin to her private state room in the lowest level of the yacht. Erin was surprised to see how immaculate it was, absolutely spotless.

"I see you're a neat freak," Erin said with a chuckle as she looked around.

"Lots of time to keep a clean room when you have nowhere to go."

"Marcy, how is it you are here?" Erin asked getting right to the point. "Are you paid? Were you taken? It's very important that we know exactly what is going on here."

"I don't know you. How do I know I can trust you?" How do I know I shouldn't kill you before you kill me?"

"I'm not here to…"

Without warning Marcy lunged at Erin, bringing her to the floor. Erin fought back with everything she had but Marcy kept coming, fighting hard.

"I'm done being a prisoner!" Marcy shouted while she continued to attack Erin.

"Marcy, stop!"

"I'll die before you and your men hurt me and my girls, you hear me!"

"MARCY!" Erin shouted as she broke free from her grasp and pinned her to the floor. "We are not here to hurt you. We are here to help you."

"That's what the other guy said!" Marcy shouted, struggling to get up. "That's what the other guy said before he beat me and raped me!" Marcy broke down and started to sob. Erin unpinned her and got up off the floor. She held out her hand for Marcy to take hold of and helped her up. As soon as Marcy was on her feet, Erin hugged her. Marcy grabbed her tightly and cried hysterically into her shoulder.

"It's over Marcy. Shhh. It's okay. You are safe now. No one is here to hurt you anymore."
Marcy cried and cried, unable to let go of Erin.

"It's been so long…"

"You are safe now, Marcy. As God is my witness, you are safe."

Up in the control room Pastor disconnected the call with the Kaiser as Jesse entered. "What's the word?" Jesse demanded, shutting the door behind him.

"There is no partner, Jesse." The Kaiser thinks the woman might be suffering from some sort of mental trauma with everything that has happened to her, possibly even some sort of post-traumatic stress.

"For this first time ever," Jesse replied with eyes locked on Pastor's, "I agree with the Kaiser."

"I actually do, too."

"Castle X yacht, come in. Castle X yacht, do you copy, over?" was heard coming though the UHF radio. Jesse and Pastor looked at the radio and then back at each other, both with a questioning look on their faces.

"Castle X yacht come in. Castle X yacht, do you copy, over?"

"Answer it," Jesse instructed pointing to the radio. "Don't tell them any more than you have to."

"This is Castle X yacht. Please identify yourself. Repeat. This is Castle X yacht, please identify yourself immediately, over."

"Pastor, this is Ted. Don't be so jumpy old friend."

"Captain Thomas, to what do I owe this pleasure?"

"Just checking in Pastor, everything okay?"

"He's not showing up on radar," Jesse said to Pastor as he studied the instruments. Get his position."

"Captain Thomas, what's your location."

"Don't you see us on radar, Pastor?"

"That's a negative, sir. There is nothing on our screen."

"Check your four o'clock."

Jesse and Pastor looked at each other and then looked out the window together. Plain as day, one thousand, maybe fifteen hundred yards away was the US Navy destroyer *Cyclone*.

"Captain Thomas, do you copy?"

"Go ahead, Pastor."

"I see you with my eyes, but I sure don't see you on radar, sir. What are you doing?"

"We're testing out the latest stealth equipment, Pastor. Works well doesn't it?"

"That's affirmative. But what are you doing? Are you following us?"

"Admiral Hoffee thought it'd be in your best interest to have back up. He knows how your missions always seem to, well, be a little more intense than you expect." Jesse chuckled to himself in full agreement with the last comment made by Captain Thomas.

"I thought Admiral Hoffee retired."

"That's funny, Pastor. He said the same thing about you."

"I'm glad you have my back, Ted."

"We've got our eyes peeled for you, Pastor. We can see a lot more and a lot farther than you can. We'll let you know if anything comes up. US Navy – over and out."

"Castle X yacht – out."

"Apparently you and Ted have a history together."

"Apparently." Pastor replied without giving up any more information.

Chapter 32

"Sir, I just received a hot message that Camper's yacht is en route, here, to the island," man one said to man two.

"Very well. That means our job here is almost done."

"Not exactly, sir. The message also informed me that we are to fire upon any and all watercraft, sir.

"Do you have the message with you?"

"Yes, sir" man one said while handing it to man two. Man two snatched it out of man one's hand. The message read:

Alert: Castle X yacht possibly in route to Castle Island. Camper not on board. Destroy any and all water craft that comes within twenty-five miles of the island for the next forty-five days, including Castle X yacht. Alert level is extremely high. Margin for error is zero.

"Did this message come from…"

"Yes," man one answered, interrupting man two. "It's the real deal."

"Load the cannons. Man the radar systems. Sink everything."

"Consider it done, sir."

Chapter 33

"I need you to trust me, Marcy," Erin spoke softly.
Marcy let loose of Erin and stepped away. She dried her
eyes with both hands and regained her composure, almost a
little embarrassed for her meltdown.

"It's one of those things that you pray about, but just
never happens."

"What's that?"

"Being rescued."

Erin suddenly remembered Savannah and the life she
had before Jesse saved her. While Erin didn't have all the
details, she knew enough to know that before she jumped
on the back of Jesse's motorcycle, her life was filled with
horrible abuse. There certainly seemed to be a pattern
emerging here with these women who had been
conditioned and kept against their will.

"I don't mean to be the one that you have this
uncomfortable conversation with," Erin said to Marcy,
talking with a very soft and compassionate voice, "but we
can't be effective in helping you through the rest of this
until we know what you know."

Marcy nodded her head, a slow gentle nod. She knew
Erin was right and she believed that she could trust her.

"I'm sorry about attacking you, Erin."

"Don't worry about that right now, it's history. You've
been through a lot."

"I don't know his name," Marcy started talking, while
focusing on a spot on the floor. "I don't know what he
looks like. All I know is his voice." Erin listened with a

keen ear while Marcy shared what she knew. "I was always blindfolded, and my head bagged with a pillow case. I was stripped naked and tied up tight before he ever came into my room. He didn't smell like a black man. He didn't smell like a white man. He had almost no smell at all that I could make out over his cologne.

His words were few, but I remember his voice. His voice was deep and sharp. I would recognize it anywhere. I'll never forget it. The smell of his cologne and the sound of his voice haunt me daily."

A tear fell from Erin's eye as she felt the pain that Marcy was reliving with her story. The two women sat down on a nearby sofa, and Marcy continued to talk.

"This man only wanted me. I was *reserved* for him, and him only. He would choke me and climb on me. He would make me…"

"You don't have to relive all of the details, Marcy. Just know that, that life is over. How do you know this man was a partner of Camper's?"

"One night he came to me a little drunk, and a little extra abusive. He told me that he had to "have me every way he wanted so his business partner would respect him." I asked him who his business partner was, and he beat me. He beat me bad, yelling at me. *Camper is my business partner, you stupid worthless whore!* he shouted at me."

"He beat me so bad I passed out from the pain. I think he thought he beat me to death. I haven't seen him since that night, and I fear that he'll be back. I fear he'll be back soon, once he knows I'm still alive."

"I can promise you this, Marcy. That man, whoever he was, won't be around while Jesse and Pastor are running this yacht. Those days are over and now you can start to put those nightmares to rest, forever."

"He's bald," Marcy added.

"How do you know that?"

"He used to like to rub his bald head on my chest."

"That's kind of creepy," Erin replied with a half-smile.

"I know, right?"

"Marcy," Erin spoke while she stood up. "will the women, the rest of the crew, listen to you?"

"Yeah. They'll listen to me, Erin. They trust me. I've been here the longest. They're loyal to me."

"How long have you been here?"

"I don't know," Marcy answered as her eyes started tearing up again.

"What do you mean, you don't know?"

"I mean I don't know. There is no sense of time on the yacht. No holidays, no seasons, no clocks, no weekends, just day and night. You forget. Time gets distorted and lost, completely forgotten about."

"Is there anything that you can tell me?" Erin asked, shocked with what she just heard.

"This is what I do know," Marcy replied. "I was with my besties, vacationing in the Dominican Republic. We were having a great time. There were hot guys everywhere and the drinks were flowing freely. We were drinking Mama Juana's. The guy I was drinking with was so hot! He'd been a perfect gentleman to me for days – never trying anything. A perfect gentleman. I had to have him, Erin. I know it sounds bad, but I had to have him."

"We've all had those moments, Marcy," Erin interrupted. "I know what you mean."

"On the fourth night we were there, the night before we were going to leave, I told him he could take me to my room and have his way with me."

There was a pause in Marcy's story. Erin waited for a moment, but still, no more words were spoken.

"What happened next?"

"I don't know. I don't even remember the sex, or if there was any. I woke up groggy and was left that way for months while I was "conditioned." I've been a hostage on these boats ever since. This is my third yacht. I was told I would be freed after I 'paid off my debt', but that day has never come."

"What debt? Debt to whom?"

"I don't know, Erin. I was set to go to med school. Another thing you might want to know is that, when Camper was 'done with the girls', they aren't let go. They were 'used' one last time, killed and tossed overboard for the sharks to feed on."

Erin was numb from what she just heard, almost lost in the horror of the story she just listened to. Camper made the Grim Reaper look like a saint. She was glad he was dead.

"Thank you for sharing that with me, Marcy. I know that was hard to do."

"It's nice to see a safe face, Erin."

"You come to me, and only me, if you need to talk, okay?"

"Thank you, Erin."

"Fix yourself up. We've got to get back upstairs."

"Erin, can Jesse really be trusted?" Marcy asked a little sheepishly. "You know, are we *really* safe with him?"

157

"Jesse is the best man I have ever met, Marcy. You can trust him with your life."

The two women gave each other a hug and Marcy was quick to straighten herself up. Like a pro in minutes, she looked perfect again. As the two ladies made their way back to the lounge to reconvene, Erin thought she'd ask one final question.

"Do you remember anything else about that night Marcy? What year it happened? The name of your guy, maybe? Anything at all?"

"I don't remember what year it was, Erin. I'm not even sure what year it is now. I think it was six or seven years ago now, if I had to guess. I do, however, remember his name. I'll never forget it. His name was Dennis, Dennis Rybka."

Chapter 34

By the time Erin and Marcy made it to the lounge, everyone else was already there and Jesse was in a hurry to get things started.

"Nice of you two to join us." Jesse started with sarcasm.

"Now's not the time," Erin fired right back, shooting him a look.

"Ladies," Jesse said, moving the conversation forward, while still eyeballing Erin, "I suspect you have been kept here, on this yacht against your will. I also suspect your captivity came with the payment of life and not a normal paycheck. Please correct me if I am wrong."

There was complete silence. Not a single woman said a word or made a move.

"That is correct, Jesse," Marcy finally answered.

"Marcy!" The women all shouted, fearful of what might happen next.

"Ladies, it's okay." Marcy addressed the group of women. "We are not slaves anymore."

The women on the yacht broke down and cried. They hugged each other and cried uncontrollably. Some of them were laughing with the joyous news. All of them were overflowing with emotion.

"What does that mean for us?" one of the women asked as the group settled down.

"Jesse, Mr. Buck as we know him, is going to explain that to us now. I ask that we all listen and wait until he's finished to ask any questions." Marcy turned and looked at Jesse saying, "Mr. Buck, the floor is all yours."

"Let's do this the right way," Jesse said as he looked over at Erin. "Let's get these ladies something to drink and get out some appetizers and have this meeting like we are all part of something grand. How does that sound?"

The women went wild clapping and cheering. Erin instantly went into 'manager mode' and instructed some of the women to work on appetizers and others to make drinks. Desi was quick to help and Georgia-Jean, well, she just sat with Bourbon and took it all in.

In twenty short minutes, the counter was completely covered with the yummiest looking appetizers one could imagine. All the women had the drink of their choice in their hand, and Bourbon was making his rounds collecting treats from anyone who would give him one.

"That was a good call, Boss," Erin said to Jesse while she stood next to him and took it all in. "If you lead them, they will follow."

"Ladies," Jesse spoke out to the group of women who seemed to be enjoying their time. "Ladies," Jesse said one more time while they settled down. "I can't operate this yacht without your help. That being said, after this trip, every one of you is free to go back to the life you came from."

"Mr. Buck," interrupted one of the women, standing up to ask the question, "I don't have a life to go back to. What's going to happen to me?" Some of the women started gossiping and agreeing with the question. There was immediate concern amongst the group.

"Let's wait until Jesse is done talking before, we bombard him with questions," Marcy shouted out. "Let's show him the respect he deserves."

Jesse and his team were impressed with how Marcy handled the crew. Marcy's women were loyal to her. Jesse thought this was an interesting observation, one that he'd file until later just in case something ever came of it.

"We aren't going to have all of the answers to all of the questions you are going to ask," said Erin as she walked across the floor in front of Jesse, talking directly to the group of women. "The main takeaway from what Jesse just told us is that you are no longer slaves to the black market. You are now paid employees."

"Too bad that didn't start with our last trip," a woman murmured sarcastically.

"I know, right? We'd already have a paycheck to spend," another woman added.

"Who said that?" Jesse questioned abruptly, startling the women into silence. "What last trip? Who said that?" As Jesse's voice got louder, the women became fearful, not wanting to answer.

"What are you talking about?" Jesse shouted.

"Mr. Buck," Marcy replied, getting up from her chair, "you want all of these answers from us. You want all of our information. Why don't you show us the respect that you are commanding we give you?" The women cheered Marcy on and stood behind the person they trusted most.

"Why don't you tell us in detail about Camper's death? Why don't you tell us who you are, where you're from and what you are doing stealing his yacht?" Again, the women went wild cheering, supporting the push for Jesse to win their trust. Jesse looked over at Erin and then at Desi. Desi shrugged her shoulders as if to say, "it's your show, you handle it."

Jesse then looked over towards Marcy at the other end of the room, still standing, waiting for an answer.

"My wife, Rachael and I stormed Camper's office with members of my former SEAL team." Jesse started with a fierce voice, not happy about reliving the experience. My wife shot Camper in the chest twice, with this pistol!" Jesse shouted as he pulled his bright stainless Colt .45 out from the back of his pants. "After we watched him take his last breath of air," Jesse continued, holstering his firearm "we left the premises."

"We left Castle X Casino in Las Vegas. On the way out, we triggered a bomb that we put in the parking garage and watched the whole building crumble to the earth, leaving nothing but a pile of rubble." Jesse's eyes were locked onto Marcy's as he slowly made his way across the floor, not taking his eyes off hers, delivering the facts.

"Some number of days ago some of Camper's thugs ran us off the road. They kidnapped my wife and my SEAL team and killed them all. Their remains were sent to me in plastic bags, and Pastor, the man piloting the yacht, and these two women" Jesse said pointing to Desi and Erin but not taking his eye off Marcy, "buried them on my property."

"They beat me and nailed me to a cross," Jesse paused and held up his hands, removing the bandages from both of them to reveal the scars that were still not fully healed. "They whipped me!" Jesse shouted, removing his shirt and tearing off the bandage's underneath, revealing the hundreds of stitches that were still covering his body. By now Jesse was only inches from Marcy, eyeballing her.

162

"I know what they did to me," he continued in almost a whisper. "I can't imagine what they have done to you."

Jesse slowly turned to walk away, but before he took his second step Marcy muttered with a cautious whisper,

"I think they're still alive."

Jesse spun around and grabbed Marcy by the arms and shouted, "What did you say?"

"Stop you're hurting me!"

"WHAT DID YOU JUST SAY?!" Jesse shouted right in Marcy's face!

"JESSE, STOP!" Erin shouted, running over to pull him off of Marcy.

"YOUR SCARING ME! LEAVE ME ALONE!" Marcy screamed!

"WHERE ARE THEY?" Jesse shouted as he shook Marcy by the arms. The other women immediately scattered in fear. Like vampires in sunlight, they were gone.

"JESSE, LET HER GO!" Erin shouted.

"TALK TO ME, DAMNIT!"

"HELP ME! ERIN! HELP ME!!"

Pastor grabbed Jesse and tried to hold him back, tearing many of his stitches open in the process. Desi and Erin struggled to help Marcy get free and as soon as she was, she bolted.

"Jesse, what's the matter with you?" Erin shouted. "WHERE IS MY WIFE?!" Jesse yelled at the top of his lungs as Marcy ran from the lounge. "WHERE IS SHE?! WHERE IS SHE?!!"

"*SLAP!*" Erin slapped Jesse across the face, hard.

"Pull yourself together, Jesse!" Erin shouted in his face. "What in the hell is the matter with you? Do you think

163

she's going to talk to you now? Do you think she is going to trust you?"

"PASTOR," Erin hollered with authority, "GET HIM OUT OF HERE, NOW!"

Jesse fell to his knees and broke down in tears. He had lost control and he was ashamed. He put his hands up over his face and cried. The salt from the tears burned the unhealed wounds in his hands as they washed blood from the re-opened wounds onto his clothes.

"Erin," Desi said looking over at her niece. "Go check on Marcy. I'll go check on the other women." Erin nodded her head and left immediately. Bourbon broke free from Georgia-Jean's grip and ran over to Jesse where he started licking his hands and face. Jesse grabbed the Aussie and sobbed into his fur, crying hysterically.

"Come on, Jesse," Pastor said softly. "Let me help you to your state room."

Chapter 35

"Things are getting dicey around here," man one said to man two, with a concerned voice. "What do we do with the hostages?"

"We don't do anything with them. Our protocol hasn't changed."

"If we are to sink Camper's yacht, our protocol most certainly has changed! Maybe we should kill the hostages and flee the island."

"We will do no such thing. We stand our post until we're told otherwise, besides, how do you plan to leave?" Man two asked to man one with a sarcastic tone in his voice. "You going to swim somewhere? I'm the only one that can fly the helicopter."

"Something's not right with this, I can feel it!"

"Our job is to keep the hostages alive and fed. They are our ticket off this place. Don't lose your cool.

"The other men…"

"Screw the other men. I am in charge and we will hold our post. Have you manned the cannons?"

"All four stations are on full alert, yes."

"Then get back to work and quit acting like a scared little kitten! Your job is to sink anything in the water, so shut your mouth and find something to sink!"

Chapter 36

"C'mon, Jesse. Get up," Pastor told his friend, trying to pull him up by his arm. Jesse yanked his arm from Pastor's grip and started to get up on his own.

"I need to talk with that woman," Jesse replied calmly, no longer crying. "I need to talk with her right now."

"I don't know that that's going to happen right now, Jesse."

"Look, I screwed up, I get it. I'll apologize," Jesse replied, now standing tall with blood seeping from some of his reopened wounds. "I need to know what she knows."

"You go to your state room and I'll find Erin. I'll see what I can do."

"Make it happen, Pastor. Make it happen now."

Jesse went one way as Pastor went the other. Pastor was reluctant to go seek out Marcy this soon but feared if he didn't Jesse would, and no one needed a repeat of what just happened. The more Pastor thought about it, the more he wanted to find Marcy before Jesse did.

Knock, knock was heard on the other side of the door to Marcy's state room.

"Marcy, it's Erin. Are you okay?"

"Go away, Erin!"

"Marcy, please let me in. We need to talk about this."

"I don't want to talk right now! Go away!"

"Marcy, I need you right now. The other women on the yacht need you right now. You need to be strong. I can try to explain what just happened. Please Marcy, open the door."

There was silence. Nothing was said, nothing was heard. Second after second ticked by until finally Erin heard a 'click' come from the door. She tested the handle; it was unlocked.

"Marcy?" she asked quietly while poking her head in. "Marcy, I'm coming in, is that okay?"

"Yeah," Marcy replied softly. "Please lock the door behind you."

Erin entered cautiously, shutting and locking the door behind her. She walked into the room and saw Marcy sitting on her sofa, with tears still falling from her eyes. Erin went over and pulled her up onto her feet and gave her a hug.

"That was completely unexpected," Erin said to her, hoping to calm her down.

"Trust him with my life, you said, right?"

"Marcy," Erin replied, stepping away to look her in the eye, "Jesse is a good man. He is very passionate about his wife, who was also my friend."

"What did his wife look like?"

"She was beautiful. She was petite with long dark hair. She was an incredible person and a wonderful friend."

"A few weeks ago, we set out with seven people." Marcy started to tell the story as she knew it, stepping away from Erin and reclaiming her seat on the sofa. "There were seven people, a few men and a few women. They looked a little rough, like they might have been in some sort of accident or something. One of the women was vocal, very assertive, almost belligerent. She snapped. She was out of control and…" Marcy started to get emotional and paused for a moment to regain her composure.

"It's okay, Marcy, you can tell me."

"They made an example out of her to keep the rest of the group in check until we got to the island."

"What did they do, Marcy? What happened?"

"They beat her in front of the others. They beat her bad, until she was nothing but a whimpering mess lying on the floor. Then to make a final statement, they broke her neck. Her body is still in the freezer in the garage."

"What garage?" Erin questioned immediately.

"The whole bottom level of the yacht is a water garage. That's where the toys are as well as the cage."

"Cage?"

"The cage that the prisoners are transported in, where they kept the hostages."

"How do you know all of this? Can you show me?"

"I've been here the longest, remember? I don't know everything, but I know a lot. That's why I know I'll never get off of this floating hell alive. I know too much."

"Take me there, now. I need to see this."

Marcy led the way to the lowest level of the yacht. It's amazing how large the vessel really was when you got the tour that no one else got, it was truly massive.

"Who killed her?" Erin asked while she followed Marcy. "Are they still on board?"

"No. The captain is... was, the only killer on board when you all showed up. Typically, the transporters, that's what we call the men that transport the hostages, do the killing. I didn't recognize the last group. They were all new."

When Marcy and Erin got to the door that led into the garage, they found it locked, not only with a door handle, but also with a deadbolt.

"I don't have a key for this door," Marcy informed her pointing to the locks.

"Stand back."

Erin took a step back and, while planting herself on her left foot, kicked the door with the bottom of her right foot, just to the left of the locks.

Wham, Wham! Wham!! – WHAM!!

Finally, after the fourth kick, the door swung open, slamming against the inside wall.

"Impressive," Marcy admitted as she followed Erin into the garage.

Erin couldn't believe her eyes. Immediately to the left was a large 12 x 12 cage made out of wrought steel. No way was anyone getting out of it, not even Houdini himself. To the right was a large floor freezer, six feet long, four feet wide and three feet deep. Erin walked over to the freezer and paused before opening it.

"That's not going to be a pretty."

"I have to, Marcy, I need to know."

Erin yanked the lid open and looked inside. "Huh!" She gasped and slammed it shut again, spinning around. Her right hand covered her mouth. While she leaned against the freezer, tears started to fall from her eyes.

"That's your friend, isn't it?" Marcy asked with a very soft, cautious voice. Erin was overwhelmed with emotion and not able to make words. Marcy walked over and gave Erin a hug.

"I'm so sorry, Erin. I'm so sorry."

"We have got to let Jesse know what's going on."

"I'm not telling him. That guy's crazy!"

"Marcy, he's not crazy. He's just been through a lot."

"Keep that guy away from me, Erin. He scares me."

"He's not the bad guy…"

"Not to you he's not!" Marcy interrupted, shouting at Erin. "He sure is to me!"

"Go hang out in your state room for a bit," Erin instructed Marcy while she headed out the door. "This is too important to sit on."

Not wanting to cross paths with Jesse at all, Marcy bolted to her state room. Once inside, she locked the door behind her and waited. Erin went straight to Jesse's room, to find it empty. She made her way back to the lounge and found only Georgia-Jean there with Bourbon, trying to ease herself of the tension that filled the air not that long ago.

"You okay, Georgia-Jean?" Erin asked in passing.

"Oh, I will be. Nothing like a little drama to get the old ticker racing."

"Yeah, that wasn't in the plan. Can I get you anything?"

"I've already got something." Georgia-Jean replied, holding up a glass with an unknown drink in it.

"One of the girls left this behind in all of the commotion, so I decided to not let it go to waste."

"Let me taste that, Georgia-Jean. We don't need you getting all loosey-goosey on us." Erin walked over to where Georgia-Jean was sitting and took the glass from her hand. Smelling the contents first, and then taking a sip, she deemed it to be a vodka tonic, on the rocks.

"Do you like the taste of this, Georgia-Jean?"

"Oh yes." Georgia-Jean replied with a smile on her face. "It's quite refreshing."

"You know that's not a club soda, right?"

"Yes, dear. I didn't just come down with the sunshine you know."

Erin chuckled at Georgia-Jean's response and thought for a moment. Maybe she should bring a couple of vodka tonics up to the control room, suspecting that's where the persons she was looking for were hiding out. On the other hand, maybe alcohol is a bad idea right now.

True to her suspicions, Jesse, Pastor and Desi were all there, almost as if they were waiting for Erin to show up. Erin entered the control room and started right in on Jesse.

"Do you have anything to say?" Erin asked as she shut the door behind her.

"Don't start with me," he replied with a sharp tone. "That woman isn't telling us everything, and there are things that we need to know, and I mean right now we need to know them!"

"Jesse, I just came from talking with Marcy, and I think you should come with me. Pastor," Erin added as she turned to head toward the door, "you might want to join us. I'll explain everything on the way."

"Desi," Pastor said while getting up from the captain's chair, "take the helm."

Jesse did a double take looking over at Desi, shocked with what he just heard. "You know how to operate this thing?"

"Just one of my many talents."

Erin led Jesse and Pastor down to the garage, recapping the conversation she had with Marcy to them on the way.

By the time they entered the garage, Jesse was in a hurry to make the discovery. Not waiting for Erin and Pastor to enter, he yanked the freezer lid open and found her lifeless body inside, frozen solid. Emotion overwhelmed him as he slowly closed the lid and fell to the floor. He covered his eyes and cried. Pastor moved around him and lifted the freezer lid to see for himself.

"Oh, Barbara," Pastor said softly while he closed the lid. Pastor and Erin hung their heads low, while Jesse sat on the floor and cried, relieved with the discovery that the lifeless beauty in the freezer was *not* his beloved wife, yet filled with anger knowing the woman in the freezer was untrained and should have never have been brought into this mess. Jesse felt personally responsible for her death, and it was surely an agonizing one at that.

Pastor reached over to hold Erin's hand and with their heads hung low, he started to pray.

"Dear Lord, oh heavenly father. It's a grim day today, that we find the…"

"Mr. Buck?" Marcy asked quietly, peeking her head through the door. Jesse looked up to see the young woman looking right at him. He slowly got up and wiped his eyes before he spoke.

"It took a lot of courage to come down here just now, Marcy. I commend you for that. I am also sorry for how I treated you. Will you please forgive me?" Jesse opened his arms inviting Marcy to give him a hug. Pausing for just a moment and looking Erin in the eye for confirmation, Marcy slowly stepped toward Jesse and hugged him. More tears came, this time from everyone.

172

"I really am sorry, Marcy. I lost control and there is no excuse for that."

"I'm sorry to interrupt, but I feel that I should have a conversation with you, Mr. Buck."

"It's Jesse. Please call me Jesse," he said letting go. "What's on your mind?"

"I was upstairs, in my state room thinking to myself, I have never met a man that was so passionate for a woman before. If someone were that passionate for me, then I would want someone to help them. You're every woman's dream."

"I don't know about all that," Jesse replied with a smile and a chuckle.

Yeah, he really is... Erin thought to herself while she listened to what was being said. ...*every woman's dream.*

"I just love my wife, and if she's alive, I need to find her."

"Not to change gears here, Jesse," Pastor chimed in. "If Barbara's body is in the freezer, then whose body did we bury?"

"Whose *bodies* might be a better question, Pastor," Erin added, racking her brain trying to figure things out.

"I suspect," Jesse replied looking at everyone in the group, "the answer to that question will present itself in time. Right now, I think we should let Marcy share her story with us."

The group of four sat down on the floor in a circle in the water garage in the bottom of the yacht while Marcy shared with everyone what she knew.

"Eight or ten days ago, maybe not that long, I don't really remember how long ago it was for all of my days run

173

together, it could have been a couple of weeks ago. Seven people were brought on board, all heavily sedated. The woman in the freezer freaked out and started punching and hitting the captors. The others tried to stop her, but the captors, the transporters as we call them, decided to make an example out of her. Word always travels fast when something like that happens. We headed straight for the island, made the delivery and came straight back. We only got back two days before you all took the boat. We just got more provisions the day before."

"What's happening on the island?" Jesse asked, trying to remain calm.

"I don't know. People have been taken there over the years. I don't know who they are, and I don't know what happens to them once they are there. The only reason I know what I do, is, well, let's say I've used my own personal resources to syphon out what little information I have from one of the transporters, which came with a private tour. I keep thinking there has to be a way to escape on the speed boat, but I have never had the opportunity."

"What speed boat?" Pastor asked, reading Jesse's mind.

"It's on the other side of the water garage. All the skis, jet skis that is, and the Chris Craft are on this side. The speed boat and the helicopter are kept on the other."

"Show me," Jesse commanded, getting up off the floor. Marcy did what she was asked and led the group to the other side of the water garage. Once everyone got through a door, separating the two sides, Marcy flipped a breaker, turning on the lights. There it sat. A 42' Lightning, built by Fountain. It shown like it had never seen the water.

"It's pretty fast, I guess," Marcy said breaking the silence. "That's what the gossip is anyway."

The boat had graphics on it that were black, white, grey and hot pink, matching the yacht. Jesse hobbled down the side of it with his fingertips on the hull. The wax was fresh, very slippery. Near the back of the boat were some steps to climb aboard. Jesse helped himself, checking out the offshore racing machine. Walking straight to the captain's chair, Jesse found the switch to raise the engine cover and proceeded to push it.

The cover lifted in two pieces, hinged on each side and lifted in the middle. No one was talking. The only noise heard was the hum coming from the electric motors. When the covers were in their fully upright position, Jesse walked back to check it out.

"Twin ten-seventy-five's" Jesse hollered back to the group. "Supercharged."

"I have no idea what that means," Marcy whispered.

"It has two, one thousand seventy-five horsepower, supercharged engines," Erin replied with a smirk.

"It means it's fast," Pastor added.

Jesse closed the engine covers and made his way back to the group.

"How often did you see Camper on this yacht, Marcy?"

"I've never seen him on this yacht. He didn't like boats. It was mainly used by the transporters and his partner."

"Yeah, about that," Jesse replied while leaving the garage area. "We have no knowledge of Camper having a partner."

"Okay, Jesse!" Marcy replied a little defensively, stopping and putting her hands on her hips and talking with sass. "You can choose to believe what you want. Apparently, everything you *thought* you knew isn't accurate. The way I see it, you *thought* you buried a body that's been in the freezer for days, so maybe, just maybe, you don't have your facts straight."

Jesse stopped in his tracts and turned around slowly, locking eyes with the woman who spoke last. Erin and Pastor held their breath as they hoped Jesse wasn't going to explode again.

"I can already tell," Jesse said, trying to keep things from getting out of control, "you and Erin are going to get along just fine." Jesse looked over at Erin and shot her a wink. The three sighed heavily and followed Jesse back up to the lounge.

That sudden burst of attitude is awfully suspicious, Jesse thought to himself about Marcy's last comment as he left the garage. *Her body language sure did get bold in a hurry.*

Chapter 37

For the next six days, the Castle X yacht cruised at 16 knots, or just over 18 miles per hour. That makes the total journey about nine days, or about twenty-nine hundred miles. Desi and Erin spent that time interviewing every one of the thirty-five crew members, finding out where they were from, what they remembered. What their parents' names were, birthdates, everything that was essential to know for their safe return to their families.

Interestingly enough, about half of the women asked about staying on the yacht as a full-time employee, stating that they had no *home* to go home to. Not knowing how to address that question when it came up, the simple answer was that it would need to be looked into, meaning the Kaiser would have to get involved.

Georgia-Jean spent most of her time with Bourbon. The two of them met all the women in the crew. Georgia-Jean became a mother to every one of them and Bourbon, well, he just became spoiled, even more spoiled than he already was. No one had ever heard of a 'yacht dog' before but Bourbon had certainly earned that title. He loved to run way out on the bow and let the wind blow through his fur. Occasionally, he'd bark at dolphins that made their way to the front of the yacht and jumped out of the water, keeping pace with the vessel, almost as if they were teasing him.

The group became comfortable with each other. The friendship between Erin and Marcy became closer, and they started to trust each other a little more each day. Marcy told Erin everything she knew, and Erin relayed it to

Jesse, Pastor and Desi. Marcy seemed to know a lot, but she didn't know everything. The information she did have was indeed interesting. The information that she provided answered some questions and created a few more.

Pastor and Desi took turns educating Jesse on how to command the massive yacht. Periodically, the US Naval destroyer *Cyclone* made an appearance letting the crew know they were still around. They even fired off a few rounds from one of their deck cannons one night, showing off the destroyer's incredible fire power, *just a training exercise*, of course. To see the flash of light followed by the *boom* from the cannons a few hundred yards away was nothing less than impressive.

Jesse spent a lot of time in his state room, pondering questions that he had no answers to. Whose bodies were mutilated and buried by Pastor, Desi and Erin? How many people are on the island? Are they alive? Are his wife and SEAL team still alive? Why would Camper collect hostages? What is the missing link here? Did Camper have a partner? If so, who is he? Where is he? Camper had a background in military intelligence. He was no fool. Now more than ever, it was becoming obvious why the Kaiser wanted Camper alive. There were a lot of unknowns. It was the unknowns that made Jesse uneasy.

Chapter 38

"Pastor," Jesse shouted as he entered the control room.

"What's our ETA and what's our plan when we get there?"

"Well Jesse," Pastor replied with a sigh, "I don't really have a plan. That's something we need to talk about."

"Well, I'm guessing you can't beach this thing, right?"

"That would be affirmative," Pastor replied with a chuckle.

"That only leaves one option."

"What option is that?"

"I'm going to have to scout out the island from another boat."

"We're set to be within 10 miles of Castle Island around midnight, tonight, maybe a little sooner."

"That's perfect," Jesse replied with a grin.

"Talk to me, Jesse. I'm not following you here."

"Visibility at sea level is only three miles. If you stay off the coast ten or twelve miles, then that provides us with some safety, some cover, a visibility cushion if you will. I can take my inflatable raft to shore while it's dark out and check things out."

"I don't like the sound of this, Jesse. Maybe I should go with you."

"It's a scouting mission, Pastor. What could possibly go wrong?"

"Everything could go wrong, Jesse! You get discovered and captured. You see your wife or SEAL team and blow your cover. You get taken out before you get to the island. Would you like me to go on?"

"I think you're underestimating my capability as a Navy SEAL."

"No, I think your overestimating your ability with your imaginary cape! Holes in your hands, hundreds of stitches, holes through your ankles. Any of this ringing a bell? You're in no condition for a scouting mission!"

"Okay, Pastor," Jesse replied sharply. "When you think of a better plan, you let me know. Until then, I'll be preparing for my mission."

Jesse left the control room, leaving Pastor scratching his head. He didn't have any better ideas and he knew Jesse was right. It was just the thought of it being so close to 'go time' and not knowing what to expect that was certainly driving the tension and uneasy feelings. *We'd better get our plan together fast, Jesse,* Pastor thought to himself. *Midnight will be here before we know it.*

At 11:47pm, Jesse burst through the door to the control room. He was dressed wearing a combat vest with several magazines of ammo, a large knife and two black Colt .45's. His arms and face were covered with black shoe polish and he was wearing a short, black wetsuit underneath.

"Where are your flippers?" Pastor asked with a smirk on his face.

"In the raft," Jesse answered, not seeing the humor in Pastor's question. "What's our position?"

"If your coordinates are correct, we're just about thirteen miles due north of Castle Island."

"Can you pull it up on the GPS?"

"It already is," Pastor replied showing Jesse the GPS screen.

"Are we confident that no one on the island will be able to see the yacht?"

"Absolutely we are!" Pastor replied excitedly. "Watch this!" Pastor reached over to a hidden control panel that he discovered while snooping around and flipped a switch that read *Phantom Mode*. Instantly, all the lights on the yacht went from white to red, making it nearly impossible to be seen at night with the human eye.

"Not bad, huh?" Pastor asked while grinning from ear to ear.

"Makes you wonder why Camper had that feature installed, doesn't it?"

"C'mon, Jesse," Pastor replied with a little sass. "All two hundred million-dollar yachts have a *phantom mode*, right?"

"Yeah, I'll bet."

"You ready to do this?"

"Yeah," Jesse answered with confidence, while handing Pastor a radio. "Here's the two-way radio. It has a range of 20 miles. Don't break radio silence for any reason at all. I'll contact you if I need to. You copy?"

"I hear you, Commander."

"I'll see you in a few hours, Pastor."

With that, Jesse was gone to scout out Castle Island, and hopefully find his wife and SEAL team still alive.

Nine hours had passed, and nothing was heard from Jesse. The sun was now shining bright and Pastor could get a visual on the island through a pair of binoculars. Erin and Desi had come up to the control room with growing concerns about his safety, thinking for sure they would have heard something by now. Knowing Jesse was the best of the best, and since it'd been such a long time, they all thought a courtesy call would have been nice.

"I'm sure Jesse is fine, ladies," Pastor re-assured them. "No news is good news."

"Knock, knock," Marcy said quietly as she tapped on the door to the control room.

"It's open," Erin told her, waving her to come on in. "Is everything all right?"

"Yeah, I believe so." Marcy replied cautiously. "Some of the crew, and myself also, were just kind of wondering why we've stopped."

"We stopped here because we didn't want to get too close to Castle Island and be discovered."

"Do you know where we're at?" Marcy asked again, very cautiously.

"Yeah," Pastor replied with confidence. We're about thirteen miles off the island's coast. Here, come see for yourself."

Marcy made her way to the GPS screen and examined it carefully. Cautious not to ruffle any tailfeathers, she worded her next question very carefully.

"What led you to believe that this island is Castle Island?"

Pastor, Desi and Erin all looked at each other and then over at Marcy, stunned with the question she just asked.

"What do you know that you're not sharing with us?"

"Well," Marcy continued, again very cautiously and choosing her words very wisely, "I think Castle Island is here." She said looking at Pastor while hitting the zoom out button on the GPS screen. "It's about 50 miles south of us. This island right here," Marcy continued while she pointed to the screen, "where we're at now, is where the Captain anchored the yacht because the water surrounding Castle Island is too deep to anchor at. There are cliffs surrounding the entire island. The only way to get on it is by helicopter."

"This would have been great information to share before now!" Desi shouted in disbelief.

"You all told me that you knew where we were going. Who was I to question you?"

"Look here," Marcy said to Pastor, pointing back to the GPS screen again. "You can anchor about five hundred feet off of this island and regroup there."

"How do you know all of this, Marcy?" Erin questioned, impressed with her knowledge.

"I've done what I've had to do to survive while trapped on this boat. Over time, I'd get a little piece of information here, a little piece there, and start to connect the dots."

"Something's not right," Jesse shouted as he came busting through the door to the control room, startling everyone.

"Nice of you to check in with us, Jesse!" Erin shouted back.

"What's the deal, Commander?" Desi added. "That's not protocol, and you know it."

"I was in no danger – this island is completely deserted. I've hiked every inch of it and there isn't so much as a foot print on it, other than my own now."

"Well, Jesse…" Pastor replied with a cautious sigh.

"What's she doing in here?" Jesse immediately interrupted, asking about Marcy.

"Sharing information that we should have asked her about sooner." Pastor continued.

"What?"

"Tell him what you know," Erin said to Marcy calmly. "It's okay."

Marcy debriefed Jesse, to the best of her knowledge. Jesse nodded his head while the dots were connecting. "That's why Camper told me I'd never find his island," Jesse said to the others. "Makes perfect sense. Thank you, Marcy," Jesse said, leaving the room in a hurry.

"Jesse!" Erin shouted, "where are you going?"

"For another boat ride!" Jesse shouted over his shoulder, disappearing out of sight.

"What do we do?" Desi asked the group. "Think we should stop him?"

"That ain't gonna happen," Pastor replied, wondering what Jesse was thinking.

"Marcy," Pastor ordered, "show Desi where to anchor this thing. Erin, contact Captain Ted Thomas with the US Navy on the UHF radio and put them on alert. I'll go talk to Jesse."

Pastor hurried down to the bottom of the yacht but, before he could catch Jesse, the 42' Fountain was backing out of the water garage.

"Jesse! Jesse!" Pastor yelled while making eye contact with the former Navy SEAL, but Jesse ignored him. On a mission to learn the truth about his wife and SEAL team, Jesse was stopping for no one.

The powerful supercharged V8's revved up fast as Jesse thrust the throttles forward. The Fountain was on plane in seconds and was headed south in a hurry, leaving Pastor with an uneasy feeling in his stomach.

"Don't get killed, Jesse," Pastor said out loud to himself as the Fountain disappeared in the horizon.

"WHOA! WOOHOO!!" Jesse screamed at the top of his lungs, grinning from ear to ear, totally impressed with the sport boats super high performance.

"I KNOW YOU'RE ALIVE, KARMA! I CAN FEEL YOU! I'M COMING TO GET YOU, LOVE! HANG IN THERE – I'M ON MY WAY!!

"Castle X yacht, come in, over. Castle X yacht, do you copy?" was heard on the UHF radio. Erin grabbed the mic and responded immediately.

"This is Castle X yacht, identify yourself."

"This is Captain Ted Thomas on the U.S. Naval destroyer *Cyclone*; We're tracking a high-speed boat at over 140 mph. Should we engage?"

"Negative! Do not engage!!" Pastor yelled entering the control room.

"That would be a negative, Captain. Please do not…"

"Give me that mic," Pastor shouted, snatching it out of Erin's hands abruptly. "Ted, this is Pastor, do you copy?"

"Go ahead, Pastor."

"Navy SEAL Commander Jesse Buck is driving that boat. Do not engage, repeat. Former SEAL Commander Jesse Buck is piloting the speed boat, copy?"

"Are you shitting me, Pastor? Commander Buck is on that boat?"

185

"That's affirmative, Ted." Pastor replied, in almost as much shock as Captain Ted was.

"That guy's a legend, Pastor. A real American badass!"

"I can promise you Ted, he's the real deal."

"How is Commander Buck wrapped up in all of this, Pastor? What the hell is going on over there?"

"Ted, you know that's classified, even for you, old friend. I need you to watch that boat with a keen eye and if anything happens to it at all, I need you to intervene."

"Copy that, Pastor." Captain Ted replied. "Nothing happens to Commander Buck on my shift! Standby."

Jesse ran the boat hard with RPM's soaring right up against redline. The powerful performance machine danced over the eight-foot swells like they were nothing, launching the boat completely into air, literally jumping over every other one. In less than twelve minutes Jesse had a visual of Castle Island. It was much bigger than the island he checked out previously. Wanting to get a look at its size from the water, Jesse decided to keep the island to his starboard side and make a lengthy loop around it.

"Sir, I'm tracking a high-speed object on radar about seven miles away, sir." Man one said to man two.

"Sink it," man two ordered.

"We don't have cannons on that side of the island, sir."

"Follow it on radar. When it comes into range of one of our cannons, sink it."

"Copy that, sir."

As Jesse circled the island, he examined it with a keen eye through a pair of binoculars. The island seemed to rise out of the water like a mountain with cliffs on every side, no beach anywhere. There were rock formations that also rose out of the water, almost like towers that encircled the island. *Those would make perfect lookouts* Jesse thought to himself as he continued to scan the coast.

On the south side of the island Jesse headed west, still nothing but cliffs. Jesse backed off the throttles and steered a little closer to the island to get a better look.

"Sir!" Man one said to man two, "the boat appears to be circling us, sir."

"Is he in range yet?"

"Negative, sir. However, if he keeps on his present path and continues to circle the island, he will be in approximately ninety seconds, sir.

"As soon as he's in range of one of the cannons, vaporize him."

"Consider it done, sir."

"*It looks pretty peaceful from here,* Jesse thought to himself, now only a couple of miles off the coast, still with nowhere to beach the boat.

Flash!

Jesse noticed something out of the corner of his eye, like a reflection off something, and he pulled the throttles back even more, now cruising about fifty mph.

"He's in range, sir," man two said to man one.

"You have your orders. You know what to do."

Chapter 39

"What's going on, Pastor?" Desi asked reentering the control room of the yacht. "Have you heard anything?"

"Negative, Desi," Pastor replied with one ear tuned to the UHF radio. "Nothing from the Navy; nothing from Jesse."

"What should we do?"

"No news is good news, Desi. We wait."

"That's crap!" Erin replied, storming out of the room.

"I agree with Erin. We can't just sit here and wait!"

"Unfortunately, ladies," Pastor replied, now only to Desi in the control room, "that's all we can do."

"What kind of game are you playing here, Pastor!" Desi shouted, jumping out of her chair. "Jesse needs some help. For all we know he's headed straight into hell!"

"You don't know that, Desi," Pastor confirmed very calmly. "Besides, Jesse brought this on himself! Until we hear from him or the Navy, we do nothing but wait."

"He could be dead by then!"

"STAND DOWN, DESI!" Pastor shouted aggressively. "WE DON'T KNOW ENOUGH ABOUT WHAT'S GOING ON TO DO ANYTHING AND IF SOMETHING WERE HAPPENING -WE HAVE NO WAY TO HELP!"

"But, Pastor…"

"I SAID STAND DOWN, DESDEMONA, AND THAT'S AN ORDER!"

"SCREW YOU, PASTOR!" Desi screamed as she stormed out of the control room.

"WE KNOW NOTHING!" Pastor shouted as Desi disappeared. "I can't make a call if I have no information to base it on," Pastor said out loud to himself, disgusted with what just went down.

With no better plan, Pastor reached for the mic on the UHF radio. "Ted, this is Pastor, you copy?"

"A little informal there, aren't we old friend?"

"Ted, we know nothing about Jesse and his whereabouts. What can you tell us?"

"Relax, Pastor. We've got him on radar. Nothing's happened. Everything's fine."

Chapter 40

You're a sitting duck out here, Buck, Jesse thought to himself. *You'd better get a move on.* Jesse slammed the throttles forward, launching the Fountain across the water. *BOOM!*

Just feet behind the Fountain was an explosion that sent Jesse to the floor of the boat, knocking the throttles into the neutral position at the same time. A storm of water rained down upon Jesse, soaking him and the inside of the Fountain.

"We missed him, sir!" man one said to man two.

"Reload and fire again!" man two shouted. "Don't miss him this time!"

"Captain Thomas, sir!" Shouted the radar technician on duty at the time. "Shots fired from the island at the speed boat, sir!"

"Can you trace the origin, lieutenant?"

"I think so, sir!"

"Trace the origin and take it out. I want total annihilation!"

"Sir, yes sir!"

"Pastor, this is Ted, copy?"

"Go ahead, Ted"

"Pastor, we have confirmation of shots fired from the island. We are taking evasive actions, over."

"Holy cow that was close!" Jesse shouted to himself as he climbed back to his feet, grabbing the steering wheel of the boat. "Think, Buck, think!" Jesse said to himself, slamming the throttles forward again.

BOOM!

A second mortar exploded, again just feet behind the Fountain, this time not only knocking Jesse to the floor but also stalling out the engines.

"Sir, we missed again, sir!" shouted man one to man two.

"Get out of the way, you clown!" man two shouted back, shoving man one to the side. "I'll take him out myself!"

"Doc!" Karma whispered, smacking Doc on the leg. "What was that noise, Doc?"

"That, Karma was a mortar from a Howitzer cannon!"

"What does that mean?" Karma asked, jumping to her feet.

"That means Jesse's here!" Recon shouted. "Be alert! Be alert! Jesse's here, and it's about to get real!"

"We don't know that, Recon," Hack fired back immediately. "These thugs could be shooting at anything, or just for fun."

"Karma," Doc ordered, "very quietly, let your parents know it *could* be 'go' time. Have them relay the message to the others, be careful not to get caught. We don't want the guards to see us stirring about. Right now, there are only shots fired and it could be nothing. The instant mortars hit the island, we're breaking out of this cage, got it?"

Karma nodded in a very nonchalant manner and did as she was told. Hearts pounded and tensions were high; suddenly out of nowhere, prayers of being rescued were about to be answered.

It just got real, Buck. Head for the island! Jesse thought to himself, getting his bearings for the second time. Jesse cranked on the boat engines. They kept turning over but wouldn't start.

"C'mon, C'mon! Start!" Jesse yelled to the boat. Suddenly engine one fired up. Jesse pushed the throttle up about halfway – still cranking on engine number two. Precious seconds passed until finally Jesse heard it - *Whoom!*

With engine two fired, he mashed both throttles to full speed - nearly launching the Fountain out of the water.

"YOU WANT A PIECE OF ME!" Jesse screamed with anger as he steered straight for the cliffs of Castle Island. "COME AND GET ME!" The Fountain accelerated like a rocket across the water with nothing between Jesse and the island but waves. "C'MON!" Jesse shouted!
BOOM!

"That's a direct hit, Captain!" shouted the radar lieutenant. "That threat has been eliminated!"

"Eliminate it again," Captain Thomas ordered, "Just for fun!"

"You hear that, Karma?!" Recon shouted from the other side of the cage. "It's 'go' time!" Twenty men locked hands on the steel bars that kept them caged and pulled against them with everything they had. Ten pulling in one direction and ten pulling in the other, they used every muscle, they had among them to try to bend the two-inch wrought steel bars that kept them caged like animals.

"C'mon! Pull!" Doc yelled with ferocity.

"Karma, look!" Savannah pointed excitedly. "They're doing it – they're bending the steel!"

Get out of the boat, Buck! Get out of the boat! Jump!!
Do it now!!! Jesse thought to himself as the Fountain sped
toward the cliffs of Castle Island at triple digit speeds.

Dive, Buck, Dive! Get out of the boat now!!

KA-BOOM!

"Captain Ted, sir!" shouted the lieutenant. "Castle
Island has a second cannon, sir. The speed boat has just
been eliminated! It disappeared off the radar screen, sir!"

"Take that cannon out now, Lieutenant! Get me a SAT
image of this island immediately! I want every threat on it
destroyed!"

"Sir, yes, sir!"

"Pastor, this is Ted, do you copy?"

"Copy Ted, go ahead."

"Pastor, the speed boat has been eliminated."

"What?" Pastor shouted. "What about Buck?"

"Pastor, I have no confirmation about Buck's well-
being. He could be alive; he could be dead."

"Judas, Ted!" Pastor shouted, stomping around the
control room. "Judas!!"

"Pastor, you copy?"

"JUDAS!" Pastor shouted out loud. *Buck's been
through a hell of a lot worse than this. I don't believe he's
dead!* Pastor thought to himself while pondering the answer
to Captain Ted's question.

"Standby, Ted"

"Copy that, Pastor."

"Sir!" man one shouted to man two. "The speed boat has
been eliminated, sir!"

"Good." man two replied with a nervous voice. "Any
sign of Camper's yacht?"

193

"Negative, sir. Nothing is showing on radar."

"Get the other four guards and bring the hostages inside. If you get any grief from any of them. Kill 'em and throw them over the cliff."

"Yes, sir!"

Chapter 41

Jesse dove as deep as he could into the pure blue water of the ocean while boat parts rained down from the explosion. Pieces of fiberglass and metal came crashing down into the water from several hundred feet above, some of them narrowly missing him. When he could no longer hold his breath, Jesse thrust to the surface breaking into the air.

"Whoa!" Looking around for anything floating, Jesse spotted a PFD, a personal flotation device, floating on the surface about a hundred feet away from him and swam over to it. He laid it under his chest and began to swim toward the rock cliffs ahead. *Couldn't be more than a mile or so away*, he thought to himself.

The distance suddenly didn't matter. The only thing that mattered was whether or not his beloved wife Rachael was still alive. If she was alive, then his whole SEAL team may still be alive for sure. These thoughts were the motivation for him to overcome the pain from his injuries and swim as hard and as fast as he could.

Chapter 42

"Just a little more!" Doc encouraged, knowing the men didn't have the strength to keep pulling as hard as they were for very much longer. "We're almost there!"

"We're good! Recon shouted. "We're there!"

"Teams of two, let's go, let's go!" Hack instructed, "Run to the north end of the island and hide!"

"Recon," Doc ordered sternly. "Do not leave Karma and her parents alone, at all."

"Copy that."

"Savannah, you ready for this?"

"Let's do it!"

Hack, Doc and Savannah hid in the bushes around the exterior of the cage and waited for the guards to show up, knowing they would. The "cage," as it came to be known, was an outdoor prison where over the years thirty-seven GHOST agents had been captured and held hostage. The perimeter consisted of two-inch-thick, wrought steel bars only twelve inches apart that were welded to a top plate and a bottom plate. The same two-inch bars spanned across the top and were covered with nothing more than palm leaves to keep the sun and weather off. The floor was dirt. There were no lights. There was no running water, no walls, no heat, no air conditioning, no nothing.

Most of the time the GHOSTS were caged like animals. If anyone attempted to break out, they were shot and their bodies tossed over the cliff into the ocean. The pounding of the waves against the jagged rocks would shred the bodies in minutes, providing quite a buffet for the local nibblers to devour. Thirty-seven GHOST agents had been captured over the years; twenty-seven were still alive.

Rice was served in the morning and on most days in the evening to eat. Once in a great while it would be accompanied with a vegetable or some kind of unknown meat. Strangely enough, there was always plenty of bottled water provided to drink. No one knew why they were being kept alive; no one knew why they just weren't killed off. *Pow, pow, pow... pow, pow* could be heard in the distance behind them as the group of twenty-four made their way to north end of the island.

"Only five shots," Recon said to Karma. "That's a good sign."

"There were six guards."

"I'm not worried about one guard right now," Recon confessed. "Our job is to build a fire, and that's what we're gonna do."

"Pastor, this is Ted, do you copy?"

"Go ahead, Ted."

"I am still waiting for instructions, copy?"

"We're moving the yacht in towards the island, Ted. We're going after Buck."

"That's a dangerous move, Pastor. You don't know what threats are out there."

"My job is to look after my team, Ted. Your job is to neutralize the threats."

"That was a lot easier than I thought it was gonna be," Savannah said as she picked up a rifle from one of the dead guards.

"It's pretty easy to fight back when you're not caged like an animal," Hack added.

"Focus guys," Doc ordered with a soft voice. "There is still one more thug on this island that we know of. There could be more."

The group of three headed toward the mansion to seek out the last of their captures. The mansion was not really a mansion at all. It was merely an enclosed version of the cage, with living quarters in the back for their keepers. There was a shower room and a few picnic tables to eat at.

The GHOSTS were only allowed in there periodically to clean up and when the weather got severe, which was rare. The one perk of being held hostage on an island in the South Pacific is that every day is a perfect 80-degree day.

"Captain Thomas, sir. Here is the satellite imagery of the island that you requested."

"Thank you, Lieutenant." Captain Thomas examined the image. "I count one, two, three, four, cannons surrounding the island perimeter, Lieutenant. Why haven't we taken all of these out?"

"We only knew where two of them were located, based on the location of shots fired, sir."

"Get rid of the other two, now."

"Sir, yes sir."

SLAM!

Jesse was slammed into the rock cliff from the ocean waves like a rag doll. Not being able to grab onto the rocks he fell back into the water where the waves picked him up and slammed him into the cliff again. This time Jesse was able to cling to a rock with the fingertips of his left hand. He struggled to not lose his grip and finally swung his right hand over to grab onto the cliff.

SLAM!

As another wave crashed into him, Jesse once again fell back into the water, only to start his climb all over again.

"C'mon, Buck, climb this wall!" Jesse shouted to himself. "Climb it!" Jesse focused hard and instead of fighting with the next wave, Jesse let the wave bring him to the wall. He prepared for the crash into it and was able to hold on. The rocks on the cliff were jagged and sharp.

They were slippery from the salty water and it was a long way to the top. Carefully choosing his footing and the placement of his hands, Jesse was able to climb out of the way of the following wave. With the wave crashing just feet below him, he could now focus on climbing.

BOOM! BOOM!! BOOM!!!

Explosions just a few hundred feet away from Jesse caused him to lose his grip and fall nearly sixty feet back down into the ocean below.

"Are you kidding me!" Jesse shouted as he focused on grabbing onto the wall one more time.

"Captain, target one destroyed, sir. Will update when target two has been destroyed.

"Nicely done, Lieutenant," Captain Thomas replied with a smile. "Keep me posted."

"Captain Thomas, copy?" Pastor said over the radio.

"Go ahead Pastor."

"What's your twenty, Ted?"

"We're six miles north, north-west of Castle Island, Pastor. Where are you?"

"Check your nine o'clock," Pastor replied with a grin. Captain Thomas grabbed his binoculars and looked due east to see the Castle X yacht floating just a couple miles away.

"You should be watching your radar a little more closely, Ted."

"Don't get any closer, Pastor. We're not done over here."

"Copy that, Ted."

"What's that noise?" Savannah asked Hack as they headed around to the back of the mansion.

"Look, over there!" Hack shouted as a helicopter was lifting off from the island. "He's running!"

Doc opened fire on the chopper hoping to damage it and send it into the ocean. Savannah and Hack joined in, spraying heavy amounts of lead at the whirly bird, but it was too far away. No real damage could be done.

"Captain Thomas, sir, we have an unidentified bogy fleeing the island, sir."

Grabbing the mic to the radio, Captain Thomas shouted for Pastor. "Pastor, we've got an airborne runner leaving the island at a high rate of speed.

"Take it out, Ted, take it out!"

"Did you hear that, Lieutenant?"

"No way he lives, Captain."

Out of ammo, Hack, Doc and Savannah watch the helicopter get further and further away. "Where is he going?" Savannah asked

"I have no idea…."

BOOM! BOOM! BOOM! were the shots fired from the destroyer, stopping Doc in mid-sentence.

KA-BOOM!!! went the helicopter. Exploding into a million pieces, nothing but debris fell into the water below. Doc, Hack and Savannah cheered wildly at the sight of their last guardian's descent into hell.

"Look!" Hack shouted as he pointed north. "The Navy's here!"

"You know what that means," Doc replied with a smile.

"That means Recon was right. Jesse's here too!"

"Let's get to the others!"

The party of three double-timed it to the other end of the island where the others were hiding, knowing in their hearts that Jesse was on his way.

"Pastor, Captain Ted Thomas here, copy."

"Go ahead, Ted."

"The known threats have been eliminated, repeat. All cannons on the island, as well as the bogy have been eliminated."

"Copy that, Ted. Please circle the island for visual report."

"Copy that, Pastor, we're on it."

Captain Ted Thomas steered the destroyer down the west side of the island to circle it, keeping an eye out for anything that might be useful information.

BEEP, BEEP, BEEP, flashed a red light as an audio alert signaled on the control panel of the Castle X yacht.

"Starboard bay door?" Pastor questioned out load. "What's going on?"

"Desi, go check this out!"

"No need to be alarmed, Pastor. Erin's taking the helicopter for a ride."

"What do you mean she's taking the helicopter for a ride? Who's flying that thing?"

"She is, Pastor, you know that." Desi replied calmly, knowing Erin had everything under control.

"Where is she going?"

"Pastor, look out the window."

Pastor grabbed the binoculars and started to scan the island. A cloud of thick white smoke was lifting into the air.

"Erin's going to get your team and bring them back," Desi continued with a smile.

A single tear fell from Pastor's eye as he watched the small six passenger chopper head straight for the column of smoke rising into the air.

"AAHHH!" Jesse screamed out loud. "C'mon Buck, you're feet from the top!" Exhausted, with bloody fingertips and a blood-soaked vest, Jesse dug deep to find the energy and the strength to clear the top of the cliff. Most of the stitches under his bandages had been torn open, soaking his vest with his blood. Failure now meant a three-hundred-foot fall to his death.

"I got you!" Recon shouted as he leaned over the edge of the cliff and grabbed Jesse by the wrist. "It's damn good to see you, Commander!" Recon said as he pulled Jesse up over the edge. The two former SEALS gave each other a hug.

"It's damn good to see you too, Recon."

"KARMA!" Recon shouted at the top of his lungs.

"Someone's here to see you!"

Karma got up off the ground and looked over at Recon, who moved out of the way so she could see her man. She sprinted over to Jesse, jumping over people on the way. Jesse, only able to get to his knees, held his arms open as his wife threw herself into his arms. Uncontrollable tears fell from their eyes as they embraced.

"I sure am getting tired of burying you, Mrs. Buck!" Jesse managed to get out through the tears.

"It's about time you showed up, Mr. Buck" Karma replied with her playful sass just before she laid a kiss on her beloved husband. The group of onlookers cheered wildly as they could all feel the love Jesse and Rachael shared for each other.

Chapter 43

"Jesse, you're a mess. Are you okay?" Karma asked, looking her husband over after their kiss.

"I am now, Rachael."

"Oh, Jesse. I love you. I love you so much!"

"I will never leave your side again, Rachael. Never!"

Vaaaarrooooommmm! went the helicopter over their heads.

"Pastor, this is Erin." Erin said over the radio. "I have a visual. Repeat, I found them, Pastor. I found them!"

"You know what to do, Erin," Pastor replied. "I'll get the Champagne ready."

"Pastor, you copy?"

"Go ahead, Erin."

"There are a bunch of people down there, it'll take a couple of trips."

"Who's flying ghetto bird?" Recon asked kneeling down next to Jesse.

"I have no idea."

"Don't you have a radio with you?"

"I did. It's at the bottom of the ocean now," Jesse replied while standing up on his feet. "Recon," Jesse commanded, "forget about the chopper. Fill me in. Where are Hack and Doc? Where is Savannah?"

"Everyone is accounted for, Jesse. Even Karma's parents are here." Recon said pointing to a couple sitting on the ground about fifty feet away.

"What?" Jesse asked, looking at Karma. "How can that be?"

"Jesse," Karma said while pulling gently on his hand.

"Ouch, ouch, ouch!" Jesse shot out pulling his hand from Karma's.

"What the matter, Buck?" Karma asked while gently picking up Jesse's hand and looking at it, seeing the wound from the hole through it.

"Oh my God, Jesse, what happened to you?"

"I had a bit of a religious experience," Jesse replied, showing her both of his hands. A look of horror came across Karma's face and tears fell from her eyes.

"I'm okay, Rachael" Jesse assured her. "I really am okay. Introduce me to your parents."

Rachael gently put her arm through Jesse's and led him over to where her parents were. Holly and Warren Meyer got up off the ground to meet the man they had heard so much about.

"Jesse," Karma said with a soft voice. "I'd like you to meet my parents, Holly and Warren Meyer." The emotion was overwhelming. Karma broke down into tears when she heard what she had just said. For so many years she thought her parents were dead, and now she was introducing them to the man of her dreams. She had to wait a minute before she could continue the introduction, just to regain her composure.

"Mom, Dad." Karma barely got out without breaking down again, "This is my husband…"
"Commander Buck," Warren interrupted, reaching out to shake Jesse's bleeding hand. It's an honor to be in your presence, sir."

"I don't know about all that, Mr. Meyer, but it's a pleasure to meet you."

"Mr. Buck, now is not the time. However, we should really have a conversation. It's an absolute honor for you to be married to our daughter, Rachael, and if I may, I'd like to call you, Son."

"The honor, Mr. Meyer, is all mine. I love your daughter with all of my heart, and I promise you I'll never leave her side again."

"I know who you are, Jesse. You have our blessing."

Jesse eyeballed Rachael's father, sizing him up. He seemed sincere enough, but still, something was a little off, maybe just a case of island fever, maybe, not.

"Jesse, this is Rachael's mother, Holly."

"It's a pleasure to meet you, Jesse." Holly said while walking up to give Jesse a hug, even in the condition he was in, Holly didn't seem to mind.

"How is it, Mr. Meyer, that both you and Mrs. Meyer are trapped on this island?" Jesse asked very cautiously.

"Jesse, my son, we're here for the same reason you are," Warren answered with authority. "We're all GHOSTS."

Chapter 44

Dust and debris were blown in every direction as Erin found a relatively safe place to land the helicopter. Not knowing who she was at first, Hack, Savannah and Doc had beads locked on their target until they recognized the pilot.

"A little jumpy for a couple of SEALs, aren't you guys?" Erin shouted as she got out of the aircraft.

"I'm not a SEAL!" Savannah shouted back, dropping her weapon and running up to Erin to give her a hug.

"Savannah!" Erin said excitedly. "Look at you, marching around with a fully automatic rifle."

"I know how to use it, too!"

"You be careful where you point that thing."

"Buck must have sent you here to get us, didn't he?" Doc asked while giving Erin a hug. With a somber look on her face, Erin stepped back and answered honestly. "Jesse's boat was taken out by the cannons while he was surveying the island. We don't know…"

"Hey!" Jesse shouted through the trees while standing hand in hand with Karma, next to her parents. "You gonna fly us out of here or what?"

"Jesse, you're alive!" Erin shouted as she ran over to give him a hug.

"Of course, I'm alive." Jesse told her giving her a gentle hug back. "You should know by now I'm not that easy to kill."

"Where's my hug, girl?"

"Karma!" Erin shouted as the tears began to fall from everyone's eyes. Hugs were passed around and emotions were flowing freely. Not being able to hold silent, Jesse finally asked Erin "Where did you learn how to fly a helicopter?"

"I flew Apaches during the war in Iraq." Erin answered as if Jesse should have already known.

"You're an Apache pilot?"

"The best there ever was!" Erin fired back with attitude. "Don't you forget it, either!"

"Pastor and I really need to work on our communication."

"How many people are here?" Erin asked.

"Twenty-seven or so," Karma answered, pointing around to the group. "How many can you take at a time?"

"I can take five at a time. Why don't you, Jesse and three others come with me first?"

"Negative!" Jesse commanded. "No one gets left behind on my shift. I'm the last to go. Take Karma and her parents first, along with two others."

"Negative!" Karma replied assertively. "I don't leave Jesse's side. If he goes last, then I go last."

"Doc, Recon!" Jesse commanded. "Organize the rest of the team into groups of five for immediate departure. You two leave before me. Karma, her parents and I will make the final trip off the island. Fall out!"

"The rest of the team?" Recon asked a little puzzled.

"Yes, Recon. The rest of the team. If we're all GHOSTS, we are all one team. Fall out!"

"Copy that, Commander!"

"Hack!" Jesse shouted over the rest of the group. Hack came running over and was eager to obey any order given to him from his commander. "I'm sorry about Barbara, Hack. I heard what happened."

"They killed her right in front of us, Commander, in cold blood." Jesse gave his teammate a man hug.

"Who did it, Hack? Who broke her neck?"

"That jerk-water, Captain, sir."

"Are you sure it was him?"

"Captain McQue did it, of course, I'm sure."

"He's dead now, Hack. We fed him to the fish."

"Thank you, Commander," Hack replied with a soft voice, hugging Jesse like a bear.

"Hack, you and Savannah get off the island. Get to the yacht. Tell Pastor and Georgia-Jean what's going on…."

"No sir," Hack interrupted. "Send Recon with Savannah. I'll stay here with you."

"Very well, Hack. Get it done."

Chapter 45

"Pastor, you copy?"

"Go ahead, Ted."

"The island is secure; all threats have been eliminated. I see white smoke. You know anything about this?"

"That's affirmative, Ted. We sent a team member to the island in a small helicopter to pick up the hostages when we discovered the smoke. It looks to be clear at this time."

"You want us to hang out for a bit, Pastor?"

"Why don't you, just to play it safe, Ted."

"Any word on Commander Buck?"

"That's a negative. I haven't heard anything yet, Ted. Pray for the best."

"Copy that, Pastor."

Chapter 46

As Erin swung the helicopter around to land on the rear heli-pad of the Castle X yacht, Pastor and Desi were quick to see who was on board. First off were Savannah and Recon, followed by three other persons. Erin was quick to fly off as the five were greeted with smiles.

"Recon, Savannah. It's good to see both of you," Pastor started with a man-hug for Recon. "What can you tell us?"

"Pastor, these people need a real shower and a real meal. There are twenty-seven or so GHOST agents on the island that Erin will be bringing back. Some of them have been hostages for decades.

"Hi, my name is Desi," she said to the three GHOSTS. "Come with me. I'll get you to your own private rooms immediately. We'll get you taken care of." Desi led the three GHOSTS off and Recon, Savannah and Pastor continued their conversation.

"Have you seen Jesse?" Pastor asked first and foremost.

"Yeah." Recon replied with a smile. "He's a little beat up, but he'll be okay."

"Karma?"

"We're all good, Pastor."

"Everyone except Barbara." Savannah added.

"We know about Barbara. We'll deal with that when everyone gets to the yacht."

"What can we do to help, Pastor?" asked Recon. "Jesse told us to get Georgia-Jean involved and start making food. We're to help people get cleaned up and…"

"Let's get Marcy involved. She'll know exactly what to do. Between her, Georgia-Jean and Desi we'll get you all settled."

"I really, really, need a shower. Like, in the worst way," Savannah said tearing up.

"Recon, you know Jesse is going to want to have a meeting as soon as he gets back here."

"He needs to, Pastor." Everyone on that island is a GHOST. There are a lot of questions to be answered."

"Recon, Savannah?" Marcy asked walking right into the conversation. "Desi asked me to come show you to a room so you can get cleaned up. If you'll follow me, please?"

"Go on," Pastor said with a smile. "Go get a shower."

Pastor watched Recon and Savannah leave with Marcy. They looked a little tired, but all things considered seemed to be in pretty good shape. Pastor made his way back to the control room with questions spinning through his head. There certainly did need to be an immediate debriefing, there were way too many missing pieces. Too many unanswered questions that needed to be addressed.

"Captain Ted Thomas, do you copy?"

"This is Captain Thomas. Go ahead, Pastor."

"Buck is alive, repeat. Commander Jesse Buck has been accounted for."

"I don't believe it, Pastor," Captain Thomas said with relief in his voice. "That guy must have nine lives."

"A hell of a lot more than nine, Ted."

"We'll stand by until otherwise instructed."

"Copy that, Ted."

Chapter 47

Erin wasted no time with the transportation of the passengers. As she left the island with the third load, Jesse walked up behind a familiar face.

"Kurtis!" Jesse shouted, startling the man that looked like he'd seen better days. "How are you doing my friend?" Jesse held out his hand to help him up off the island floor. Kurtis, glad to see Jesse, stood up and responded with a gentle man hug.

"I don't think I want to play in your sandbox anymore, Jesse." Jesse chuckled.

"Not always an island of paradise, is it?"

"This is certainly not my game, and I don't want to play it anymore."

"I'm glad you're alive, Kurtis. Your wife must be going crazy. We'll get you in touch with her once we're back on the yacht."

"Thank you, Jesse."

"I'm sorry you had to go through this, Kurtis. It wasn't part of the plan."

"Seeing you here, helps a lot."

"In a few days, this will all be nothing more than a bad dream."

"You mean a nightmare."

The two men gave another man hug and Kurtis was on the next flight to the yacht. Not long thereafter, Erin was landing on Castle Island for the very last time. Jesse, Karma and Karma's parents climbed aboard in silence and watched as Erin lifted off the ground with effortless precision of the aircraft.

"Does this radio work?" Jesse asked Erin while reaching for the handset. "Can I reach Pastor on this thing?"

"Just key the mic."

"Pastor, this is Jesse, copy?"

"Good to hear from you, Commander. What can I do for you?"

"Tell your Navy buddies to destroy the island."

"Come back, Jesse? Destroy the island?"

"Affirmative, Pastor. Level it. Burn it. Destroy it. Everything they have. Blow it off the map."

"You don't want to keep it? Not staying there anymore?"

"I'm keeping the yacht. Burn the island down."

"You got it, Commander."

Pastor jumped on the radio and informed Captain Thomas of the new plan, target practice on Castle Island. A little overzealous, Captain Thomas did exactly that. The destroyer sent hundreds of rounds of missiles and mortars into the island until the entire thing was a raging inferno. The show was quite spectacular from the air and when Erin landed the helicopter on the Castle X yacht, everyone on it was clapping and cheering, watching the show in the background.

"You do know how to make an entrance, don't you Mr. Buck."

"That wasn't for me, Karma. That was for everyone else."

Chapter 48

The crowd that greeted the party on the last flight was amazing. Almost everyone on the boat was cheering for Jesse and Karma. Hugs were given to Erin from total strangers and *thank you's* filled the air. Pastor and Desi helped move everyone down to the main lounge area where the crew had put together the most incredible buffet that many had ever seen. To no one's surprise, Savannah and Bourbon had found each other, and Bourbon was eager to show Savannah how much he missed her.

"Ladies and Gentlemen," Jesse shouted above the crowd. "Ladies and Gentlemen." As soon as the crowd silenced, Jesse began talking.

"Everyone should have their own state room by now, is that correct?"

Marcy nodded her head from the other side of the room while many in the group answered with a *yes*.

"If for some reason there are not enough state rooms to go around, let me know. Some of my team and I can bunk together."

"Mr. Buck," a man said loudly, stepping forward from the crowd. "Mr. Buck, you don't know me. My name is Rich Nelson, former Army intelligence and black ops commander. If you don't mind my saying so sir, from where I'm standing, we're all part of your team now."

All the GHOST agents clapped and whistled, cheering wildly. Tears of joy fell from some of their eyes while others chuckled with emotion.

"Mr. Buck," Marcy shouted from the back of the room. "Everyone has their own state room, sir. You and your wife don't have to share."

"I have a lot of questions," Jesse continued. "I want to talk with everyone. However, the rest of today and tonight are for celebrating." Everyone on the boat burst out into cheers one more time. The crew cheered for the rescued GHOSTs and the rescued GHOSTs cheered for their rescue.

"Eat, drink, socialize," Jesse continued. "You are all safe. The crew is no longer captive on the yacht and the GHOSTs are no longer captive on the island. The Castle X yacht is no longer a slave ship!"

The emotions that filled the room were intense. Laughter, tears of joy, clapping – it was an amazing sight. A successful mission beyond everyone's imagination, but a mission that Jesse feared was yet to be over.

"Hack," Jesse shouted, over to his friend at the buffet, "can I see you for a moment?"

With plate in hand, Hack walked straight over to Jesse.

"Yes, Commander, what's up?"

"Will you and Erin fill a couple of plates for Karma and me and meet us in our state room immediately?"

"Absolutely, Commander. Is everything all right?"

"Just do it, and please tell Georgia-Jean to come with a first aid kit. I need some sutures."

"I'm on it, Commander."

"Mr. and Mrs. Meyer," Jesse said to Karma's parents, "if you'll…"

"Stop right there, Commander," Warren interrupted Jesse.

"It's Mom and Dad, if you're okay with that." Karma squeezed Jesse's arm and looked her man in the eye. He looked down at her smiling and followed up with a peck on the cheek.

"Mom, Dad, your state room is right next to ours. I'll show you where it's is."

"We're going with you, Jesse," Warren fired back sharply. "We were trapped on that island for a long time. Whatever is going on here, I want to know about it."

Jesse was too tired to argue with his new father-in-law. Running through options in his mind, he decided he didn't have any.

"Very well," Jesse said reluctantly. "If you want some food…"

"No need for that," Erin said joining the group with authority. "I'm having some food sent to your state room for all of us right now."

"Who's all of us?"

"You'll see. Follow me."

Gently grabbing Karma by the hand and trying to keep up with Erin; Jesse, Karma and her parents headed straight for Jesse's state room.

"Mr. and Mrs. Meyer, this is your state room," Erin said as she opened the door to the room. "Jesse and Karma are the very next door on the right. We're going to get started in about half an hour, maybe forty minutes, if you'd like to meet us then. I'm sure you'd like a shower before we get started, and I have placed some fresh clothes on your bed that should fit. There will be food and drink waiting for you over there."

Just like her Aunt Desi, Erin was all business and continued down the hall to the next room, not waiting for anyone.

"C'mon, Warren," Holly told him, pulling on his arm. "Let's take a shower and get cleaned up. Rachael and Jesse would probably like to do the same." Karma's parents headed into their room, locking the door behind them.

When Jesse and Karma followed Erin through the door to their state room, Pastor and Desi were already there with three crew members that had just finished setting up a mini version of the buffet and were on their way out.

"Has it occurred to anyone that I might want some private time with my wife?" Jesse immediately started in.

"Jesse, this can't wait," Erin started to reply. "It's important that…"

"I DON'T TAKE ORDERS FROM YOU, ERIN!" Jesse shouted at the top of his lungs. "NONE OF THIS HAS TO HAPPEN RIGHT NOW!!"

"Jesse, honey," Karma said to her beloved husband with a soft soothing voice, trying to calm him down. "Erin isn't the enemy here. Let's take a deep breath and have a conversation. No matter what happens, Mr. Buck, I'll be lying in your arms tonight."

Jesse looked at his wife and pulled her into his arms. "I have missed you so much, Rachael. We buried you, again. I thought you were dead." Tears started to fall from the tough Navy SEAL's eyes as he gently held his wife in his arms.

"But I'm not dead, Jesse; and I love you more than ever."

"I can't handle burying you again, Rachael."

218

"I love you, Buck."

"I love you, too."

The couple shared a real kiss while the others in the room remained silent. When the kiss was over, Erin assured Jesse the meeting was necessary, but they'd keep it short and sweet.

"I'm sorry I'm late," Georgia-Jean said as she popped through the door. "Jesse, honey, I can't find any sutures for you. There aren't any in the first aid kit."

"I've got that taken of," Erin replied before anyone could say anything. "Here," she said reaching into her pocket. "Use this." Erin tossed a spool of red *SpiderWire* fishing line over to Jesse while a devious grin spread across her face. "It seems to work well."

"What do you need sutures for?" Karma asked with a concerned look on her face, seeing the humor in the fishing line but not reacting to it. "Are you okay, Buck?"

Jesse took a step back and removed his black combat vest, still wet with seawater and blood, only to reveal blood-soaked bandages that were wrapped around his entire upper body.

"Huh!" Karma gasped when she saw the bandages.

"It gets better," Jesse replied. While looking her in the eye, he slowly unwrapped the bandages from around his chest cavity, revealing the hundreds of stitches that had torn free that were once holding together the wounds from being whipped.

"Oh my God, Buck!" Karma shuttered as she started crying. "What happened to you?"

Desi and Erin looked away when they saw Jesse's wounds, not knowing he had been beaten and whipped as badly as he was.

"I'm okay, Rachael."

"No, you're not! You have holes through your hands and your body has been shattered! Huh!" Karma stopped herself mid-sentence. Placing her hand over her mouth, she started to cry uncontrollably. She moved towards her husband slowly as she just realized what they had done to him.

"Please tell me they didn't."
Without saying a word, Jesse looked down at his feet.

"They wanted me to die a Christ-like death." Jesse admitted softly.

"Jesse, I want to hug you so badly right now, but I'm afraid I'll hurt you."

"Rachael, I really am okay." Jesse assured her. "Look, baby – they nailed the stakes right below each ankle, not through the top of my feet. They didn't even do it right!"

"Don't call me baby, Mr. Buck." Karma whispered to him while she clamped her fingers over his lips and kissed him on the ear lobe. "I'm not your baby."

"I'm sorry, love." Jesse spoke out of the side of his mouth. "We really need to get these wounds restitched so they won't scar any worse than they're already going to."

"Georgia-Jean," Karma said, now leading Jesse into the bathroom, "I'm going to get Jesse cleaned up. We'll be right back for you to stitch, is that okay?"

"That's just fine, dear," Georgia-Jean answered, "I'll be right here."

220

In just a matter of minutes, Karma led Jesse back out to the main area of the state room where he sat in a chair at the dining table. With his back toward Georgia-Jean, she started to restitch the open wounds. Recon and Savannah entered the room just a few minutes later, followed by Hack. By the time Karma's parents got there, Georgia-Jean was done with Jesse's back and was stitching up his front.

"That looks painful, Jesse." Warren said as he walked over to take a closer look.

"It's not as painful as burying my wife was."

"But you haven't buried your wife, Jesse, she's right there." Warren replied, pointing to his daughter, not knowing the whole story."

"He's buried her twice, actually," Pastor said handing Jesse a Scotch on the rocks.

"Let's cut to the chase, shall we?" Jesse said getting right to the point. "Hack, do you remember the envelope I gave you some time ago and the instructions that were in it?"

"Absolutely I do, Commander. Those tasks were completed that night."

"Good." Jesse replied with a head nod. "I'll have another envelope for you before we get off this yacht."

"Copy that, Commander."

"What's this all about, Jesse?" Pastor asked.

"I want to know how thirty-seven of the best trained Navy SEALs, Army Green Berets, and others can be captured and why they were being held in a non-hostile situation on a deserted island," Jesse continued. "What happened to the ten that were not rescued?"

"If you tried to escape, they killed you," Holly replied entering the conversation. "We believe we were being held for collateral. That's the only reason we were kept alive."

"Collateral, for who? Collateral for what?" asked Erin.

"Any time a GHOST agent was on to Camper, he captured us. He shot us with tranquilizers, and we ended up on his island." Warren added. "That's how he got Holly; that's how he got me. That's how he got Rich Nelson and the others."

"Warren," Jesse started, "tell me about the mission you were on when you got captured."

"Holly and I suspected he was a king pin in the human trafficking arena, so we posed as buyers. He was flying us to the Philippines on one of his private jets to 'look at the merchandise.' The next thing we knew, we were shot with tranquilizers and when the drugs wore off, we were in the cage."

"We've been in that cage for twelve years, Jesse." Holly added.

"Yeah, about that," Jesse commented. "Who knew all of these GHOST agents were there?"

"I don't think anyone did, Jesse," Pastor chimed in. "I think everyone, including myself, thought these GHOST agents were all dead."

"What does the Kaiser think?"

"Why don't you ask him when he gets here. He'll be here in a day or two," Pastor commented.

"Why is the Kaiser on his way here?" Jesse asked. "I don't want to see him right now. That guy gives me a headache. I don't want to deal with him."

"You just found twenty-seven missing GHOST agents, Jesse. That's kind of a big deal and he wants to thank you, personally."

"Thank you, Georgia-Jean," Jesse said as he got up from the chair, he was sitting in. "These look perfect!"

"Especially with the red fishing line." Karma added with a smile.

"Don't run off now, Jesse. I need to put some antibiotic ointment over these and get you bandaged up," Georgia-Jean added.

"Desi, Erin," Jesse ordered, "I want interviews started on the GHOST agents first thing in the morning. If the Kaiser is on his way here, and I'm sure he is, he's not coming to pat anyone on the back. He's coming here for answers. It's our job to have them ready."

"We already have a lot of those answers, Jesse," Holly told the group.

"Good," Jesse replied, now reaching for his wife's hand. "Then the two of you can help Desi and Erin."

"What do you want us to do, Commander?" Recon asked of him and Savannah.

"Do what you do, Recon." Jesse replied with a smile. "We'll talk soon."

"Anything else, Jesse?"

"Yeah, one last thing," Jesse said looking into Karma's eyes. "Meeting's over; it's time to go to bed."

Chapter 49

"Oh my gosh, Buck!" Karma said while draping herself over her man. "How do you always know just what to do to make my body tingle?"

"It's just what I do, Karma love."

"We didn't tear any stitches out, did we?"

"I don't think so, honey, but if we did, it was well worth it. That's the best sleepless night I've ever had!"

"I'm not here to injure you, Buck."

"You're not injuring me, Karma."

"I'm not here to reinjure you either."

"Rachael," Jesse said while kissing his wife on the forehead, "the pain I felt in my heart when I thought you were dead was far worse than the injuries to my flesh, back then or last night."

"Oh, Jesse, you're going to make me cry."

"What about you? Did you ever think I was dead or that we weren't going to see each other again?"

"Honestly?" Karma asked while sitting up in bed and looking over at her husband. "I knew in my heart that you'd come to my rescue. I didn't know when, I didn't know how, but I knew sooner or later you would find me and it was that thought, that belief, that kept me sane the whole time."

"What was it like on the island? You all seem to be in relatively good shape, other than a little stressed. Not exactly what I expected to find when I arrived."

"We were just caged, Jesse. We weren't abused. We weren't beaten. We were fed. It was really weird. The only time anyone got injured was when they tried to escape, and they were killed. If you just went with it and didn't rock the boat, it was just like being a hamster in a cage. It wasn't a great experience, don't get me wrong, but it certainly wasn't a hostage experience like you would imagine. To be honest with you, Jesse, it really *was* almost like we were being held as collateral."

"That was mentioned before," Jesse said to his wife, while thinking that would add a new dynamic to the scenario. "We'll come back to that. Tell me about your parents. How are they involved in this?" Jesse asked while sitting up in bed, now facing his wife. "I thought you told me your mother was a teacher."

"I never really knew what my father did growing up and you are right. I thought my mother was a teacher. Apparently, what really happened, they met in the Army. She was Army intelligence and he was a Green Beret. After falling in love, they both resigned from the military and were recruited as GHOSTs. Why? What's up, Buck? What are you thinking?"

"I'm thinking something still isn't adding up. I just can't put all of the pieces together."

"What are you talking about?"

"Karma, the island was the only place you could have been hidden."

"I'm not following you."

"Why was Camper stockpiling GHOST agents?" How did he know where to find them? How did he know they were GHOSTs? Why did he kidnap you?"

"Jesse, Camper was dead before we were taken. The GHOST agent questions are great questions. These are also questions that I don't have answers to."

"This isn't over yet, Karma."

"Why do you say that?"

"Okay, there were boxes of mutilated body parts shipped to our Lost Lake residence. Every box had someone's name on it. Pastor, Desi and Erin buried you. They buried everyone from the limo accident that night, except me. Where did those body parts come from? Were they even human remains? Why weren't DNA tests run on them? How do I know Pastor isn't playing me? These are all questions racing around in my head and I can't get them to stop."

"Jesse, really?" Karma questioned, almost disgusted with Jesse's last comment. "Pastor is not playing you. That man is not the bad guy."

"I don't know, Karma. Pastor seems to know more than the next guy, all the time. I have to question him."

"Who do you trust, Jesse?"

"Other than you and my SEAL team? No one."

"What about the Kaiser? He's a shady, untrustworthy creep."

"The Kaiser, is certainly a creep, and I don't like him, but he's not the bad guy. That guy is wound so tight and is so strait-laced, look at him. He eats and breathes his job. It's his life. I may not like the guy, but I seriously doubt he's the enemy. You don't rise to that kind of power position, while working on a second agenda at the same time."

"Jesse, I can't read your mind and I don't think I have all of the pieces here."

"Marcy, one of the women on the boat, told Erin that Camper had a partner."

"Why didn't you just come out and tell me that?" Karma asked, a little frustrated. "How would she know? Is she a credible source of information? What did she say about Camper's partner?"

"I don't know. Erin should have more info about that."

"What do you want me to do, Jesse?"

"Talk with Erin. Get a real introduction to Marcy. Win her trust and friendship and pick her brain. If Camper had a partner, someone could be hunting us right now, someone with unlimited funds and unimaginable resources."

"I'll make it a priority, Jesse."

"I also want a meeting with your parents. They were on that island a long time. It's time I have a chat with them.

"Me, first, in the shower, now!" Karma replied with a seductive smile while grabbing her husband by the fingers. "Then you can have your meeting with my parents!"

Chapter 50

After their shower, Karma went to find her parents while Jesse headed down to Doc's state room. Just as he was about to knock on the door it opened, and to his surprise Marcy stepped out, wearing just enough clothes to cover herself and holding the rest.

"Oh!" Good morning, Mr. Buck. You startled me," Marcy said, shocked to find Jesse standing there.

"I'm sorry Marcy. I thought this was Doc's room."

"It is my room, Commander." Doc hollered from the other side of the door. "Come on in."

Jesse stepped aside to let Marcy out, a little shocked with what he discovered, and proceeded to watch her scurry up the hall and disappear. Jesse then went on to enter Doc's state room and closed the door behind him.

"I do hope someone has told you about Sue?"

"Yes, Commander," Doc answered as he continued to get dressed. "Erin told me about Sue last night. Marcy overheard the conversation and we got to talking."

"That must have been some conversation," Jesse replied with a smile.

"Jesse, while Sue's death is tragic, she wasn't the woman for me. She told me the last night I saw her that she was going back to the Philippines to be with her family as soon as I got back. She was only there to watch your dog."

"I'm sorry about that, Doc. Things certainly got messed up."

"It's not your fault, Commander."

"Doc," Jesse said immediately, changing the subject, "I am meeting with Karma's parents in a few minutes and I want you there. If you hear anything that would make you suspicious, make a note of it."

"You mean suspicious like, mentally unstable, suspicious?"

"Yeah."

"Commander, they've been trapped on an island for how many years?"

"That's exactly why I want you there."

"You know I will be."

"In fact," Jesse thought out loud, "get Recon and Hack up there as well. We'll be in the control room until we find a better place to converse.

"I'm on it."

"And, Doc,"

"Yeah, Jesse."

"I really am sorry about Sue."

"Don't be, Jesse. Marcy is amazing!"

Jesse rolled his eyes and left the room. On his way up to the control room he crossed paths with Erin who was on her way to find him.

"Jesse, we'll be meeting in the conference room."

"Conference room?" Jesse questioned. This thing has a conference room?"

"Absolutely it does," Erin answered as if that were a foolish question. "You'll like it as well. I'm having breakfast brought up from the galley so we can take our time with the meeting."

"You sure do think of everything, Erin."

"I've got your back, Jesse. Isn't that what you pay me for?" Erin asked with a wink. Jesse knew the small salary she was making on Lasso payroll was nothing in comparison to what she had made as a GHOST agent.

When Jesse and Erin arrived at the conference room, Jesse was stunned to see all the GHOST agents there.

"Good morning, Jesse," Warren said, greeting Jesse with a man hug. "When word got out that you wanted to meet with Holly and me, everyone else wanted to be there. I hope you don't mind."

"Not at all," Jesse replied, looking over the GHOST's in the room. "We'll get started in just a few minutes."

True to his word, Recon, Hack, Savannah and a few other stragglers were there a few minutes later. Erin encouraged everyone to get a plate full of food, and Jesse was delighted to see some familiar items from the Lasso menu, such as the Eureka style eggs and his somethin' sassy hash brown potatoes. With everyone eating, the room was quiet enough for Jesse to start speaking his mind. It was time for the meeting to begin.

"There are a lot of questions that I have about what has been happening," Jesse started out. He paced back and forth in front of the room with a cup of coffee in his hand. His voice was stern and his eyes were sharp. You could see the gears turning in his head.

"You people, sitting in this room," Jesse continued, "are the baddest of the bad, and you people, all of you were captured. How did this happen? How could this possibly have happened?"

The room was silent. Eye contact was being made by everyone, to everyone, but no words were spoken.

"Jesse," Erin spoke out, getting up from her chair and heading to the front of the room. "Let's try a different approach to this, shall we? Jesse, why don't you get something to eat and I'll lead the meeting for a bit."

Jesse was reluctant to give Erin the reins. However, his growling tummy overrode his initial thought and helped convince him to see where Erin was going with this.

"The Kaiser is going to be here…"

"What about our lives?" One of the GHOST agents interrupted.

"Screw the Kaiser!" another shouted out.

"Did he *finally* send you to find us, Commander Buck?" another voice shouted.

"I've been on that island for twenty years! I'm done being a GHOST!"

"SILENCE!" Warren shouted, jumping out of his chair. "You will give Commander Buck and his team the respect they deserve! You'd still be there if it wasn't for him!"

"I know," Jesse started speaking with a gentle tone of voice, hoping to calm the situation. "All of you have been through a lot. You should know a few things before this goes any further. All the cash that we seized from Camper, will be divided equally among everyone who was on the island and got rescued. Each one of you will meet with Hack sometime before we get back, and he will set up your offshore account and the money will be transferred to you before you leave the yacht. That makes every one of you, everyone in this room, a very wealthy individual."

Smiles and sighs filled the room and suddenly the tension just got a little less nerving. Erin reclaimed her seat and let Jesse continue.

231

"The next thing is, I am going to recommend to the Kaiser that anyone who wants out, gets out. Please remember when you signed up to do this, you signed up for life, no matter what the consequences. That being said, anyone who wants out can get out and you will still keep your paycheck from Camper's bust. In fact, if you want out of the GHOST agency, you can leave the meeting now. No hard feelings. No questions asked."

Jesse was stunned to see no one moving. He waited for a moment, and no one left. Another minute passed by and everyone remained seated.

"Instead of us asking how you got captured, why don't you share with us what you know and let's see how much information we have," Erin said to the group taking over the meeting.

"Erin, we've had this conversation hundreds of times amongst ourselves," Holly chimed in. "We were all taken basically the same way."

"And what way was that?" Pastor asked from across the table.

"At some point in time while we were on our different assignments, we all felt a little off. Dizziness set in, slurred speech and just like that, the lights went out. When we woke up, we were on the island. Some of us were shot with a tranquilizer and some of us were drugged, but the end result seemed to be the same."

"This is an inside job." Doc blurted out. "There is no other way the best of the best could be taken so easily."

"Some of you were drugged?" Jesse asked. "I thought you all were shot with tranquilizers." Jesse continued while looking at Holly for confirmation.

"Only five or six of us were tranquilized. The rest of us were drugged," an unknown man added to the conversation. "What difference does it make? We've all been shot with tranquilizers at one point or another. It's how they maintained control in a non-lethal fashion."

"You, sir," Jesse said, pointing to the man who was just talking, "tell me your name and where you were when you were taken."

"My name is Pankow, Justin Pankow. I'm a Special Ops Marine. I was taken while on a mission in Cairo, sir. I was hunting a Soviet spy. One night I had invited myself to an elite party and while I was there, it happened just like Ms. Holly said."

"You," Jesse said pointing to another, "name and mission."

"My name is Mike Avis," the man said, getting up from his chair. "I'm also a Special Ops Marine. I know about your mission back in Desert Storm, Commander. I know about you and three others living off the grid for forty days just to make your capture. Very impressive."

"Where were you when you got captured?" Jesse continued, ignoring the compliment.

"I was in Seoul, South Korea. I was targeting Kim Jin Su, a North Korean rebel that was eluding the government for identity theft of highly ranked military officials with top secret clearances. I too, was at a dinner. I felt dizzy and barely remember hitting the floor. I woke up, lying in the dirt on the island."

"Thank you, Mike, and it was only thirty-seven days."

"You, sir," Jesse said pointing to yet another, "name and mission."

233

"My name is Alan Pierce. I'm an Army Green Beret, trained in military intelligence and guerilla warfare. I was in Australia on vacation. I passed out in the sand with the most beautiful woman on the planet. When I woke up, I was surrounded by these ugly mugs." There was a slight chuckle amongst the group, and a few comments were made in self-defense.

"Holly," Erin asked, "where there any other women on the island?"

"Holly is the only female GHOST agent that was ever in the field," Pastor answered before she could.

"I didn't ask about GHOST agents. I asked about women in general," Erin fired right back, not taking her eyes off Holly.

"To my knowledge, yes, Erin. I was, however, very well protected."

"I guess so."

"You." Jesse said pointing to another, while looking at Erin and wondering where she was going with that last question to Holly, "what's your story?"

Again, and again, the stories all had a common link. These people were all on mission all over the globe when they were drugged and smuggled to the island, with the exception of Alan Pierce who was apparently on vacation.

"Who's the traitor?" Jesse finally asked. "Who set you all up?"

That's when the room fell silent again. Eyes wandered the room, waiting for a response from anyone.

"Is it you, Pastor?" Jesse finally asked. "You seem to know more than anyone else, all of the time."

"Knock it off, Jesse," Karma fired back. "Let's be a little more proactive here, okay?"

"What about the Kaiser?" Jesse asked the group. "Is he the goat?"

Nothing but silence filled the room again. No one was talking.

"Why is no one saying anything?" Jesse asked, getting a little frustrated. "Will someone say something? Anything?"

"We're just tired, Mr. Buck," a lone voice spoke out. "We want this situation to be over and this meeting is proof that it's not."

"What's your name?" Jesse asked as he took his seat. "My name is Ransom. Cliff Ransom."

"Help me out, Cliff. What are your thoughts on all of this?"

"Well, Mr. Buck, I think the part that bothers me the most is I don't know who I can trust, and unfortunately, that includes you."

There were agreements that softly filled the air. Heads nodded and arms folded. Jesse suddenly felt a little outnumbered.

"Jesse is not the guy you should be questioning here," Warren spoke out in Jesse's defense.

"You say that because he's supposedly married to your daughter, who just happens to be a GHOST agent as well?" the man continued.

"Really?" Jesse shouted as he jumped out of his seat with anger-filled veins.

"Jesse," Karma said to him, "let the man speak his mind. We know what the truth really is."

"Hack, Recon," Jesse said while eyeballing the man who spoke with a reckless tongue, "Camper was paying someone. Someone on the inside, someone on the outside, it doesn't matter. Find out who that person was."

"We're on it, Commander," Hack said as he and Recon immediately left the room.

"Meeting adjourned."

Chapter 51

The conference room emptied in seconds and everyone scattered. Wondering what happened to Georgia-Jean, Kurtis and others, Jesse and Karma headed to the lounge on the main deck. By the time they arrived, Pastor was there, starting to give a sermon to the ship's crew. He was explaining to them the importance of following Christ and making good decisions. Jesse and Karma, along with her parents, found a place to sit and listen. Word traveled fast about Pastor and his sermon. Minutes later, the yacht was on autopilot and everyone on board had an ear bent towards Pastor and his words of power.

"Following Christ isn't an option," Pastor explained with emotion. "It's a commitment. Christ never gives up on you! Why would you give up on him? Not all of life's lessons are easy ones. Not all of life's lessons are short ones. Ask the ladies on this yacht. Ask the GHOST's rescued from the island. Ask Savannah. Ask Moses. Ask Paul. Often times the life you are living isn't about you. It's about someone you are helping, or someone Christ wants you to help. Maybe he wants you to grow.

Maybe he wants you to help another cause. Maybe he wants you to see a bigger picture. Following Christ isn't a joy ride. It's a challenge. When you follow Christ, you will have to make tough decisions. You will have to be honest. You will have to be dedicated. You will have to be loyal. The disciple Paul was eventually beheaded for following Christ. How dedicated are you? How loyal are you?"

The women that made up the yacht's crew were teary-eyed. Pastor guessed that many of them, maybe all of them, had never heard a sermon in their life. Everyone was listening. Pastor, once again, delivered a powerful message.

"When you follow Christ, you think about the consequences of your decisions before you make them. How will that decision affect you? How will it directly affect those around you? How will it indirectly affect those around you? When you follow Christ, you won't always see the big picture, however, when you follow Christ, you are protected, when you follow Christ, you are blessed..."

By the time pastor had finished, many of the ship's crew were sobbing, all of them crying. Most of the GHOST agents were a little emotional as well. A much-needed sermon to help heal some deeply rooted wounds.

The rest of the day was pretty low key. Jesse told Karma, along with her parents, about everything that had happened in Eureka. The house, the Lasso, everything being destroyed again, and suggested that when their *cruise* was over, they settle down at Jesse's Virginia estate and move forward with the Aussie rescue plan. Karma was ecstatic and Holly and Warren were all in.

Kurtis made a satellite phone call to his wife. They cried together for over twelve minutes before they could get into their conversation. Getting back to each other was all that mattered to them. Kurtis told Jesse that he had retired from being the limo driver, and that Jesse's *sandbox* had too many *fleas* in it.

Recon and Savannah stumbled across a large trunk that had numerous cases of clay pigeons inside it. Along with the birds was a pair of Benelli 12-gauge semi-automatic shotguns with dozens and dozens of boxes of ammo. It didn't take long for a group of GHOSTs to blow off some steam by shooting trap off the fantail of the yacht. Savannah again proved to be a deadly accurate shot, only missing one out of fifty.

As the sun was setting, Jesse grabbed Karma by the hand and led her up to the upper deck to watch the sunset where they discovered Pastor and Georgia-Jean in one of the hot tubs, alone. Their bathing suits and robes were hanging over a nearby railing, and they watched Pastor pouring some sparkling wine into their glasses.

"Karma," Jesse whispered, "go get the group and tell them to quietly meet us back here."

With an evil grin spreading across her face, Karma disappeared. While she was on her way to get the others, Jesse snuck up behind Pastor and Georgia-Jean and swiped their bathing suits and robes from the railing and returned to the meeting place completely undiscovered. Karma returned with the group - Desi, Erin, Recon and Savannah, Hack, Doc, everyone including a few others that wanted in on the shenanigans.

Jesse gave a loud whistle, startling Pastor and Georgia-Jean. As they turned for their clothes, members of the group held them up and sang out "Hey Sinners!!!" They bolted, laughing hysterically, leaving Pastor and Georgia-Jean naked in the hot tub, with nothing to cover themselves with when they got out.

"Animals!" Pastor yelled as the group disappeared.

"Forget about them," Georgia-Jean said to Pastor, not worried about their clothes being gone. "Let's do what we came up here to do."

"You're not worried about being labeled a sinner?" Pastor asked with a raised eyebrow.

"Pastor," Georgia Jean replied playfully, "Matthew 22, verses 36 through 40."

Pastor thought for a moment and then recited: "(36) Teacher, which is the greatest commandment in the law? (37) Jesus replied: 'Love the Lord your God with all your heart and with all your soul and with all your mind. (38) This is the first and greatest commandment.' (39) And the second is like it: 'Love you neighbor as yourself.' (40) All the Law and the Prophets hang on these two commandments."

"Shut up and kiss me!"

Before Pastor could make another comment, Georgia-Jean wrapped her arms around Pastor's neck and the couple proceeded with their evening.

Chapter 52

The next morning, Jesse and Karma were having breakfast with her parents when Desi, Erin and Pastor walked into the lounge and sat down.

"How was the hot tub last night, Pastor?" Jesse poked hoping to get a rise out of the man.

"The Kaiser will be here early this afternoon." Pastor responded, completely ignoring Jesse's comment. "He wants to meet with us first, then the GHOSTs, and after that, the crew."

"What's his agenda?"

"Who is the Kaiser?" Warren interrupted, wanting to know.

"What do you mean, who is the Kaiser?" Jesse questioned.

"I mean, *who* is he? Is it the same guy that recruited Holly and me years ago?"

"I don't know, I guess so. I don't know what his real name is. I only know him as the Kaiser."

"Pastor," Warren asked, "Do you know what his name is? Do you know if it's the same guy?"

"I don't know," Pastor replied. "I guess it's the same guy.

"Does anyone have a real name for the Kaiser?" Holly asked, jumping into the conversation."

"Does anyone have a fake name for the Kaiser?" Karma questioned.

Everyone in the group traded looks with each other. The pause in the conversation was all the answer everyone needed.

"Jesse," Warren started to respond, "I can tell you the assumed names of all of the other GHOST agents that were in the field when we were captured. How is it that none of us has any kind of name at all for the man giving us orders?"

"Pastor," Jesse replied, "I do believe this is a question that if anyone should have the answer to, it'd be you."

"I don't have a name for the Kaiser."

"I've got a bad feeling about this guy," Holly said, looking Jesse in the eye.

"What did the Kaiser look like when you met him?" Jesse asked looking at both Holly and Warren.

"He was a very distinguished looking African-American gentleman," Holly answered.

"I remember him having a deep voice. He was a man of few words.

"Bald guy?" Jesse asked.

"Yes," Holly answered while Warren nodded his head.

"It's gotta be the same guy," Karma added.

"I'm not convinced the Kaiser is in on this," Jesse said, looking around the group. "What are your thoughts, Pastor? Then again, how do we know you're not Camper's partner?"

"Jesse, stop!" Karma said, smacking her husband in the leg. Jesse had a stern look on his face. Everyone could see the gears turning, wanting to know what he was thinking.

"Be cautious of what you eat and no booze. Only drink the bottled water in your rooms and don't leave your rooms unlocked."

"Jesse, what are you thinking?" Karma asked, not sure where this was going.

"Trust seems to be an issue right now. Let the others on our team know, but don't start a panic with everyone on the yacht. Let the rescued GHOST agents relax. They've earned it, and they need it. There isn't anything my team can't handle if something should go awry."

"Commander," Warren replied crossing his arms, "Aren't you overreacting a little bit?"

"Yeah, Jesse," Karma agreed. "There isn't anyone on this yacht that has malicious intent. Everyone is happy. Everyone is having a great time."

"A savvy enemy will strike when you least expect it, when you have your guard down the most. The Kaiser deems it necessary to get on board this yacht, to immediately hold meetings and get answers to questions. What's with the urgent urgency?"

The group had no answer for that question. They just took it in.

"Just be cautious and be aware of your surroundings."

Chapter 53

Jesse, Recon, Pastor and Doc were searching for Georgia-Jean after the meeting to let her know the Kaiser would be there in just a few hours. When the four men checked the sun deck, they found Georgia-Jean along with Savannah and Marcy. All three of them were basking in the sun, soaking up some vitamin D while the others were in the meeting. Bourbon, of course, was by Savannah's side, also enjoying his leisure time on the expensive mega yacht.

Doc was quick to grab Marcy by the hand and head off somewhere, more than likely to get some private time. Recon peeled off his shirt and took Marcy's place on the lounge chair, showing off his incredible physique, Savannah took this opportunity to straddle his lap and rub suntan lotion all over his chest and arms.

"Remember, Chris," Savannah spoke quietly while her soft hands rubbed lotion into Recon's skin, "you're not on the menu."

"You're the only woman for me, Savannah," Recon assured her with a kiss. "Like Karma is to Jesse, you'll soon be my wife, until death do us part."

"I love you, Chris."

"I love you too, Savannah."

"Why don't you two get married while you're on the yacht?" Georgia-Jean asked out of the blue. "Pastor could do it. Jesse could do it. Why wait?"

"That's a great idea, Chris. Why don't we get married now?"

"We don't have our rings, baby; don't you want them when we get married?"

"We don't need rings to get married, Chris. We'll get them soon enough."

"It's up to you guys. I don't have a problem with it." Jesse added.

"Don't have a problem with what?" Karma asked while walking up to Jesse and putting her arms around him.

"Marrying Chris and me while we're on the yacht," Savannah answered while leaning over to give her man another kiss.

"Oh, Jesse, that's a great idea!"

"It wasn't his idea, honey," Georgia-Jean fired back. "It was *my* idea."

"That's why it was such a great one G-J. None of us thought about it!"

"Chris, we could get married this afternoon!" Savannah spoke just loudly enough to be heard by the others. Her hands were on Recons chest and her lips moved gently around his face. Recon was so involved with her; he never heard her words.

"The Kaiser is coming in this afternoon," Jesse reminded the group. "Today may not be the best day. However, as of now, there is nothing on the schedule for tomorrow.

"What schedule?" Karma asked with a playful tone. "We're two thousand miles from anything."

"Tomorrow will be just fine, Commander," Recon replied, wrapping his arms around his soon-to-be wife.

Jesse looked at Georgia-Jean and nodded his head to let the two lovebirds be. The three quietly made their way off

245

the sundeck and left Recon and Savannah to have some privacy.

Chapter 54

"Captain Thomas, do you copy?" Pastor asked into the radio.

"I copy, Pastor. What's on your mind?"

"Just checking to see if you are still out there. I can't see you."

"That's the whole point of stealth mode, Pastor, to not be seen or heard."

"Are you expecting any visitors on board today, Ted?"

"That's affirmative. I guess your guy the Kaiser is leap-frogging across the ocean. Hopping from Navy ship to Navy ship just to reach your yacht."

"Yeah, he's a very driven man."

"That guy sure does have a lot of power, to control the Navy."

"You have no idea. Do me a favor, Ted. Let me know when he leap-frogs off you and is headed this way, just so he doesn't surprise us."

"You got it, Pastor. Over and out."

"Over and out, Ted."

As soon as Pastor got off the radio with Captain Thomas, he notified the others that they were closing in on crunch time. The crew made sure the conference room was ready for the meeting and then made their rounds touching up the yacht. The plan was, when they saw the Kaiser's helicopter coming in, the crew would vanish to their rooms to get cleaned up while Jesse and his SEAL team, along with the rescued GHOST agents, debriefed the Kaiser in the conference room. After the debriefing, the Kaiser would meet the rest of the crew. Each minute that passed could be counted as the tension in the air thickened, for it seemed that everybody had their own agenda for the debriefing.

Chapter 55

True to his word, Captain Thomas radioed Pastor regarding the Kaiser's departure from the destroyer. It would only be ten or twelve minutes before he got to the yacht. Jesse and Pastor waited near the forward helicopter pad and watched with binoculars while the others waited in the conference room.

"I have a visual." Jesse announced, locking his eyes on the incoming chopper.

"Help me out, Jesse. I see nothing."

"You're looking up too high," Jesse said noticing where Pastor's binoculars were pointed. "Check the horizon."

"I see him. He's coming in low and fast."

"Like he's late for a meeting."

"How long do you think he'll stay on board?"

"Well," Jesse started to reply with a sigh. "Since there is one cabin available, and we have plenty of food and alcohol, and the crew is nice to look at, I imagine he'll ride it back with us."

"I was afraid you were going to say that."

As the chopper approached the deck, Jesse and Pastor stood back far enough to let it land. The chopper stayed still just long enough for the Kaiser to get out. He was carrying a small duffel bag and a briefcase. No sooner than he was clear of the chopper, the pilot lifted off and high-tailed it out of there.

"Gentlemen," the Kaiser announced with his stern voice and handshakes for both. "Well done gentlemen, take me to the meeting. Let's get started."

As if the yacht were just another boat, the Kaiser made no comments about it. He simply followed Jesse and Pastor to the conference room. When they arrived, Karma and her parents were there to greet them.

"Holly, Warren." It's been a long time. So glad you are safe," the Kaiser said, as he entered the room. All of the GHOST agents got up from their chairs and stared at the Kaiser. The room was cold and silent. Tensions were extremely high. Everyone's heart was pounding, waiting for someone else to speak first.

"How is it that one man can capture all of you and keep you hostage?" the Kaiser spoke out aggressively. "You were all the best of the best, yet all of you have been presumed dead."

The room was silent. No one spoke a word. Everyone had eyes locked on the Kaiser. "That question was not rhetorical. I want some answers!"

"Maybe that's not the best way to start this meeting," Holly suggested.

"Maybe you'll let me run my meeting the way I want, Mrs. Meyer."

"KAISER!" Jesse shouted. You owe these people a little more respect. If I were you Kaiser, I'd take caution with your tone."

"All of you know the game," the Kaiser continued, pointing to everyone in the room. "Your cover is not broken. You are on your own. There are no rescues, that is until Mr. Hero, over there deemed it necessary to embark on his own mission."

"You told me…"

"I'll deal with you later, Commander Buck!" the Kaiser interrupted.

"Christensen, you were the first one on the island. You got caught having drinks with a Russian spy. Harris!" the Kaiser shouted, pointing to another GHOST agent. "You got caught having drinks off duty in Amsterdam. Daniels!" the Kaiser continued aggressively, "you got captured in a cat house in Las Vegas. Really?" All of you together couldn't find a way off of the island?"

The room remained silent. Some GHOSTs were sweating and biting their lips. Still nothing was said.

"Damn it! I want some answers!" shouted the Kaiser!

"We were caged like animals, SIR!" Daniels replied, eyeballing the Kaiser, showing no fear at all and possible aggression towards the man. "If we tried to escape, we were shot and our bodies were thrown over a cliff into the ocean below. Those of us who did try to escape met that very death."

"But they fed you, and kept you alive."

"Why would they do that Mr. Kaiser?" The GHOST agents started firing questions out at random, one at a time.

"Why would they keep us alive?"

"How did they find out we were GHOSTs?"

"How did they know where to find us?"

"Who's the insider, Kaiser!" Daniels shouted as he started to walk towards the man dressed in black. "From where I'm standing, it was you!"

"That's enough!" The Kaiser demanded. I did not set any of you, and certainly not all of you up. That's hogwash and you know it! Your error put you there. Your mistake

251

got you captured. Tell me, who did you trust that you shouldn't have?"

"YOU!" an unknown voice shouted.

"From my perspective, you're the only guy that could have set us all up," another GHOST added.

"We've had a lot of time to sit and talk, Kaiser. You're the rat and you're gonna pay!"

"SILENCE!" the Kaiser shouted. "YOU KNEW THE RULES. YOU PLAYED THE GAME. I SET NONE OF YOU UP! IT'S YOUR CARELESSNESS THAT GOT YOU CAUGHT!!!"

"How did all of us end up in the same place?" Holly asked with a very normal tone in her voice. "Who is the only person that knew all of our whereabouts?"

The room fell silent while they waited for the Kaiser to answer. He looked around the room and the faces were angry. They were tense.

"You tell us, Kaiser, how is it that we were all drugged and captured?"

"There is one man who I…"

"That's crap and you know it Kaiser!" a voice yelled.

"There is no other man!" It's you!!" added another.

Sensing the meeting was rapidly getting out of control, Jesse made eye contact with Recon and Doc and gave them a head nod to get the Kaiser out of the room.

"STOP!" Jesse commanded. "The Kaiser is not the enemy here."

"Screw you, Buck!" shouted a hostile GHOST agent getting up out of his chair. "Shut your mouth or I'll send you overboard with him!"

"STAND DOWN, AGENT!" Jesse shouted at the top of his lungs. The unidentified GHOST agent locked eyes with Jesse but held his ground.

"I SAID STAND DOWN!" Jesse commanded again. Karma and Savannah walked up on either side of the man, ready to drop him if they needed to, as the situation was definitely getting out of control.

"Would you like us to remove you from the meeting?" Karma asked very politely.

"Get him out of here!" Jesse ordered Recon and Doc. The two men escorted the Kaiser out of the room immediately while Jesse demanded order.

"Quiet!" Jesse shouted above the rising noise levels. "I SAID QUIET! SIT DOWN. SHUT YOUR MOUTHS!"

The group reclaimed their seats and gave Jesse the respect he commanded.

"I know many of you are angry and frustrated. The Kaiser is not the bad guy. He is not the enemy."

"How do you know that, Commander?" shouted the same hostile GHOST agent.

"Your next outburst will find you swimming. Do you understand me?" Jesse replied to the man while pointing his finger at him. "See those two women next to you?" He continued, pointing to Karma and Savannah. "They are lethal. Got it. Sit down and keep your mouth shut!"

The man took a swing at Savannah, who blocked it and dropped him with a swift kick to the gut.
"What some more?" she asked with a smile. "That wasn't even my best shot." The rest of the group was shocked with the responsiveness of the stunning red head.

"Answer the girl, or take your seat." Karma added, ready to pounce if she had to.

"This meeting is not about Kaiser." Jesse addressed the group with a calm voice. "He didn't do this. We need to find the man who did. If it wasn't him, then there is a leak. Leaks need to be fixed."

"I speak for the group," a man said getting up from his chair. "We've had many a day to ponder this, and all of the evidence points back to the Kaiser. You can pick your side, Commander, but if you're with us, then you're not with him."

"I don't have all of the pieces to the puzzle, and we don't need to jump to conclusions."

"Don't be so naïve, Commander."

"The Kaiser is off limits until we know for sure what's going on," Jesse said raising his voice. "Is that understood?"

"Who put you in charge?"

"He's the guy that saved you. All of you." Warren finally spoke out. "You'd all be on that island if it weren't for Jesse. It's time to work with him and give him the benefit of the doubt. Can we do that?"

"The Kaiser is off limits." Jesse reiterated. "Tonight, there will be a dinner party to celebrate the return of the GHOST agents. I will be packing and I promise you, if there is any aggression towards the Kaiser, I'll shoot you myself. Is that understood."

No one said a word. The room was silent with looks of disgust on everyone's face.

"IS THAT UNDERSTOOD?" Jesse shouted.

Everyone in the room mumbled that they understood, against their will, but agreed to keep the peace.

"Meeting adjourned."

"Jesse," Warren whispered as the group left the room, "if you have an extra sidearm, I'd like to be carrying as well."

"When's the last time you fired a sidearm?" Jesse asked with a smirk.

"It's like riding a bike, Commander. You never forget."

"Go see Recon; he'll set you up."

"Thank you, Jesse. I'm on my way."

Chapter 56

Karma, Savannah and Holly made their way out the door and talked with each of the GHOST agents. They helped iron out the tensions and assured everyone that there was no reason or evidence to believe that the Kaiser was involved in this in any way. Jesse didn't like the man, but there was no reason to doubt his innocence. Not knowing who to trust or what to expect, Jesse had a meeting with his SEAL team, Pastor and Warren right before dinner.

"Here's how tonight is set up," Jesse said as he started passing out fully loaded clips to everyone. "Tensions are high. Some of the GHOST agents are angry. They want blood. They want to blame the Kaiser for their captivity. While I don't think he's involved, we can't rule him out. Everyone's a suspect. Keep your eyes peeled. If you see something suspicious, question it. If you see something obvious, act on it. No mistakes gentlemen. Got it?"

"Got it," the men replied.

"Let's go, and remember guys, try to enjoy your evening. This is for you as much as it is for everyone else."

The men made their way to the main dining area. The ladies in their group were already there socializing with the crew. The evening had started out on the right foot and everyone seemed lighthearted. The GHOST agents arrived right after Jesse and his team and mingled effortlessly. Everyone could finally catch their breath. The spread looked fantastic. The buffet must have been sixty feet long and had everything you could ever want to eat. The group wasted no time making their way to the food. When Jesse deemed it safe for the Kaiser to join them, he sent Hack to get him and bring him in. All possible precautions were taken, just in case.

Jesse had asked his group to spread out through the room. Pastor and Georgia-Jean sat at one table, Recon and Savannah at another and so on. Doc sat with Marcy near the back and Hack had a seat reserved for himself at a table of all female crew members from the yacht. As soon as Hack returned with the Kaiser, Jesse took control of the crowd and stood up to make an announcement.

"Ladies and gentlemen," Jesse spoke over the crowd. "Ladies and gentlemen," Jesse said again to settle the group down. "The reason all of us are here tonight is to celebrate the coming home of our peers and the freedom of the ladies who have been captive on board this yacht. This was all possible because of this man right here standing to my left." Out of respect for Jesse, the group stood up from their chairs and started to clap. "He goes by the name of Kaiser and he would like to have a brief word with us."

"I know many of you have been through a lot..."

As soon as the Kaiser started talking, Marcy got pale. Every word she heard coming from the Kaiser's mouth filled her with fear. She started to tremble, slightly at first. Holding Doc's hand, her trembling got his attention. Her trembling turned into shaking.

"Marcy, are you okay?" Doc whispered down to her.

Slowly ducking behind Doc, careful not to make a scene, Marcy managed to whisper back.

"That's him."

Recon noticed the movement and watched her closely from a few tables away.

"That's Camper's partner," Marcy whispered in fear. "Don't let him see me. He'll kill me if he sees me."

Recon made eye contact with Doc and he nodded down towards Marcy's legs, noticing the stream of urine puddling on the floor.

"JESSE, THAT'S HIM!" Doc shouted, pointing directly at the Kaiser. His booming voice filled the room instantly, followed by utter chaos. "THAT'S CAMPER'S PARTNER! GET HIM!"

"Clear the room!" Recon shouted as he charged towards the Kaiser. Jesse instinctively backhanded the Kaiser with his fist, knocking him to his knees and grabbed him in a headlock.

"You lying bastard!" Jesse shouted. You're done! DO YOU HEAR ME, YOU'RE DONE!" Jesse dragged the Kaiser out of the room, punching him in the face every chance he got.

"You've been playing us this whole time!

"Let go of me, Commander!" the Kaiser shouted as he struggled to free himself from Jesse's grip.

"I didn't do it! Release me, Commander! It's not me you fool! Let go of me or your life is over! Do you hear me!"

"Your life is over, Kaiser. Mine's just beginning!" Jesse shouted back, punching him one more time, knocking him out. When Jesse got him outside, he dropped the unconscious man on the floor by the railing of the boat. Recon and Hack were right there while most of the others scurried away. Karma and Savannah worked to settle the group down while Doc took Marcy to her state room to calm her down and get her cleaned up. Pastor grabbed Georgia-Jean by the hand and got out of there as well.

"What are we going to do Commander?" Recon asked while looking at the Kaiser.

"We send him overboard," Doc replied, joining the others.

"How's Marcy?"

"She's scared out of her wits, Jesse."

"Do you believe her?"

"Yes, Commander, I believe her."

"So, do I," Hack added.

"I never did like this guy," Jesse replied cautiously, calculating his next move. "We have to be sure about this. What does Marcy have to gain from lying to us?" Jesse asked the group.

"Nothing, she's a nobody."

"Exactly."

Just then a half dozen GHOST agents caught up with Jesse, Recon and Hack.

"Throw that son-of-a-bitch overboard!" one of the GHOST agents yelled while kicking him in the gut.

"Take him back to the island and cage him! Leave him there to rot!" Another GHOST shouted.

"Knock it off!" Jesse commanded. "I'll deal with him."

"You'll deal with him?" another angry GHOST hollered. "Why don't you let us deal with him? You know he's the guy, Jesse. He's the only one it could be."

"We don't know that for sure," Jesse replied, trying to keep a level head about the situation.

"You weren't trapped on that island, either."

"I'm not saying he's not. We just need some answers first."

"We've all had plenty of time to think about it, Commander. Besides, I saw the fear in that woman. I've got all the proof that I need!" another added.

"If you won't do it, I will!" shouted the GHOST agent as he moved in towards Jesse.

"Stand down," Jesse ordered the GHOST. Showing signs of aggression towards Jesse, the GHOST took a swing at him. Jesse stepped back, yelling "I TOLD YOU TO STAND DOWN!" The GHOST agents were all teaming together. The situation was rapidly moving from out of control to completely chaotic. Jesse, Recon, Hack and Doc were surrounded, and attacked by the GHOSTs. Mob mentality set in as Jesse and his SEAL team were ambushed. Six on four. Punches were being thrown; kicks were being landed. The skilled GHOSTs were no match for the younger SEALs, but it was still a situation that Jesse never wanted.

With all of the commotion going on, no one saw the Kaiser climb to his feet and, before anyone could stop him, he grabbed Jesse from behind, with his arm around Jesse's neck, keeping him in a chokehold, the Kaiser grabbed Jesse's pistol and pressed it against his head.

"THAT'S ENOUGH!" The Kaiser shouted. "I didn't have any part of this Commander Buck!" the Kaiser continued, speaking loudly into Jesse's ear. The men all tried to get the Kaiser off of Jesse but Jesse intervened.

"STAND DOWN!" Jesse yelled as loudly as he could, fighting for air.

"DO AS HE SAID OR I'LL PULL THE TRIGGER!" the Kaiser shouted aggressively.

The men kept trying to get the Kaiser, but the Kaiser held Jesse between them and him.

"I SAID STAND DOWN!" Jesse yelled again.

"BACK OFF OR HE'S A DEAD MAN!" the Kaiser reiterated.

"STAND DOWN!" Jesse shouted one more time.

"I see they listen to you, Mr. Buck," the Kaiser said loudly again, squeezing his arm tighter and tighter around Jesse's neck, pressing the pistol hard against Jesse's temple. "Tell them to step back."
"STEP BACK!" Jesse commanded. "Give us room!" The men moved cautiously and did what they were asked. Jesse saw Recon and Hack moving in.

"Recon, Hack – stay put."

"Tell your men to…",
WHACK!

Jesse brought his elbow up under the Kaiser's face and spun out of his chokehold, grabbing his pistol right out of the Kaiser's hand. Before the Kaiser could react, Jesse had his left hand locked around the Kaiser's throat and had him pinned backwards against the railing of the yacht. His right hand tightly clenched his bright stainless colt .45 where Jesse held it just inches from the Kaiser's face. With a clenched jaw, Jesse was asking the questions now.

"Why, Kaiser? Why!?" Jesse shouted angrily in the man's face. "It was you who sent the boxes of bodies to my property, wasn't it?!"

"They… were… Does." The Kaiser barely got out. "They were John Does… I had to… motivate you…"

"Why would you recruit us to capture us?" Jesse shouted in the man's face. "WHY?"

261

"It... w-asn't – me..." the Kaiser tried to get out. "I'm not the guy."

"Then who's the guy?" Jesse asked. "WHO'S THE GUY?" The men in the background were yelling and carrying on. "Throw him over, shoot him, kill that loser! That guy is a traitor!" were just some of the things being yelled by the GHOST agents.

WHAM! SMASH!

Jesse drove his knee up into the Kaiser's groin area and followed it with a right elbow to the face.

"DAMN IT! TELL ME WHO THE GUY IS!" Jesse commanded.

"Ron... Tis.. chon..." the Kaiser tried to get out, gasping for air and in great pain. Jesse's anger grew from within. He had to restrain himself from killing the Kaiser right then and there. The number of men surrounding him grew and they all shouted for him to finish off the man who had betrayed them all.

"YOU'RE A LIAR!" Jesse shouted, elbowing the Kaiser in the face one more time. "WHO IS HE?"

"Ron..e Tish...on" the Kaiser squeaked back. "Ronnie Tischon, Ronnie Tischon!"

POW! POW! was heard by everyone and the crowd went silent. The Kaiser looked down at his abdomen where Jesse had just pumped two rounds into the Kaiser's gut.

"You shot me," the Kaiser gasped.

"I did," Jesse admitted. "And now I'm going to throw you overboard."

The group of GHOSTs cheered wildly as Jesse lifted the Kaiser up over his head.

"I'm telling you the truth!" the Kaiser hollered. "Ronnie Tischon!"

"You're a liar, Kaiser! I hope you burn in hell!"

"Commander…"

SPLASH!

The Kaiser smacked the water hard. Everyone was watching over the railing when Karma and her parents came running after hearing the gun shots.

"Jesse!" Karma yelled out. "Jesse, wait! Here!" Jesse moved aside and let Karma up to the railing of the yacht.

"Give him this!" she shouted as she tossed a throwable life ring hanging from the railing, overboard. "Don't let him drown," Karma continued with a smirk on her face. "Let the sharks get him."

"Commander!" the Kaiser shouted from the water as the yacht left him behind.

"The excitement's over guys. You have all been relieved of your duties. The GHOSTs are no more. We're retired. All of us."

The gathering on the deck dissipated immediately and in seconds only Jesse, Karma and her parents remained there.

"I would have done the same thing, Jesse." Warren said with approval.

"How long do you think he'll survive out there?" Holly asked.

"With the life ring he *could* survive for several days. It'll be painful, but he could survive," Karma replied not looking away from the water.

"I imagine the predators will show up a lot sooner than that," Jesse added. "C'mon, let's go join everyone else. I feel like we really have something to celebrate now."

Floating in the ocean with pain rippling from his abdomen outward, the Kaiser bobbed in the water, fearful of what was about to happen next. The amino acids in his stomach were burning and eating away at his insides while the salt water was burning his wounds on the outside. The Kaiser watched in great pain as the yacht got smaller and smaller, leaving him behind. Before the yacht was out of sight, the first fin protruded up through the water. Circling him. Watching him. Then the second. Minutes later he was surrounded by fins. One shark nipped at his left foot, shearing it right off his ankle. As pain and fear set in, he struggled harder and harder. Screaming like a little girl, he thrashed wildly in the water, which only enticed the sharks to toy with him that much more. Nip by nip, bite by bite the Kaiser was eaten alive by some of nature's most perfect predators.

Chapter 57

"Jesse! Jesse! Jesse!" could be heard long before the group got to the parlor. Everyone on the yacht was chanting Jesse's name, knowing that the Kaiser had been put out to sea. The missing link had been discovered and the problem had been solved. There would be no more missing GHOST agents. There would be no more GHOSTs at all. When Jesse, Karma and her parents walked into the parlor, everyone started cheering and clapping. Crew member after crew member lined up to give Jesse a hug. The GHOST agents that had been held captive on the island were finally at ease, drinking and toasting.

"C'mon Buck," Karma whispered into Jesse's ear. "let's get out of here. This isn't our party."

"I'm with you," Jesse replied. Grabbing his wife by the hand the couple headed for the door. Warren and Holly followed without saying a word. Recon and Savannah saw this and headed in the same direction with Hack close behind.

"Commander," Recon shouted, leaving the parlor. "Commander! What's up? Why are you leaving?"

"We're just going to do our own thing, Recon."

"All four of you?"

"It's not a sex thing, birdbrain!" Karma shot out, laughing.

"I didn't mean it like that!"

"We're just going to sit in the piano room and enjoy some downtime."

"Well, do what you want," Recon replied surprised that Jesse wasn't going to join them. "There's a party going on and we're not going to miss it!"

Recon and Savannah turned around and vanished into the parlor to rejoin the party that was getting wild fast.

"Jesse," Karma said while grabbing onto her man's arm. "You should go let Kurtis know about the party. He's been locked in his stateroom since he got on board. Maybe this is what he needs."

"That's a great idea, Karma. Why don't you and your parents head on upstairs and I'll catch up with you shortly."

"Sounds great, Buck!"

"Kurtis!" Jesse shouted as he rapped the back of his hand on the door to Kurtis's stateroom. "Open up buddy! There's a party going on upstairs."

When Kurtis opened the door, he looked a mess. He hadn't shaved since he'd been on board. His clothes were wrinkled and his halitosis could have knocked a buzzard off a shit wagon one hundred yards away. Jesse could tell he needed to relax a little bit.

"I don't want to play in your sandbox anymore, Jesse," Kurtis said, walking away from the open door. Jesse chuckled as he entered the room.

"C'mon Kurtis. Go get shaved. Get yourself a shower, and please, please brush your teeth!"

"I'm not going up there, Jesse. I just want to be home. I miss my wife."

"You did get ahold of her, didn't you? She does know you're coming home, right?"

"Of course, she does, but I just can't get there fast enough!"

"Is that all that's bothering you?"

"You mean, other than my businesses are failing, I'm behind on my bills, and I was almost killed. Hell, Jesse! I don't even know what day it is anymore!"

Kurtis was now sitting on a sofa sipping Johnny Walker Blue straight from the bottle, and Jesse could tell he had no intentions of changing his current state of being.

"Gimme that!" Jesse said, swiping the bottle of Scotch from Kurtis's hand. Jesse locked eyes with his friend and took a swig, then set the bottle down on an end table next to the sofa.

"I'm not asking you to play in my sandbox, Kurtis," Jesse told him with a stern tone in his voice. "The bad guy is dead. Everyone on board is celebrating upstairs. I'll bet anything you could use a breath of fresh air. Get your butt in that bathroom and get cleaned up now. I'll be back in fifteen minutes with some clean threads for you to wear, and Kurtis…"

"Yeah Jesse?" Kurtis replied while dragging himself into the shower.

"You have been well paid for your inconvenience. See Hack when you get upstairs. I'm absolutely, positively sure that'll put a smile on your face."

Jesse got together with Desi and Marcy and got Kurtis a fresh set of clothes to put on, a pair of white shorts and a white polo shirt that had a multitude of colors on it. It almost looked like paint was thrown on it from afar to give it a splattered effect. It was one of those shirts that looked really cool on the hanger, but when Kurtis saw it, he loved it and better yet, it actually fit! Jesse led Kurtis to the party and then proceeded up to the piano room where Karma and her parents were chatting quietly.

"Here he comes now, Rachael," Warren said, pointing to Jesse entering the room.

"What took you so long, Buck? Everything okay?"

"Hi, Love." Jesse greeted Karma with a kiss. "Everything's fine, Kurtis just needed a little help getting motivated."

"Get yourself a drink," Holly said pointing to a well-stocked bar. "This conversation is just getting good."

"Really?" Jesse asked as he dropped jagged shards of ice into a rocks glass. "What'd I miss?"

"Daddy was just telling us a little bit about your past, Commander." Karma replied with a sexy little smile stretched across her face. "Apparently, you *are* an American badass!"

"With all due respect, sir." Jesse said heading over to the couch. His voice was stern and the look on his face was unsettled. One could tell immediately that Jesse was not happy about being the topic of conversation, and he wanted to know exactly what was said.

"I highly doubt you know as much as you think you do. That being said, there is a reason I don't talk about my past and expect you to not talk about whatever it is you *think* you know as well. Do I make myself clear?" By now Jesse was standing in front of Warren, looking down at him sitting on the couch. Warren was not fazed by this and very calmly handled the situation.

"I mean you no disrespect, son." Warren spoke soothingly. "Have a seat and hear me out." Warren waved for Jesse to sit next to Karma on the couch. Jesse slowly sat down next to her, not taking his eyes off Warren, waiting to hear what her father had to say.

"Jesse," Warren started while reaching over and putting his hand on Holly's knee. "We're all here because we're the best at what we did. The very best. We all are highly trained and intelligent people."

"Smart enough to get caught and caged like rats!"

"Jesse! Stop!" Karma told him smacking him in the arm. "Let him talk!"

"Commander," Warren continued, ignoring Jesse's rat comment. "One of our jobs as GHOSTs is to study those coming up behind us. To seek out new agents. Half the GHOSTs on this yacht have heard about your heroics. The soldiers you've saved. The hostages you've freed. The villains you've brought down. I know about your desert mission. I, Jesse, am the one who first noticed your potential when you saved your drill instructor's life. Remember? The mortar? The landmine? The hummer you were driving?"

"I don't need to relive that day," Jesse replied sharply.

"You went against direct orders to fall back to save your team that day, and against all odds, you did. I'm the one, Jesse," Warren said getting up off the sofa and walking over to where Jesse and Karma were sitting. "I'm the guy that first told the Kaiser about you twenty years ago. I'm the guy, Jesse, that made sure you always got the best medical treatment when you needed it, I'm the guy, Jesse, who always had your back behind the scenes, I'm the father, Jesse, that is honored to have you as my son-in-law."

"You were Army. I'm Navy. I'm not buying that. Besides, how could you protect me when you've been caged on this island for how long? Ten years? Fifteen years?"

"Really, Jesse?" Warren asked with great deal of sarcasm. "We both know that the Army and Navy often work together on special ops assignments. Don't pretend you don't know that. Everyone knows who you are. When we were recruited, I told the Kaiser that we needed you on our team, he agreed. After we were captured the Kaiser took over, looking after you."

"If the Kaiser was such a great man, why did he betray all of you?"

Thud, thud, thud, thud could be heard coming from the floors below. The sound of some serious bass was now penetrating throughout the yacht.

"I don't know, Jesse," Warren replied, reclaiming his seat. "I see the trail of bread crumbs leading over to him, but I can't wrap my head around as to why."

"Do you think I was wrong in doing what I did?"

"No!" Warren and Holly both answered simultaneously. "It needed to end, and from where I'm sitting, you ended it."

Boom, boom, boom, boom. The pounding of the bass coming from the music was getting louder and more pronounced…

"From where I'm sitting, Warren," Jesse said while reaching over to hold Rachael's leg. "The GHOSTs are no longer." Jesse held up his glass of Scotch to make a toast. "To freedom." Karma, Warren and Holly all reached over and clinked glasses with Jesse.

270

"To Freedom."

"Karma!" Savannah shouted out excitedly as she busted through the door. "You have got to come see this! The Kurtis guy found some DJ equipment and he's rockin' the yacht!"

"Savannah, honey…" Karma started to reply.

"Erin's getting ready to sing!" Savannah interrupted. Karma jumped to her feet.

"C'mon Buck, let's go!" She grabbed her husband's hand and headed for the door.

"Rachael!" Holly shouted abruptly. "We're in the middle of a conversation here."

"We've got to go check this out, Mom!" Karma replied tugging on Jesse's arm.

"This should be worth watching," Jesse said looking back at Warren and Holly while being dragged in the opposite direction. Just like that, the conversation went unfinished and the group of five were on their way to the party a couple of floors below.

When Jesse, Karma and her parents got to the party, it was a sight to see. The main lights were dimmed, the glass doors were open to the back, and party lights illuminated the entire area. The weather was perfect and everyone seemed to be having a fantastic time. Kurtis was wearing a headset and dancing behind a pair of electronic, computer-controlled turntables. He really was in his element. Apparently, *this* sandbox was okay to play in. He was rocking the place like no one had ever seen or heard. The base was pounding so hard that the yacht was making ripples on the glass-like ocean surface.

On one of the two 85" monitors that were mounted on the wall, the words for the current song were being projected. On the monitor that was adjacent to that was the official music video for that song. There was a series of lights surrounding the entire room that were synced to the music that Kurtis could control from where he was operating everything. Apparently, Kurtis wasn't kidding when he told Jesse *he could spin some records.* As it turned out, Kurtis really *was* the party guy.

It only took Karma a few seconds to lock eyes with Erin, who was wearing a devilish grin. She whispered something into Kurtis' ear and then regained eye contact with Karma.

"What's going on?" Holly asked, picking up on her daughter's body language.

"Karma and Erin have a *thing,*" Jesse replied while looking over his shoulder at Karma's parents. "They are very competitive with each other."

"What do you think she's going to sing, Buck?" Karma asked, not taking her eyes off Erin."

"I have no idea, Karma. I wouldn't even begin to know where to guess."

When the song ended Erin was quick to take command of the room by talking through a wireless microphone.

"I knew you'd show up," Erin said, pointing to Karma across the room.

"What's the deal tonight?" Karma shouted back across the floor with gusto. "What's the challenge?"

"What's going on?" Holly whispered to Jesse.

"Just watch," Jesse answered without looking away. "This ought to be good."

"Kurtis picks the artist," Erin started to speak into the mic. "Marcy picks the song. Would you like to sing first?" Erin asked as she tossed the wireless microphone across the room to Karma. Like it was nothing, Karma reached up with one hand and picked the microphone right out of the air, ready to go toe-to-toe with Erin one more time.

"You know I will!" Karma answered confidently. "What's the song?"

"Ladies," Kurtis addressed Karma and Erin through his own mic, "the artist for karaoke tonight is:" Kurtis let the suspense simmer for a moment before dropping the answer, "Lada Gaga!"

Karma and Erin both looked over to Kurtis, wondering how he came up with that. "Can't find anything a little more..." Erin started to say.

"It's my choice," Kurtis interrupted into the mic. "The album will be the 2011 album titled "Born this way!"

"Give me a song, Marcy!" Karma shouted as she pushed those closest to her back so she had room to do her thing.

"The song I have chosen for you is *Edge of Glory*."

Being stranded on the island and out of touch with the real world, most of the GHOSTs had no idea who Lady Gaga was and had certainly never heard of that song. The ship's crew, on the other hand, knew exactly who Lady Gaga was and cheered wildly when they heard the song selection. All eyes were on Karma as Kurtis cued up the music.

"I love this song, Buck!" Karma said as she turned to her man and grabbed him by his shirt with both hands. "I've got this!" Karma stood on her tip toes and pecked Jesse on the lips. "This is for you, Jesse!"

273

Karma nailed the song right out of the gate. Perfect pitch, perfect tone and made no hesitation to give it all she had. Seconds into her performance Karma was standing on a table and dancing somewhat provocatively, letting the entire audience know she was dancing for her man. She pointed to some of the GHOSTs to slide another table towards her. As soon as the tables were touching, Karma stepped forward. Table after table was soon pushed together as Karma danced, using every one of them. No matter what table she was on, she made it clear that she was not only performing to win, she was singing and dancing for Jesse.

"Oh my gosh!" Holly shouted out, grabbing Warren by the arm. "I can't believe how good she sounds!"

"I can't believe she's dancing like that!" Warren replied, somewhat embarrassed. His little girl had grown up to be all woman. Karma was beautiful, sexy, smart and apparently dancing and singing were two talents that her parents never knew she had. While Warren was very impressed with Karma's singing gift, the provocative dance she was giving Jesse was a little rough on his eyes.

"She's not doing anything wrong!" Holly replied as she elbowed Warren lightly in the ribs. "You don't mind it when I dance like that for you!"

"Don't say that so loud!" Warren whispered into Holly's ear, a little bashful that she would mention that in public. "Besides, it's not exactly the same thing."

The crowd was really getting into the performance, clapping to the tempo of the music and cheering Karma on. Lady Gaga is a tough performer to try to duplicate, but Karma was not at all intimidated and was certainly holding her own. When the song was over, right after the final lyric was sung, Karma finished off by saying "I love you, Buck" into the mic. Jesse reached his arms up and Karma stepped off of the table into them. Wrapping her arms around his neck, the couple embraced with a hot passionate kiss.

"That was amazing, Rachael! I'm so proud of you!" Holly told her with tears of joy falling from her eyes as she turned Jesse and Karma's kiss into a group hug. Warren was quick to join and equally proud of his daughter's performance.

"Very impressive performance there, Mrs. Buck," Marcy spoke into the mic. "How'd she do guys?" Did you like that little song and dance Karma gave us?"

The crowd went wild cheering for Karma, completely shocked with the level and quality of the performance.

"Shall we keep this competition moving forward?" Marcy continued into the mic.

"Yes!" The crowd shouted excitedly.

"Where is Erin?"

"Here I am!" Erin shouted from in front of the bar. "I need a mic!"

Karma picked right up on that and chucked her microphone over the crowd right into Erin's hands. Erin reached up and grabbed the microphone right out of the air and never took her eyes off of Karma's, insinuating that she was just as cat-like as Karma was.

"Nice catch!" Marcy cooed into the mic.

"What's my song?" Erin demanded, wanting to get singing.

"The song for you, Erin," Marcy responded looking right at her, from the same album is *You and I.*"

"That's not my song!" Erin shouted back with disapproval.

"That's the song I chose for you."

"She's going to sing the cover." Karma said leaning into her man.

"I'll sing *Born This Way* Erin continued with a deviant grin. "I'll sing the cover. It's the only way I'll be able to beat Karma."

"Give it your best shot, honey!" Karma shouted at the top of her lungs. "You can have the cover!"

"I get to pick the song, ladies." Marcy intervened, a little perturbed that she had been removed from the equation.

"Cue it up, Kurtis!" Erin said shooting him a wink and holding up her hand to Marcy, as if she was telling her that *she* was in control of this situation, not her. When Kurtis cued up the song *Born this way* Erin propped her hands on either side of her and hopped backwards, sitting on the bar. She kicked off her boat shoes one at a time and unbuttoned the top few buttons of her blouse. The whistling and cheering started almost immediately as Erin was getting fired up to sing.

When the lyrics appeared on the screen, she also pegged them, like a professional singer. Erin was on her "A" game. Just a few words into the song and Erin was standing on the bar. Holding her mic with one hand, she unbuttoned her blouse with the other, all while she was singing.

"She is *not* gonna to take her clothes off!" Desi said to the others, watching her niece in shock and awe.

"Looks like she's going for it!" Jesse whispered into Karma's ear as he held her close.

276

"She sounds good, too." Warren said, enjoying this show much better now that it wasn't his daughter up there dancing.

By the time the chorus was being sung, Erin was swinging her blouse over her head, wearing nothing on top but a very sexy black satin bra. Her dance moves were seductive and her focus was strong. She wanted to be the center of attention and she was going to make it happen. Erin let her top fly into the crowd and unzipped her shorts. With a gentle push over her sexy hips, they fell to her feet. She stepped one foot out of the shorts and flicked them into the crowd with the other. Erin was covering her lower half with only a black pair of satin panties, equally as sexy as her bra. She sang and danced, touching herself, much like Lady Gaga was doing in the video.

"That's pretty hot!" Savannah told Recon. "Watching her is making me want you to have your way with me!" she whispered into his ear. "Let's go spend the rest of our evening in our room. Take me, Chris. Show me I am your woman!"

Not having to say a word, Recon led Savannah by the hand out of the party and straight to their room.

"What was that all about?" Karma asked Jesse as they watched the two of them leave.

"They probably need a lust break," Jesse replied not taking his eyes off Erin. Erin was undoubtedly a very sexy woman with an incredible figure. Jesse had to agree with many that night, Erin did look very hot up there.

"When are you going to dance like that for me?" Doc asked Marcy as he approached her from behind, grinding on her a little, wanting her to feel the invitation in his pants.

"Right after I strip you and tie you up!" Marcy replied not missing a beat.

"I'll let you tie me up, baby!"

"Be careful what you wish for, stud!" Marcy replied with a smile and a wink.

"You should tie me up tonight!"

"No worries there! I can't wait to do it!"

The music ended and so did Erin's performance. The GHOSTs were all chanting *Erin* and most of them were probably very aroused from what they just saw, especially after being trapped on an island for years and years.

"Sexy, sexy, SEXY!" Marcy shouted into the mic. "How did you all like that?" The level of cheering from such a small group was impressive by anyone's standards. Erin had one-upped Karma tonight.

"That was one hot little show you put on for us, Erin!"

Erin, who had just reclaimed her clothes and was getting dressed, couldn't erase the smile from her face. She knew her performance was hot!

"I don't know," Kurtis interrupted. "I don't know what I liked watching more, Lady Gaga in her video or Erin on the bar!"

"Erin, Erin, Erin!" most of the group chanted.

"Looks like we have a winner!" Marcy announced, pointing over to Erin. "To celebrate, we have Jell-O shooters for everyone!"

"Erin can have tonight, Buck," Karma told Jesse as she clung to his arm. "Let's get back to our room and have some *us* time."

"I'm all for that. Wait," Jesse interrupted his own train of thought, "has anyone seen Pastor and Georgia-Jean?" No one in the immediate conversation said a word. Just a few heads shaking "no."

"They're adults, Buck. Let them be."

"What about Bourbon?"

"What about us, Jesse?"

"Jesse," Warren added, "It's a boat. No one can go very far."

"I guess you're right. Let's go finish our conversation."

"The conversation can wait!" Holly immediately replied, grabbing Warren's hand much like Karma grabbed Jesse's. "I've got some dancing of my own to do tonight!"

"Mom!"

"What's the matter, Rachael?" Holly asked with a bit of surprise. "Do you think that your father and I don't like to…"

"Enough!" Karma shouted. "I don't need to hear any more, nor do I need that image burned into my head. See you in the morning!"

After a few looks were shared, Warren and Holly headed in one direction while Jesse and Karma headed in the other. There was a feeling of ease in the air and everyone wanted to take advantage of it.

Chapter 58

"Are we allowed to just take this boat out?" Georgia-Jean asked Pastor as she climbed aboard the 30' *Chris Craft Corsair* down in the water garage of the yacht.

"Of course, we are, honey!" Pastor answered with gusto. "We can do whatever we want!"

"Tell me again why we are driving off in the middle of the night?"

"The ocean is a flat calm tonight, Georgia-Jean. We're going to drive a few miles away from the yacht and watch the sun rise of a lifetime," Pastor continued. "Trust me, my dear, you're going to love this!"

"What about Bourbon?" Georgia-Jean asked as the Aussie barked at the couple getting on the boat.

"C'mon Bourbon!" Pastor shouted. "C'mon boy!"

Pastor clapped his hands and the Aussie leaped onto the open bow of the boat, claiming his seat.

"We're not going to get lost, are we?"

"No, my love," Pastor assured Georgia-Jean. "We're drifting in the same current the yacht is, we're just going to experience this on our own."

"Okay, Tom." Georgia-Jean said with a twinkle in her eye. "I'm all yours."

Pastor was shocked to hear Georgia-Jean call him by his birth name, and this made him smile as he fired up the Chris Craft. The threw-hull exhaust was music to Pastor's ears. The deep, throaty sound echoed in the bottom of the yacht as he backed the vessel out for its evening run. Pastor could tell there was a powerful V8 under the engine cover just by hearing the lope in the cam as it idled; 400hp minimum was a good guess. If the engine was supercharged it could be a lot more. Whatever the horsepower was, the engine sounded really nice.

Moments later, Pastor piloted the boat away from the yacht on the glass-like surface of salty water. Gently pushing the throttle forward, the *Chris Craft* stepped up onto its plain and glided across the ocean. The full moon and clear sky gave plenty of light to see by. The yacht got smaller and smaller behind them as Pastor and Georgia-Jean looked forward to their time away from the party, quiet time with Bourbon underneath a heavenly sky.

Chapter 59

"Oh, my gosh, you are such a good lover," Marcy told Doc as she sat up on his naked lap, catching her breath one more time.

"I'm glad you like how I handle your body," Doc replied while pulling on the nylon ropes that secured him to the bed. "Are you going to untie me now? These ropes are a little uncomfortable, you have them so tight."

SMACK! Marcy backhanded Doc across the face as hard as she could.

"Hey! What the hell was that for?"

"That was an attention getter, Doc." Marcy's facial expression turned ice cold as she climbed off Doc's body and walked over to the closet.

"I need you to listen to what I have to say very carefully." Marcy continued as she stepped into a wet suit. "I have good news for you and bad news for you." She continued. "The good news is you are such an amazing lover that I can't bring myself to kill you like I had originally planned."

"Yeah?" Doc replied a little worried. "If that's the good news, what's the bad news?" Doc asked, wondering if he should have.

"The bad news is, this yacht has a self-destruct mechanism on it. Only I know where it is. I took the liberty to set the timer for three minutes. Once I flip the switch, the lights will go out and you'll start living the longest three minutes of your shortened life."

"You're out of your mind!"

"You and your team will soon be nothing more than fish food, those of you who aren't already dead, that is."

"You're one crazy bitch!"

"That's *exactly* what my late husband, Cameron used to tell me. You know who I'm talking about, right? Cameron? Cameron Perzel? Went by Camper?" There was a sort of twinkle in Marcy's eye that was as truthful as it was sinister. Marcy ran and jumped onto Doc's lap, landing hard on his groin, and slapped him across the face just as hard as she did the first time.

"What are you talking about?"

"That's right, Doc!"

Smack! A second backhand was landed across Doc's face.

"When I heard about you bringing my casino to the ground and killing my husband, I was actually okay with it. He was fat and out-of-shape. He was a lousy lover, not built like you at all. Not above the waist and certainly not below."

Smack! A forehand slap to the other side of Doc's face was landed, this time leaving his cheek with a red hand mark.

"You hit me again and I'm gonna…"

"Your gonna what?" Marcy interrupted.

Smack! Another backhand was landed right across his face.

"I have you bound tight. You're not gonna do a thing; nor are you going anywhere. You'll die in this bed and there is nothing you can do about it. You men are all so predictable. Always thinking with the wrong head. To think, you never saw this coming. You're such a fool."

283

Marcy got off Doc's lap and positioned herself next to the bed while she continued her story, putting her hair into a ponytail at the same time.

"When you seized all my assets and took all my money, that made me want to seek revenge. Sure, I have lots of insurance money to live on, but still, how far will a couple hundred million go? That's poverty. I can't survive on that for very long, however, I'm not worried, Doc. I will get my money back; I promise you that."

"There is definitely something wrong with you."

"Pay attention, Doc. Since you figured out that Camper was the ringleader in the largest human trafficking organization on the planet, I knew it was just a matter of time before you'd come looking for the island, and the only way to find it was to take *my* yacht. It's a beautiful yacht, isn't it? It's a shame I have to sink it."

"You'll never get away with this!"

"On the contrary, Doc. I already have. See Doc, no one knows who I am and those that did know me at one point in time believe me to have been dead now for many years. I'm a nobody. I don't really exist. I guess you could say, like you, I'm a ghost."

Chapter 60

Knock, knock, knock was heard at the door of Jesse and Karma's state room followed by Recon's voice.

"They're all dead, Commander." Jesse sat up in bed like he was spring-loaded.

"Recon, what?"

"They're all dead, Commander, the GHOSTS and some of the crew, maybe all of the crew. They're dead sir."

Jesse jumped out of bed and pulled some shorts on while hurrying to the door. He yanked it open and stepped out of the way letting Recon and Savannah in. With a quick peek down either side of the hall, he then shut the door and locked it behind him.

"What do you mean everyone's dead?" Jesse asked for confirmation.

"There are bodies all over the parlor, Commander. They're dead."

"Karma," Jesse said tossing her some clothes. "You're gonna need these."

"How?" Jesse asked. "Did you see any bullet holes in anyone?"

"No, none. It's like everyone was poisoned."

"The Jell-O shooters," Karma said as she popped out from underneath the covers with her clothes on.

"I didn't see that one coming," Jesse replied surprised.

"Why the shooters?" Savannah asked innocently enough.

"Because we're not dead," Karma replied immediately. "What does that mean, Buck?"

"Where are Hack and Doc?" Jesse asked Recon.

"Doc left with Marcy last night, and I'm not sure where Hack is."

"Doc's in trouble," Jesse said while pulling a large black duffle bag out from underneath the bed. "I want teams of two." Jesse spoke with authority as he opened the bag and handed out Colt .45 ACP's to everyone. "No one, absolutely no one, leaves their teammate unless they are dead. Got it?"

"That's a comforting thought," Savannah said, rolling her eyes.

"Hey, Red!" Jesse snapped. "This is the real deal. Don't screw around and remember what you have learned. It just might save your ass right now! Karma," Jesse ordered, "bang on that wall and see if your parents are responsive." Karma hurried over to the adjoining wall between the two state rooms and did what Jesse asked.

"Mom, Dad!" Karma shouted through the wall. "Wake up!"

Holly blinked her eyes and looked over at the clock on the nightstand.

"Rachael, honey," Holly replied with a groggy voice. "it's 4:48 in the morning."

"Mom, now!" Karma asserted as she banged on the wall a few more times. "It's an emergency!"

"We'd better get over there," Warren added, tossing the covers off and planting his feet on the floor. "This sounds serious."

In just a few short moments, Holly and Warren were next door in Jesse and Karma's state room, eager to get filled in.

"This is what we know," Jesse started as he handed side arms to both of Karma's parents. "The GHOSTs are dead; we don't know if it's all of them or most of them. Some of the crew is dead as well. Again, we don't know exact numbers but we're guessing most of them. Our hunch is they were poisoned."

"The Jell-O shooters," Holly added.

Jesse paused for a moment and looked at Karma.

"What can I say?" Karma smirked. "Great minds."

"We have no whereabouts on Doc, Hack, Pastor, Georgia-Jean or…"

Bam, bam, bam, was heard on the stateroom door.

"Jesse, it's Desi and Erin. Let us in!"

Recon ran over to the door and let the two ladies in.

"Well," Jesse smiled, "We know where Desi and Erin are."

"We're not dead," Desi answered, reaching into the duffle back and grabbing a couple of pistols, handing one to Erin. "What's the plan, Jesse?"

"How is it that you all are just up at this hour of the morning?" Holly asked, dumfounded that everyone was coincidently up and wondering around the yacht."

"It's too quiet." Recon replied.

"That's exactly right," Desi added. When it's too quiet, you need to know why."

Holly just shook her head. *I was enjoying the quiet,* she thought to herself.

"We don't know who's a good guy and who's a bad guy," Jesse addressed the group. "We have to assume that anyone left alive is part of the problem. We need to eliminate, or at the very minimum neutralize the problem and find our missing team members. Right now, we have to believe that all crew members still alive are in on this. In groups of two – Desi and Erin," Jesse commanded, "You two look for Doc."

"Doc left with Marcy last night," Erin interrupted.

"We know, and that's not a good thing."

"Recon and Savannah – go find Hack."

"We're on it."

"Warren and Holly – you two seek out any surviving GHOSTS and Karma and I will search for Pastor and Georgia-Jean."

"Where's Bourbon?" Savannah asked

"At this point in time," Jesse said with eyes locked on Savannah, "Bourbon is not a concern. Let's move!"

Chapter 61

"It's beautiful out here," Georgia-Jean said softly to Pastor as she nestled up against him on a back corner of the *Chris Craft*. "It's amazing how many stars you can see, even with a full moon." she continued.

"Look at our yacht over there," Pastor told her pointing across the horizon. "It's got to be what, a mile or two away and you can still see it on the water."

"Thank you for bringing me out here, Pastor," Georgia-Jean whispered as she turned around and gave Pastor the kiss of a lifetime. "Do we have some time to burn before sunrise?"

"You bet we do, honey!"

Chapter 62

"Well, Doc," Marcy said as she climbed onto his lap one last time, "this is the end of the line for us." Marcy planted her hands on either side of Doc's face and forced a goodbye kiss on him. Marcy sat up and followed the kiss with one last *SMACK!* A final, hard slap across the face.

"You have been an absolute pleasure!"

As if nothing had ever happened, she headed for the door. "Don't worry, Doc, your nightmare will soon be over, oh, yeah. I almost forgot. One last thing." Marcie told him as she paused at the door of the state room.

"Did you like my performance last night? What do you think, best actress maybe? Do you know how long I had to hold it, and how hard it was to keep from peeing myself, just so I could do it when the time was right? Watching you guys go after that poor innocent bastard was so worth it! You killed my husband. I killed your Kaiser. Cameron would be proud." Blowing Doc a kiss, Marcy left her state room.

"Going somewhere, hussy?" Erin spoke with authority as she and her Aunt Desi watched Marcy leave her state room from the hallway.

"Yes, I was just about to go look for Doc."
"Liar!" Desi said as she dropped Marcy to the floor with a throat jab.

Without saying a word, Marcy started defending herself and attacked Desi and Erin. All three women displayed excellent martial arts skills and strength. Punches and kicks were thrown and blocked by all of them. Marcy, apparently, had been expertly trained.

"Desi! Erin! "I'm in here!" Doc yelled from inside the room, hearing the commotion in the hallway. That was just the opportunity Marcy needed for her to slam Desi and Erin's heads together like symbols, knocking them both senseless and dropping them to the floor.

"Who are you two bitches calling a hussy?" Marcy spoke sarcastically as she stepped over the two women and proceeded up the hallway.

"Marcy!" Rita shouted coming down the hall. "Some of the crew who weren't poisoned are starting to move about. What would you like me to do?" Rita, who was one of the crew members and loyal to Marcy, was obedient but not very intuitive. She was deadly when set in motion but never took any initiative on her own. Her weapon of choice was a knife, which she always kept with her. Rita didn't like guns.

"Do you have your knife on you?"

"Of course."

"Let me have it," Marcy told her, holding out her hand but never making eye contact.

The instant Marcy felt the handle hit the palm of her hand, she swung her hand back across Rita's throat, cutting deep into her neck.

"Your services are no longer needed," Marcy said without turning around or looking behind her. A smile crept across her face when she heard Rita's dying body hit the floor. "I'm done with all of you."

Chapter 63

"Hack!" Recon shouted through the door to the stateroom. "Hack!!"

"Kick it open," Savannah said, moving out of the way. *Wham! Wham!! WHAM!!!*

Recon kicked the stateroom door so hard that it came right off its hinges and landed flat on the floor with a loud crash!

"Recon! Dude!! What the hell?" Hack shouted while the couple abruptly sat up in bed.

"Who's the broad?" Recon answered as he pulled a bead on the head of the woman that was sitting next to Hack."

"Recon! Put that gun down!" Hack demanded. "Have you lost your mind?!" The woman tried to cower behind Hack as she whimpered in fear.

"All of the GHOSTS are dead, Hack."

"They were poisoned," Savannah added stepping next to Recon while being on full alert.

"Tabitha is not one of the killers, okay?"

"Prove it," Recon replied with eyes locked on his target. "She's one of them; she's one of the crew."

"Marcy's girls are loyal to Marcy." Savannah added while trying to size up the woman. "She's playing you, Hack."

"Get dressed old friend and come with us. She can wait for you here."

"Hack, don't leave me here!" Tabitha cried while clamping onto his arm. "You have to believe me, I'm not part of that group!"

"Do it, Chris. Shoot her." Savannah instructed.

"I ought to."

"Recon, Stop!" Hack shouted, leaning in front of her.

"She's not one of them! I believe her!"

"She's your baggage," Recon said lowering his pistol. "If she so much as flinches the wrong way, she's done."

"Got it, chick?" Savannah asked rhetorically.

"Both of you, get dressed, let's move."

Chapter 64

"Aunt Desi, are you okay?" Erin asked as she picked herself up off the floor.

"Yeah, I will be," Desi replied, holding her head, trying to shake off her confusion.

"Erin, Desi – I'm in here!" Doc shouted. "I'm tied up!"

"Give us a minute!" Erin shouted back, still shaking off the dizzies.

"Desi, Erin!" Karma shouted as Jesse and she spotted them in the hallway. "What happened? Are you okay?"

"We just got taken by the queen bee," Erin told them.

"Who did this?"

"Marcy," Desi replied, still holding her head. "She's tougher than she looks."

"What are you doing here? Where are Pastor and Georgia-Jean?"

"We can't find them anywhere," Karma informed them.

"Jesse, you need to untie me!" Doc hollered, hearing the voices in the hall. "The boat is rigged to blow!"

Just then, everybody in the hallway traded looks as they silently confirmed with each other what they had just heard.

"Jesse!"

"I'm coming, Doc!"

"Aahhh! The door's locked!" Jesse screamed pounding his fist against the door. "Stand back!" Jesse shouted to the women while he stepped back and rammed the door with his shoulder.

Wham!, wham!!

The second time Jesse rammed the door it broke free, sending both Jesse and the door to the floor. The women quickly hurried, stepping over Jesse to assist Doc.

"Holy cow, Doc! You are butt-naked!" Erin shouted, closing her eyes and turning away.

"A little help, please?" Doc shouted.

"I'm not going over there!" Karma shouted, walking back to Jesse.

"C'mon, Doc!" Jesse shouted. "Put some clothes on! We've gotta get out of here!"

"Jesse, quit making jokes! The boat is rigged to blow!" Doc shouted.

"I'll untie you, Doc!" Desi said, smiling at the sight of Doc lying there completely naked. "You're no good to me tied up!!"

"Aunt Desi, really?"

"Jesse, Marcy is Campers wife!" Doc continued. "This whole thing was a set up! We've got to get off this boat now!"

The instant Doc's feet hit the floor the lights went out. Not a single light was on, anywhere on the yacht.

"She just cut the power!" Doc shouted. "In three minutes, we're dead!"

Chapter 65

With all power cut to the entire yacht and the self-destruct timer counting down, Marcy was now strapping herself into her own personal nuclear-powered submarine. The submarines name was *Project X;* it was a prototype that was built for her to "shut her up" as her late husband would have put it. It was only fourteen feet long. It had a seating capacity of two and could run for up to one full year without needing service. There were enough supplies on the sub for two people to sustain life for up to nine months on minimal rations.

The desalination system meant you'd never run out of drinking water. The *Project X* had a hull crush depth of 770 feet and a maximum underwater speed of thirteen knots per hour. It was complete with sonar, radar and GPS. The sub even carried with it, UHF and VHF radio capabilities. Because it was so small, it could easily be mistaken as a shark or a small whale when it showed up on someone else's sonar screen. Marcy descended into the depths of the ocean from the belly of the yacht, leaving everyone on board to perish with less than 150 seconds until "boom" time.

Chapter 66

"Pastor?" Georgia-Jean asked while sitting up on the boat seat. "Where did the yacht go?"

"Not to worry, Georgia-Jean," Pastor started to reply. "It's right over…" Stopping mid-sentence, Pastor was a little alarmed that he could no longer see the yacht himself. He turned around and saw nothing. Nothing to the left, nothing to the right, nothing anywhere.

"We must have drifted a little bit. That's okay, the sun will be rising shortly, and we'll be able to see it then. I wouldn't worry. We can't be that far away."

"Let's go, let's move, now, now, now!" Jesse shouted as he helped the group through the doorway into the hall.

"I can't see anything, Buck!" Karma told him, tripping over herself.

"Follow the hallway with your hands!"

"Jesse, who's with you?" Recon shouted, hearing the others coming up the hallway.

"Erin, Desi, Karma and Doc. Who's with you?"

"I'm with Savannah, Hack and Tabitha."

"Who's Tabitha?" Doc asked.

"Recon – about face - get off the boat! It's gonna blow!"

"What about my parents, Buck?"

"Karma, let's go! Off the boat! Let's move!"

The group fumbled their way up to the parlor where the deck was illuminated only from the light of the full moon. Everyone knew the timer was counting down and stress levels were extremely high. Finally, being able to see a little bit, Jesse was in a hurry to get everyone off of the yacht before it blew.

"Rachael, is that you?" Holly shouted to the group.

"Holly, Warren, get off the boat now!" Jesse shouted. "It's gonna blow! Get off the boat! Get off the boat!"

The group hurried toward the fan tail of the yacht and stopped as they looked over the edge into the water.

"That's a thirty-foot drop, Jesse!" Holly shouted at him. I'm not…" Before Holly could finish her sentence, Warren picked her up and tossed her over the side of the boat into the 80-degree water.

"Dad!" Karma shouted.

"Rachael, let's go!" Warren shouted back as he dove off himself.

Like an orchestra of bass drums, the bombs started going off.

Boom, boom, boom, boom-boom-boom!

"Go, go, go!" Jesse shouted.

Everyone started jumping into the water and swimming away from the yacht as fast as they could, hoping it wasn't too late. Jesse made sure he was the last in the water for he'd never leave a man behind again.

"There it is, Pastor!" Georgia-Jean said, pointing to the yacht in the distance. "Look," Georgia-Jean said referring to the flashes of light coming from the structure bombs going off. "They're having a light show! It's beautiful!"

When Pastor looked up and saw what was happening his mouth dropped.

"Jesus, Mary and Joseph!" he shouted. "That's not a light show!"

"Swim for your life!!" Jesse shouted to the group. "Swim! Swim! Swim!"

Pastor and Georgia-Jean could now hear the rumbling from the structural bombs going off; then suddenly the entire yacht blew apart like burning matchsticks. A mammoth ball of fire and burning debris illuminated the water as it reached up into the early morning sky, being seen for miles.

"Huh!" Georgia-jean gasped! Pastor!"

"I know Georgia-Jean, I see it. That's not good!"

Bourbon had his paws of the side of the boat and started barking at the scene in the distance. Georgia-Jean grabbed Bourbon and wrapped her arms around him. Pastor fired up the *Chris Craft* and headed in the direction of the yacht, fearful of what he was going to find.

"Captain Thomas" reported one of the crew members on the destroyer. "We've lost the yacht, sir. It just disappeared."

"What do you mean it just disappeared?"

"It's not showing up on radar, sir. It vanished."

Captain Ted Thomas reached for his binoculars and immediately started scanning the horizon in the direction of the yacht.

"Oh my God!" he said in shock when he saw the burning yacht off in the distance. "Get us over there, now! Be sure to make your approach carefully. We don't know what we're going to find."

"Get under the surface and stay together!" Jesse shouted. Grabbing Karma's hand, Jesse took a deep breath and dove as deep as he could. He could only hope the others followed his lead as the debris started raining down upon them.

Chapter 67

Debris flew hundreds of feet into the air from the explosion. The blast was so powerful and intense it literally shattered the yacht into splinters. It rained tiny pieces of debris down on the water with nothing larger than the size of a dinner plate. One at a time the group popped their heads out of the water in desperate need of air. One by one, they swam to each other to huddle together until everyone was accounted for.

"Karma?" Jesse asked, still holding his wife's hand. "Are you okay?"

"I'm okay, Jesse. Where are my parents?"

"Over here, Rachael!" Warren shouted. "We're heading your way."

"Whoa! Yeah!" Recon shouted as he came shooting up out of the water. "We're not in Kansas anymore, are we Commander?"

"There is something wrong with that guy," Holly said, shaking her head.

"Is Savannah with you, Recon?"

"I'm here, Jesse."

"Where are the others?"

"I'm here," Doc said as he swam to the group, speaking for the first time without his French accent. "Hack and Tabitha are bringing a floating cushion."

"What happened to your sexy French accent, Doc?" Savannah asked immediately.

"I thought you were from France." Karma added.

"I believe I told you I was French, not from France." Doc replied with a grin.

"Why don't you clarify that for us old, buddy," Recon added to the conversation.

"I'm from Chicago," Doc said laughing. "I just speak with my French accent to impress the ladies."

"Well, how about that," Recon said looking over towards Jesse. "Just when you think you know someone."

"C'mon, grab hold," Hack said to the group as he and Tabitha swam over with the floating cushion.

The group made their way to the cushion and grabbed onto it, needing the rest and the chance to catch their breath.

"Head count." Jesse shouted. "Who's here? Are you injured?"

"I'm okay, Jesse," Karma started.

"Doc, I'm good."

"Holly, I think I'm okay."

"Warren, no injuries."

"Erin, I'm here Jesse."

"Desi, here."

"Hack, good."

"Tabitha, I'm okay."

"Savannah, I'm okay."

"Yeah, Baby! Whoa!!" Recon shouted.

"You still love the rush, don't you Recon?" Doc asked from across the cushion.

"It's not the job, Doc. It's the adventure!"

"Over here!" Shouted an unknown voice. "I'm over here!"

"Identify yourself!" Jesse commanded.

"Pankow," the voice shouted across the water. "Justin Pankow, Special Ops Marine, sir!"

"Doc, go bring him in."

"On it, Jesse." Doc left the cushion and swam over towards Pankow to help bring him back to the group.

"Look, there is goes." Warren said about the last of the yacht's burning hull dropping below the water line, starting its descent to the bottom of the ocean.

"That's something you don't see every day," Holly said with a somber voice.

Before Justin Pankow had a grip on the cushion, Jesse was firing questions.

"Are you all right?"

"Yes, sir," Justin answered. "I believe so."

"How is it you're alive?"

"Well, for starters, I don't like Jell-O." Justin answered as he gripped the floating cushion. "I was tired and headed to bed when they started passing the shooters around. The next thing I knew some crazy bastard was shouting *get off the boat, get off the boat* so I grabbed my shorts and a t-shirt and jumped off. I swam as far away, as fast as I could."

"You swam the wrong way, buddy," Hack poked.

"Glad to have you with us, Pankow," Jesse said with a tension-filled voice. "Now I am troubled with who else we left alive on that boat."

"All things considered, Buck," Karma said, talking directly to her man but addressing the whole group, "I think we should be grateful we're alive and not dwell on who didn't make it."

"Commander!" Hack said from the other side of the cushion. "What do we do now?"

Chapter 68

The reflection of sunlight was just barely starting to make its presence on the horizon, glistening across the glass-like surface of the ocean.

"Listen," Holly said, quieting the group! "Do you hear a boat?"

"I don't hear anything," Tabitha answered.

"I hear it, too." Karma added.

"Ssshhh!" Doc shushed, trying to hear where it was coming from.

"I don't see anything," Savannah said as she looked around in all directions.

"It's not light enough yet, but I hear it as well," Jesse said scanning the horizon.

"That's a V8," Recon said with a look of concern on his face. "A boat that size couldn't make it out here on its own."

"JESSE, Jesse, jesse. KARMA, Karma, karma," Pastor shouted across the water as the boat idled near. "CAN, Can, can, YOU, You, you HEAR, Hear, hear ME? Me? me?" His voice, echoing across the water, was like a gift from the heavens.

"CAN, Can, can, ANYBODY, Anybody, anybody HEAR, Hear, hear ME? Me? me?"

"That's Pastor! Karma said excitedly to the group. "How in the world?"

"PASTOR! Pastor, pastor. OVER, Over, over. HERE, Here, here!"

Bark! Bark! Bark! Bourbon's sharp eyes honed in on the group of survivors floating in the water about 100 yards away.

"I hear Bourbon!" Savannah started to cry. "He's alive!"

"Do you think Georgia-Jean is with him?" Karma asked Jesse with a devilish grin on her face.

"Undoubtedly."

"How delightful!" Georgia-Jean shouted excitedly to Pastor. "I can hear them! I can hear them!"

"Answered prayers!" Pastor replied easing the throttle up just a tad.

"Wave your hands! I see the boat!" Holly said as she started waving frantically. The group of friends started shouting and hollering, waving their arms uncontrollably, relieved to see the *Chris Craft* approaching.

"I don't believe it," Jesse said shaking his head.

"Like magic, huh," Recon added.

"This ought to be a good story," Desi muttered.

"I see them! I see them!" Georgia-Jean shouted while pointing over to the right a little bit.

"I've got 'em,'" Pastor confirmed. He pulled the throttle back into the neutral position and shut the boat down. He coasted right up to the floating cushion. The group of friends were all cheering and relieved to see Pastor, now saving them from the water. Pastor immediately helped everyone get on board the *Chris Craft*. Women first, then the men.

Of course, Bourbon immediately lavished Savannah with puppy love. Once everyone was out of the water and in the boat, the questions started to fly.

"How is it that you weren't on the yacht?" Jesse questioned, almost angrily, wondering if he had something to do with the explosion.

"Really, Buck?" Karma fired back in Pastor's defense.

"Jesse!" Georgia-Jean interrupted. "Pastor asked me if I wanted to watch the sunrise away from everyone else, that's all."

"Bourbon followed us, so we took him along," Pastor added calmly. "You still don't trust me, do you, Jesse?"

"Trust is earned, buddy," Jesse fired back immediately. "You've got a long way to go."

"Are there any more survivors?" Pastor asked, ignoring Jesse's last comment.

"We haven't really looked for any," Erin answered. "Everyone on the boat was poisoned."

"Anyone left alive on the boat when it blew is surely dead now," Jesse continued.

"Do you think that includes Marcy?" Tabitha asked.

The group was silent, and all looked over to Doc for confirmation."

"I was tied up! I don't know where she went!"

"There were no other boats in the garage when we took this one," Pastor said, trying to connect all the dots.

"I don't see her floating around anywhere," Jesse said, sort of hinting to everyone to keep their eyes peeled.

"She won't last long out here by herself if she's not already dead," Hack said, not really worried about the Marcy situation.

"We kind of have bigger things to focus on right now, like how to remedy the current situation."

"Not to worry, Jesse." Pastor said grinning from ear to ear. "Look behind you."

Jesse and the others on the boat turned to see what Pastor was referring to. Like a unicorn that popped up out of nowhere, the Navy destroyer *Cyclone* was inching its way towards them.

"That your buddy Ted?

"Hell, yes, it is!" Pastor replied smiling.

"Are we ever going to have a normal day together?" Karma asked Jesse while she leaned up against him.

"Mrs. Commander," Doc replied with a chuckle, "this is a normal day with Jesse."

"Jesse?" Karma asked noticing her man looking just a little sad. "What's the matter?"

Jesse looked around one more time for confirmation but knew in his heart, he was gone.

"We lost Kurtis."

"Huh!" Karma gasped as she covered her mouth with her hand.

"The limo driver?" Pastor chimed in. "No, we didn't. He's on a floaty about 100 yards over there." Pastor acknowledged, pointing in the direction of Kurtis. "He insisted we pick you guys up first. Said he needed a moment to clean out his shorts."

Just then, the group heard Kurtis shouting in the distance as he struggled to paddle his way over to the *Chris Craft*.

"Jesse! Come and get me! I don't want to play in your sandbox anymore!" The group chuckled together at Kurtis's comment.

"Let's go pick him up!"

Chapter 69

Later that afternoon, everyone was onboard the Navy destroyer, *Cyclone*. The group met down in the chow hall with Captain Thomas not only to get something to eat, but also for a debriefing.

"First things first," Jesse started after taking a bite out of his sandwich. "Kurtis, how in the world did you get off the yacht?"

"I jumped!" Kurtis answered with a chuckle.

"We all did, brother," Hack told him looking for the long answer.

"I didn't do any of the shooters. I don't like Jell-O. I was passed out on the sofa, and when I heard Jesse yelling *get off the boat, it's gonna blow*, I ran outside and jumped into the water. I swam away as fast as I could."

"You and Pankow, both. I'm glad you made it off, Kurtis."

"Yeah, I'm done playing in your sandbox, Jesse."

The meeting went on with Doc telling everyone what Marcy told him and Pastor explaining how he and Georgia-Jean ended up on the *Chris Craft* to watch a romantic sunrise together.

"Where does that leave us?" Warren asked. "Where are we as far as GHOSTs?"

"There are no more GHOSTs" Jesse answered. "We're retired, all of us. The GHOST agency has been put to rest."

"I don't think you have that kind of power, Jesse," Pastor responded.

"Don't underestimate the power of the man holding all of the cards," Jesse replied sternly, wanting Pastor to remain seen, but not heard.

"So, what do we do when we're dropped off in San Diego?" Hack questioned.

"Whatever you want," Jesse assured the group. "Karma, her parents and I are going to head to Virginia until we figure out what our plan is. Any of you are free to join us."

"If you two are going to Virginia," Doc added, "then I'm gonna head back to Fiji."

"I'm going back to Eureka," Erin announced to the group. "That's where home is. That's where we belong, all of us."

"I'm with you, Erin," Desi commented. "We'll be *there* if you want us for anything."

"So that's it? This was our last hurrah?" Recon asked, a little bummed out. "I thought we were this group of hero's that swooped down and saved the day."

"How many more casinos do you want to bring down, Recon?" Jesse asked with compassion. "How many more burning yachts do you want to jump off of?"

"I waited for you in Eureka, Commander!"

"Recon, you are more than welcome to come to Virginia with us. However, it's time for you and Savannah to focus on each other. Take your money and go enjoy life."

"I want to go to Eureka, Chris." Savannah told him. "I like it there."

"Guys, our war is over," Jesse told them. "Go live your lives."

Chapter 70

Three months later…

"Hey, Buck!" Karma shouted to Jesse as he was putting some steaks on the grill at the Virginia estate. "It's Pastor," she told him handing him his phone.

"Pastor!" Jesse answered cheerfully. "It's great to hear from you! We're about to have steak and eggs for breakfast. Wish you were here!"

"Jesse, I need to talk with you."

"It's awfully early out there, Pastor," Jesse said, noticing the time in Virginia was only 7:15am. "What's the matter? Is everything okay?"

"We need to meet, Jesse."

"I'm not going to Eureka, Pastor, but you're more than welcome to come out here any time you want."

"We're pulling in the driveway right now," Pastor said right before he disconnected the call.

Jesse put away his phone and looked down the hill towards the end of the drive. He saw three black Chevrolet Suburbans entering the driveway at a rather high rate of speed. Jesse removed his apron and headed through the house to meet them out front. He knew this was not good. Anytime you see black Suburbans in Northern Virginia traveling in groups, you need to proceed with caution. It was a red flag for potential trouble.

"What's going on Jesse?" Warren asked, seeing the seriousness in Jesse's face.

"Pastor's here," Jesse answered, focused on where he was headed. "Apparently with some friends."

"Feds?" Warren questioned as he followed Jesse.

"Looks like it."

Jesse, Karma and her parents all walked out front together. As the vehicles stopped at the top of the drive, Pastor was the first to exit, followed by several Secret Service agents, two US Marshalls and then the President of the United States, himself.

"What's going on here?" Jesse asked sternly.

"Jesse," Pastor said as he walked towards him, "I'd like to introduce you to the President of the United States of America. Mr. President, this is Navy SEAL Commander, Jesse Buck."

"Yeah, it's former Navy SEAL Commander *and* former GHOST agent," Jesse said, eyeballing the President.

"I know who he is," the President replied.

Without shaking hands or even showing the slightest emotion about being there, the President got straight to the point.

"Commander Buck," the President started with a very stern, unpleasant attitude. "You killed a top-secret government official."

"No, I..."

"I'm talking about the Kaiser!" The President interrupted angrily.

"Your top-secret government official was nothing more than a shady thug. He was a liar!!" Jesse fired right back. "He was in on it the whole time!"

"Commander Buck!" The President's shouting continued. "The Kaiser was not in on anything. He was a very highly respected individual who was a master at doing his job. You were on a need to know basis and you didn't need to know. You, Mr. Buck, have been played for a fool!"

"Mr. President, sir! I suggest you tell me why you are here or get off my land."

"I'm here to tell you what your next assignment is."

"I don't answer to you!" Jesse shouted in the President's face. "There are no rules to this game, remember? I owe you nothing. I'm retired."

"I don't think you understand the magnitude of your situation," the President continued with a slightly lowered voice. "Your only options are GHOST agent or federal prison for murder. I'm sure Pastor told you that once you are a GHOST, you are a GHOST for life. You, Mr. Buck, are the best. You're the best there has ever been."

"What are you getting at?" Jesse asked angrily, stepping into the President's personal space. The Secret Service agents all pulled their side arms out and drew beads on Jesse's head, fearing aggressive actions would be taken towards the President.

"On the contrary, Commander Buck. There are rules to this game. I make the rules and you do answer to someone. You answer to me. You killed the Kaiser," the President told him with a clenched jaw. "You're the Kaiser now."

"Screw you!" Jesse shouted. "I'll take door number two! I'll take federal prison."

"Very well. Arrest him!" the President ordered while snapping his fingers.

"No!" Karma shouted as she and her parents moved towards the group. Warren grabbed Karma and tried to hold her back, but she fought against her father's grip.

"You can't do that!" Warren shouted. "He's no criminal!"

"Stand down!" one of the Secret Service agents shouted while they all pulled beads on Karma, Warren and Holly.

The threesome stopped and watched helplessly, nervous over what was about to unfold.

"It's okay, Karma," Jesse told her as the two US Marshalls moved in and took Jesse into custody. "Get my lawyer Bobby Morgan on the phone. He'll take care of this."

With Jesse in handcuffs, the President held up his hand ordering the US Marshalls to hold up for a moment as he started to speak.

"Commander," the President spoke with a snide attitude, "your lawyer cannot help you. No one can help you. You no longer exist, remember? You have thirty seconds to make up your mind. You either honor your contract as a CIA GHOST agent or spend the rest of your life rotting at ADX in Florence, CO. What's it gonna be?"

"Jesse, don't do it!" Karma said softly with tears falling from her eyes. "Don't leave me, Jesse. We'll figure it out."

"What's it going to be, Mr. Buck? You have twenty seconds."

"I'm sorry, Karma."

"Take him!" The President ordered the Marshalls, while snapping his fingers again. "Put him in the vehicle."

Karma turned into her father's shoulder and wept while her parents stood there in silence, in complete disbelief over what unfolded right in front of them.

"Mr. President," Pastor said before the President got into his vehicle. "Mr. President!"

"What is it, Mr. Cary?"

"We have no one else."

"That's not my problem, Mr. Cary. That's your problem, and I suggest you get started figuring it out."

"He is not the criminal, here!" Pastor shouted, but the President and his team ignored the words that were just spoken and proceeded to leave with Jesse in custody.

"Move in!" Pastor shouted at the top of his lungs, waving his hand over his head. "Move in now!"

Hearing this, Jesse struggled to escape but was forced into the back of one of the Suburbans. Warren pushed Karma and Holly to the ground as they watched Jesse's SEAL team rise like magic from the grass. They were surrounded and never knew it. Weapons were drawn and the threat was real. Blood was sure to be spread.

"Stand down!" Doc shouted at the group of feds with his monstrous voice. "Stand down immediately or you will be fired upon!"

Karma and her parents watched with pounding hearts, wondering what they could do to help.

"Get me out of here!" the President shouted, diving into the lead Suburban.

The three Suburbans fled the scene and headed down the hill at a high rate of speed, hurrying to try and escape the ambush.

"Fire!" Doc commanded the SEALs with authority.

"It's go-time ladies," Pastor said ferociously into a handheld radio. "Stop those vehicles! Jesse's in the middle!"

Pow! Pow! Pow! could be heard in the distance. The unmistakable crack that can only be made from a high-powered rifle echoed across the northern Virginia hillside. While the SEALs were pumping hundreds of rounds of ammunition into the vehicles' trying to disable them, Erin and Desi were placed on an adjacent hillside with instructions to take out the drivers.

"Savannah!" Pastor yelled into a two-way radio. "Stop the lead vehicle!"

Savannah, who was sitting on standby in Jesse's armored Hummer, slammed the gas pedal to the floor on a mission to take out the lead vehicle. She guided the armored vehicle as it sped down the street towards the entrance to the driveway.

The driver of the middle vehicle was shot and killed. His lifeless body lay hunched over the steering wheel and his foot lay heavy on the gas pedal, causing it to pin itself against the lead vehicle. Savannah saw the vehicles leave the driveway and, with her foot still on the floor, she rammed them both right where they were touching, sending them both into violent spins. The two Suburbans spun into rolls and tumbled off the road and into the ditch. The driver of the third Suburban, also killed, just missed Savannah and crashed into the ditch as well.

As the SEAL team moved in to surround the vehicles, the government agents opened fire on them, spraying lead frantically to eliminate the threat. The SEAL team returned fire, determined to not lose the battle.

"Cease fire!" Pastor shouted, but the SEAL team kept shooting.

"Cease fire!!" Pastor ordered, but still the SEALs continued to pump hundreds and hundreds of rounds into the vehicles and the agents, until they were no longer fired upon.

"CEASE FIRE! CEASE FIRE!!" Pastor shouted at the top of his lungs. "STOP SHOOTING NOW!!!"

Doc held his fist up, ordering Recon and Hack to stop firing their weapons. Instantly, the shooting stopped, the noise silenced and the smoke from the barrels dissipated as everyone watched and listened intently.

Warren, Holly and Karma came running down the hill shocked with what they saw. The vehicles looked like Swiss cheese and there were no signs of life, anywhere.

"Jesse!" Karma shouted with tears falling from her eyes.

"Stay back!" Doc yelled to everyone as he was not sure if the situation was safe or not.

Wham! Wham! Wham! The group could hear some sort of banging coming from one of the vehicles.

"Jesse!" Karma shouted again.

Wham! The back door of one of the vehicles was kicked open and Jesse climbed out. He was still wearing the hand cuffs but managed to bring them to the front of his body. In his hand he clenched a Glock .40 caliber pistol from one of the government agents. Oblivious to everything around him, Jesse was on a mission, a mission to find the President.

"Jesse!" Doc hollered at him. "Jesse, watch your back!"

317

"Find the keys!" Jesse shouted back still marching towards what was left of the lead vehicle. "Get me out of these cuffs!"

"Secure the perimeter!" Doc shouted to the SEALs as he waved his hand in the air.

Jesse marched over to the front vehicle, which came to rest on its roof and kicked the passenger side window, shattering the glass.

"Vehicle three, clear!" Recon shouted in the background.

"Vehicle two, clear!" Hack immediately confirmed. "I've got the keys!"

The government agents, every one of them, dead. There were only two survivors amongst the carnage, Jesse and the President. Jesse reached into the Suburban, dragged the President out through the window and slammed him down on the asphalt where he started to beat on him.

"I don't report to you! Do you hear me! None of us report to you!!"

"Jesse, stop!" Karma shouted as she ran over.

"Pull him off! Pull him off!" Pastor added. Doc and Hack ran to the scene and tried to pull Jesse off the President.

"WE'RE DONE! DO YOU HEAR ME?! LEAVE US ALONE!!" Jesse fought with everything he had, beating on the President, slamming him into the asphalt. Yelling and screaming in the man's face. Jesse was so out of control, Doc and Hack couldn't pull Jesse off him.

"Recon! Help them!" Pastor ordered.

"LEAVE US ALONE! DO YOU UNDERSTAND ME?!" Jesse yelled in the President's face again. "I'LL

318

BRING DOWN A WAR ON YOU SO SWIFT AND SO
SEVERE THAT YOU'LL WISH YOU DIED IN THAT
VEHICLE RIGHT THERE!"

"Get him off!" Karma shouted. "Get him off! Dad,
Pastor – help them pull Jesse off!"

"THIS NEVER HAPPENED! YOU HEAR ME!! THIS
ENDS RIGHT NOW – DO I MAKE MYSELF CLEAR!!
IT'S OVER! THE CIA GHOSTS ARE DONE!! THIS
ENDS RIGHT NOW!!!"

Jesse slammed the President into the asphalt one last
time and finally let go of him. It wasn't until then that the
other SEALs could pull Jesse off the President.

"Get off of me!" Jesse commanded his SEAL team,
breaking free from their clutches as he walked calmly
toward Karma.

"Keys!" he shouted. Without saying a word, Hack
handed Jesse the keys to unlock the hand cuffs he was still
wearing.

"Recon, Doc, Hack!" Jesse commanded. "Rendezvous
point. Three days. Fall out, now!!"

Without saying a word, the SEALs headed over to the
Hummer and got in. The armored Hummer was hardly
scratched from the impact of ramming the Suburbans.
With Savannah still behind the wheel, the foursome sped
off.

"Jesse, what rendezvous point? You're bleeding! Are
you sure you want to just up and leave?" Karma's words
were almost desperate as she tried to get into her husband's
mind. "Jesse, talk to me!"

"Warren, Holly – you have the house," Jesse told them as he walked right past, now tossing his handcuffs and keys into the bushes on the side of the road.

"Jesse, maybe you should…" before Pastor could finish his sentence, Jesse spun around and landed a hard righthand hook across Pastor's face. He hit Pastor so hard that it knocked him clean off his feet. Jesse stepped over him and looked down at Pastor lying on the ground.

"That's for fouling up my life!" Jesse spoke as he towered over him. "You're lucky I don't bury you." Jesse just glared at Pastor for a moment. He watched Pastor lay on the ground as he knew Pastor didn't have the nerve to try and get up.

"I suggest you find a way to clean up this mess you got us all in. Get it figured out or our next mission will be you."

"Karma!" Jesse said to his wife as he took her by the hand and headed up towards the house. "Get what you need, we're out of here in ten."

When they got up to the house, the couple went in separate directions. Jesse and Karma wasted no time gathering needed supplies. While Karma was in the bedroom putting a bag of clothes together for the two of them, Jesse was downstairs in the vault putting together a duffel bag with other needed necessities when Warren walked in.

"You have a plan, Jesse?"

"We've got to get out of here before anyone comes looking for the President."

"Where are you heading?"

"That's not important right now. It's a safe place, only my team and I know where it is," Jesse told him as he continued to stuff his bag with guns, ammo and money.

"Karma will be safe, Warren. You don't have to worry about that."

"Holly and I worry about the both of you."

"I don't know where this is going to lead, Warren."

"I know you have to leave, Jesse, I get it. Just keep in touch from time to time. We'll be here, with the dogs."

"Thanks, Warren." The two men gave each other a man hug. They both understood the current situation and knew there were no more words to be shared, only actions to be taken.

"Jesse's a good man, Rachael," Holly told her daughter as she gave her a hug. "We know you'll be safe with him."

"I'm sorry, Mom. I must go. He's my man and I'm not leaving his side."

"Good men are hard to come by, honey. I know you have to go."

"KARMA – LET'S GO!" the ladies heard from the other end of the house.

"You'd better get out of here, Rachael. I love you!"

"I love you too, Mom!"

The two women gave each other a hug and shared a single tear as they headed toward the other end of the house. They found Jesse shirtless at the kitchen sink, washing off the morning's excitement. Taking a wet towel, he washed the blood off his face, hands and arms. When he dried off, Warren tossed him a clean t-shirt that he got out of the laundry room. The t-shirt was solid black. The back of the t-shirt boasted a large cross with the words *Jesus has got my back.*

"Figured someone should have your back for the next few weeks," Warren told him with a chuckle.

"Karma, let's go."

Jesse headed to the garage. He put the duffel bags in the trunk and opened the door for Karma to get in.
"We're taking this?" she asked out of curiosity. "We've never taken this car anywhere."

"Just in case we need something fast," Jesse replied with a smirk. Once inside the car Jesse depressed the clutch and hit the start button. The powerful performance Cadillac came to life and once again purred like a predator, waiting to be unleashed with the odometer still reading 217 miles on it.

"Sounds nice, Jesse. Does this thing really move?"

"We're about to find out!"

Karma blew a kiss to her parents as Jesse backed out of the garage and before the car had stopped moving, Jesse revved the engine and dumped the clutch in 2nd gear. The rpm's soared as the back tires roasted themselves in a growing cloud of grey tire smoke. As Jesse launched the Caddy down the driveway, it pushed him and Karma deep into the Recaro seats with impressive acceleration.

"Whoa!" Jesse hollered. "Does that answer your question?"

"Hell, yes, it does!" Karma answered, grinning from ear to ear. At the end of the driveway, Jesse slowed just enough to maneuver the Caddy through the wrecked vehicles and the debris on the roadway. Pastor was standing there with his hand up, signaling for Jesse to stop.

"Jesse! Jesse, wait a minute!" Pastor shouted.

"Looks like Pastor wants to talk to you," Karma said, wondering what was about to happen.

"I have nothing to say to that guy right now," Jesse commented, driving right past him. Once Jesse was clear of the debris, he dropped the hammer in the Caddy. The CTS-V climbed into triple digits as if it were nothing and begged to be pushed for more. The Cadillac accelerated like a Z06 Corvette and handled like a slot car.

"I like the Caddy," Karma told her man with a smile. "I like my Corvette better, though."

"Glad you like it. You'll be in it for a few hours."

"A few hours? I thought you told Recon three days?"

"That was secret squirrel talk to throw Pastor off our trail."

"Then where exactly are you taking me, Buck?" Karma asked looking over at her man.

"To the rendezvous point."

"And where is this rendezvous point exactly?"

"Pikes Peak."

Chapter 71

"Mr. President, are you okay?" Pastor asked cautiously as he approached the man who was finally getting up off the ground.

"Am I okay?" the President shouted angrily. "That animal is on the loose! He's killed all of my men and he tried to kill me, and you're going to ask me if I'm okay?"

"How exactly did Jesse Buck try to kill you while he was handcuffed in the back of another vehicle?" Pastor asked with a bit of attitude.

"You set this whole thing up, didn't you, Tom?"

"I set up nothing, Mr. President. Jesse Buck and his team are always on full alert. I had no way of knowing this was going to happen."

"You should be arrested!" the President shouted. "You have obviously forgotten on which side of the fence your loyalty should lie.

"Mr. President," Pastor replied, calmly handing him a handkerchief from his pocket to wipe the blood off his face, "Jesse Buck and his team will never be found, that man is gone. You need to let this go."

"Let this go! Look at this mess!"

"Looks like a training exercise that went horribly wrong, if you ask me."

"A training exercise that went wrong?" the President shouted at Pastor. "Are you out of your mind? I want that man caged like the animal he really is!"

"How do you cage a man that doesn't exist?" Pastor shouted back at the President. "We've stripped that man of his life and dropped him into a pit against his will. He gets the job done. This *mess* just shows you how incompetent *your* men really are. Let it go. He's the best there is, and he's been through a lot. I suggest you take a good hard look at this carnage and take heed. Jesse Buck doesn't know how to lose. Let it go!"

"Go spit!" the President shouted.

"Then I'm out as well, Mr. President." Pastor turned away and started walking up the driveway towards the house, hoping Desi and Erin were smart enough to continue to lay low and not be seen or get caught. Pastor knew that reinforcements for the President were not far away and was surprised that they hadn't already shown up.

"Tom!" The President shouted. "Tom!!"

Not wanting to show any disrespect, Pastor stopped and turned around, waiting for him to speak.

"I am the President of the United States…"

"Maybe you should think about that for a moment," Pastor interrupted. "Maybe you should think about the freedom Jesse Buck and his team gave the people that voted you into office, so you could have that title. Without leaders like Jesse Buck and the team that follows him, you sir, would be the animal in the cage."

"I will not be…" the President started to reply.

"This is your mess to clean up, Mr. President, not mine," Pastor interrupted again. He could hear several vehicles coming down the road a high rate of speed and knew it was the President's cavalry.

"You can contact me when you come to your senses, Mr. President. In the meantime, I suggest you take a moment to remember what's *really* going on here and get your head right." Pastor proceeded to calmly walk up towards the house wondering if he would be taken into custody or if the President would let well enough alone. Pastor looked up toward the sky and prayed out loud, saying "Dear Lord, please keep Jesse and his team safe. Amen!"

Chapter 72

Five hours up the road where the interstates I-70 and I-77 intersect is the sleepy little town of Cambridge, Ohio. Cambridge is not a very big place and easily overlooked on a map unless you need gas. Just off the highway is a Wal-Mart shopping center that Jesse proceeded to head toward and, once he pulled into the parking lot, he immediately spotted his black Hummer and the passengers inside waiting for him.

"What's going on, Buck?" Karma asked, needing some clarification.

"Well, Karma," Jesse started with a sigh, "we're about thirty minutes away from camp. This is the best place to pick up some groceries and supplies."

"Camp? Supplies?" Karma asked almost with disapproval in her voice. Are we really going camping, Buck?"

"Have I ever lied to you, Baby?"
Smack! Karma slapped Jesse in the leg hard telling him "Don't call me Baby!"

"Haha," Jesse chuckled. "Karma, you know I only do that to get a rise out of you."

"Well, don't!" Karma snapped back angrily "or you'll be *camping* by yourself!"

Jesse parked the Caddy next to the Hummer and the party of six exited the vehicles and headed towards the door.

"Let's break up into two teams," Jesse ordered. "Recon, you go with Karma and Savannah to get groceries. Doc,"

Jesse continued while reaching down to hold Karma's hand, "you and Hack come with me."

"What kind of groceries should we be buying?" Karma asked, hoping for some instruction.

"Anything you want. We'll be here for a few days."

"Do we have anything to cook on?" Savannah asked prodding for details. "We're *camping*, is it?"

"We're actually glamping," Jesse replied with a smile. "There is a full kitchen and a grill. We even have running water; we just don't have any food. It's been awhile since I've been here."

Not sure of much, the group broke off into two teams and completed their shopping spree. With the vehicles loaded up, the group was once again on the road.

Chapter 73

Salt Fork State Park is located in southeast Ohio about 10 miles north of where interstate highways I-70 and I-77 intersect. There is a huge lake, a lodge to stay in, cabins to rent, a beautiful golf course and more. It's a tranquil place to visit and spend some quality time with not only the ones you love, but also with nature, and if fishing's your thing, the lake has plenty to offer every angler.

Not far from Salt Fork rests an RV campground known to the public as Whispering Oaks. It's a gated community where all walks of life gather. It's the kind of place where backgrounds don't matter as much as friendships. The kind of place where trust goes a long way and there is no room for liars or unethical people.

The members actually own their lots and pay annual HOA dues, and they like it that way. It's a lot less transient with lot ownership and one gets the opportunity to really know their neighbor and the fellow campers.

It's a safe place. One doesn't worry about their kids taking off on their bicycles or running around to go play for hours at a time, and to date it doesn't even show up on a GPS.

"Where's he taking us, Chris?" Savannah asked as she followed Jesse through the gate at the entrance to the campground.

"I have no idea, baby," Recon answered back just as curious as she was.

"You know how Jesse is," Hack added. "He's got a port for every storm."

"I'd hardly call this a port in the storm," Savannah continued, "This place looks a little…"

"A little, what?" Doc interrupted.

"Casual, maybe?" Savannah whispered with caution.

"What in the world is that supposed to mean?" Hack chimed in. "It's a campground, Savannah. People here are *supposed* to be casual."

"I don't know, it's just a little…" Savannah stopped mid-sentence and took it all in while the group of four followed Jesse and Karma in the black Caddy to their destination. In just a few moments, the two vehicles pulled up to a campsite that was occupied by two trailers. One was an older mobile home and the other was a newer 30' camper.

"Is this what you call camping?" Karma asked, questioning Jesse's decision to bring everyone here. The grass was almost waist-high, and the place looked as if it hadn't been touched in years.

"I guess no one has been here since before my father died."

"Jesse, are you serious? This is where we're staying?" Karma asked getting out of the car.

"Karma, will you please have a little faith in me?"

"Yo, Commander!" Recon shouted, getting out of the Hummer. "We've stayed in some rough places before you and I but…"

"Stop!" Jesse commanded. "Doc, Hack, you two are up in the camper." Jesse said, tossing a set of keys over to Hack. "Open it up, get it plugged in, hook the water up to the back. Let me know if you have any questions."

"We're on it, Commander." Doc replied, heading up the hill.

"Recon, Savannah, the two of you are with us here. You get the guest room. Karma and I get the master suite. Karma, you and Savannah check out the inside while Recon and I get things hooked up out here. DOC! HACK!! We're on yard cleanup detail in 15 minutes!" Jesse shouted.

"Karma," Jesse said holding out his hand. "Trust me."

Karma took Jesse by the hand and together they walked up the stairs and onto the deck. The mobile home was completely covered by a roof-over that had a large deck running the length of it. There were two glass top patio tables and chairs on the deck, along with a grill under a cover. Everything was covered with dust and pollen. Jesse proceeded to unlock the sliding glass door and slide it open.

"After you, my love," Jesse said as he stepped aside to let Karma enter first. To Karma's surprise, the interior of the mobile home was beautiful. It was a 1960 Princess home that had been totally remodeled just a few years before. Hardwood floors glistened. Beautiful white cabinets in the kitchen were complimented with grey and black granite countertops. The stainless-steel appliances accented everything perfectly.

"This is lovely," Savannah said, entering behind Jesse.

"Jesse, I am impressed," Karma said humbly. It's a little dirty, but I'm very impressed."

"It took us a long time to get this place looking like this," Jesse replied with a kiss. "I'll tell you all about it later. You and Savannah get to work cleaning up in here. Recon and I will bring in the groceries and then we'll jump on the yardwork. In a couple of hours, we'll all be sitting on the deck laughing, waiting for the grill to warm up."

"Get to work, Buck." Karma said, smacking Jesse on the butt. "We've got this!"

"C'mon chick," Karma said to Savannah as Jesse and Recon headed outside. "It's time to roll our sleeves up and lay down some elbow grease."

In less than fifteen minutes, both trailers were hooked up to water and the power was on. The women were wiping everything down on the insides and the four men were frantically cleaning up the yard. Hack was on stick detail, picking up sticks and yard debris from the trees and tossing them into the fire pit. Jesse and Recon were both using mowers to cut the grass, Jesse on a little red riding mower and Recon was using a push mower. Doc was out of control with the weed eater, almost having too much fun.

True to Jesse's word, in less than two hours the chores were done and "Camp Jesse," as Jesse called it was in tip top shape.

"Okay, Buck." Karma started in as she handed Jesse a Johnny Walker Blue on the rocks, "start talking. How is it that you own property in an RV campground on the other side of the country?"

"Now this is a story that I can't wait to hear!" Recon added, wondering why Jesse had never mentioned this before.

"That makes two of us," Doc injected into the conversation.

"Three of us," Hack agreed while clinking glasses with Doc.

"The short story is," Jesse started, "my grandmother was an original lot owner up here in the 70's and my father thought it would be a good land investment for me. I bought it when I was 18, and through the years either my father or I took care of it."

"Your father took it over when you went into the Navy, didn't he?" Hack questioned. "Yeah, and he's probably the one who restored it," Doc continued.

"Call it how you see it," Jesse replied with a smile. "It's a port in the storm."

"A cozy one at that!" Karma said while leaning over to kiss her man.

"Isn't this a little, well, redneck, up here?" Savannah asked very cautiously.

"That's coming from a woman out of Texas," Recon said in disbelief.

"What do you know about rednecks, Dallas?" Savannah fired back, sending the group into a hysterical laugh.

"Why do you say that, Savannah?" Jesse asked looking for specifics.

"Look at all of these people riding around on four-wheelers. They all have beers in their hands."

"That doesn't make them rednecks, Savannah," Doc answered before Jesse could respond.

"Savannah," Jesse started, "take a good look at these people. These are not rednecks up here. These people are not labeled Democrats or Republicans. These people are Americans."

"Yeah, baby!" Recon shouted while Hack and Doc whistled and cheered to Jesse's response. "These folks work hard all week and they play hard all weekend. These folks get it done. They're good people. It's safe up here. Let 'em nurse a beer while they ride through the park or visit fellow campers. It doesn't bother me at all. Besides, it can't be that redneck up here. We even have our own celebrity!"

"HEY JESSE!!!" a man shouted from his golf cart, holding up his beer as he rode by the campsite. "IT'S GOOD TO SEE YOU AGAIN, BROTHER! WOOHOO!!"

"Who in the world was that?" Karma asked with a laugh.

"That's Cleveland," Jesse responded with a chuckle and a wave to the fellow camper. "I don't know his real name. Since he's such a huge Cleveland Browns fan, he's been dubbed with the nickname, Cleveland. The whole campground knows him as Cleveland."

"Is he sober?" Savannah asked, again with caution.

"Haha," Jesse chuckled. "Probably not. But a better question is, how is it you all were hiding on my property, ambushed the Presidential parade and escaped up here with me?"

"That is a good question," Karma said, supporting her man.

"Jesse," Recon started, looking Jesse square in the eye. "Pastor brought us in on this just in case things went awry, which they did. He told us the President wasn't happy with you, and he didn't want to see you get taken away."

"Well, screw the President," Karma replied, taking a sip of Scotch.

"Yeah, well, we all have targets painted on our heads now. We've got to figure this out." Jesse added.

"Jesse," Savannah started again very cautiously. "Who's the celebrity that camps up here with you? What's their name?"

"You don't believe me, do you?" Jesse asked with a smirk.

"No, I don't."

"Who is it, Buck?" Karma asked, more for Savannah than anything.

"Our celebrity is an author," Jesse replied with a pause, intentionally dragging out the suspense. "You probably don't know him Savannah, his name is Waddell."

"You're telling me Thomas Waddell camps up here with you?" Savannah asked with a sassy attitude. "The Thomas Waddell?" The famous writer, Thomas Waddell?"

"Yeah, Savannah. That's what I'm telling you."

"You know who that guy is?" Recon asked his woman, not knowing she was much of a reader.

"Hell, yes, I know who that guy is!" Savannah answered excitedly. His books are amazing!"

"I've never even heard of him," Doc said not having a clue as to who they were talking about.

"He writes thrillers!" Savannah exclaimed, almost giddy. "It doesn't matter what he writes; they are all good! I'm his biggest fan!!"

The group chuckled together as it seemed "Camp Jesse" was okay after all.

"So, what's the plan, Jesse?" Hack asked eager to get back to work.

"Enjoy my steak and grilled veggies with you fine people," Jesse answered deliberately avoiding Hack's question. "Sit by a campfire and sip Scotch with my beautiful wife after that."

"You always say the nicest things," Karma whispered into Jesse's ear with a kiss to his earlobe.

"That's not what I meant, Commander."

"I don't have a plan, Hack. Not yet anyway." Jesse answered almost honestly, not wanting to get into the nitty-gritty of what happens next. "I don't even have the micro SD card. It's in Bourbon's collar, so I can't review any information to come up with a plan."

Hack reached down into his pocket and pulled out a thumb drive. "Here, catch." He told Jesse as he tossed it over to him. "I made copies of the micro SD card, and there's a laptop in the Hummer."

"Nicely done, Hack," Jesse replied with a smile. "Very nicely done."

"Back to the original question - what's the plan?"

"The plan right now is to enjoy the evening; we'll worry about a plan tomorrow. No one's going to find us here. We're safe."

Just then an orange 1971 Corvette convertible pulled off the road and right up onto the grass. It was a beautiful machine. It had chrome side-pipes and custom wheels. The hood told the Corvette world that it boasted a 454 underneath it and the revs to the engine before it was shut down told the group it was matched with a manual gearbox.

"Oh my gosh!" Savannah whispered loudly to the group. "That's Thomas Waddell right there!"

"I know who he is, Savannah," Jesse replied nonchalantly. "Tom and I go way back."

"You know Thomas Waddell?" Savannah questioned in a whisper.

"Tom!" Jesse said getting up from his chair and stepping off the deck to greet his long-time friend, ignoring Savannah's question. "How are you doing old friend?"

"Jesse, it's been a long time," Thomas replied, giving Jesse a man hug. "It's good to see you!"

"Damn good to see you too, Tom. C'mon on up, join us. What can I get you to drink?"

"You still drinking Scotch?" Thomas asked as he followed Jesse up the stairs to the deck.

"You know it."

"I'm on it," Recon said, jumping up from his chair to fetch a rocks glass and some ice for Thomas.

"Mr. Waddell, may I please have your autograph? I'm your biggest fan!" Savannah said, standing eagerly with her hand held out to shake.

"I don't have anything to write on or with, honey," Tom replied with a smile. "If you have your phone handy, I'll take a selfie with you. How's that?"

Seconds later Savannah had a selfie that was undeniable proof that she had met her favorite author and she was giddy from ear to ear.

After introductions, everyone was settled around the table sipping their favorite beverage and enjoying the company. There were lots of questions for Tom about being an author, and there were lots of questions from him about being a SEAL. In what seemed to be no time at all, the steaks were coming off the grill.

"Tom, we have plenty of food, please stay, have dinner with us." Jesse invited.

"I didn't bring anything, Jesse. Are you sure?"

"Buddy, we go back a long time," Jesse insisted. "Of course, I'm sure."

"Thank you, Jesse. Don't mind if I do."

Dinner passed gracefully. Everything was cleaned up and the group was sitting around a campfire listening to Jesse and Tom catch up. Every so often a fellow camper would pass by on a golf cart or a four-wheeler and throw up a wave and a shout, showing their welcome.

"So, Tom," Jesse started, looking over towards his car. "That's a pretty hot looking Corvette you're sporting over there.

"Jesse," Tom replied, grinning from ear to ear, "that my friend, is an original, thirty-two-thousand-mile car. Its color is known as Ontario Orange. Of course, it has a 454 under the hood. Jesse, that's one of 12 ZR-2's produced, ever."

"That's a ZR-2?"

"Not only is it a ZR-2, it's the *only* ZR-2 produced in that color."

"What's a ZR-2?" Savannah asked not knowing much about cars.

"In 1971," Karma answered, showing off her car knowledge a little, "there were a couple of high-performance options available on the Corvette. The ZR-2 package consisted of special high-performance suspension, high performance brakes and a close ratio four speed transmission. It also came with a heavy-duty cooling system. You had the ZR-1 option for the 350, and the ZR-2 option for the 454."

"That's exactly right, Karma. I'm impressed," Tom told her. "Jesse, you want to take it for a spin?"

"I do!" Karma fired right back.

"I wanna go!" Savannah added immediately, following Karma's lead.

"Go ahead ladies," Tom replied with a smile. "The key's in the ignition."

"Ah, Mr. Waddell," Recon replied cautiously, as the women were already up and walking toward the car, "are you sure you want to do that?"

"That's a pretty rare car," Hack added, following Recon's lead.

"Sure, why not?" Tom questioned. "They seem harmless."

Jesse, Recon, Doc and Hack burst into uncontrollable laughter when they heard Thomas's comment.

"Harmless is not exactly the word I would use to describe either one of them," Jesse barely got out over his laughter.

"Animals," Karma said to Savannah while rolling her eyes.

"They'll be fine, Jesse, I'm not worried."

"Karma!" Jesse shouted to the ladies who were now fastening their seatbelts. "Don't over drive it."

"I've got this, Buck! I love you!!"

"Thanks, Mr. Waddell!" Savannah hollered right before the 454 erupted with life.

"The gate card is in the pouch!" Tom hollered back.

Savannah looked in the pouch located on the dashboard right in front of her. Seeing the gate card, she pulled it out and held it up, confirming that they had it. Seconds later the two women were gone.

"Hey, Commander," Doc said entering the conversation, "not that I'm at all *not interested* in listening to you and Mr. Waddell here catch up, but is there anything else to do around here?"

"Now you're talking," Hack added, a little bored himself. Jesse looked over at Thomas and thought for a moment. "It's been a while since I've..."

"Send them over to Leslie's," Thomas interrupted. "There's always a good crowd over there. Good people. I'm sure they'll enjoy themselves."

"How do we get there?" Recon asked, implying he was looking for directions.

"Start humping, buddy, just like being back in the desert," Hack replied getting up from his log.

"Doc," Jesse said as he tossed him a small ignition key from his pocket, "there's a golf cart in the garage next to the trailer you and Hack are staying in. You guys can take that."

"Thanks, Jesse!" Doc replied with a smile, snatching the key out of the air without ever taking his eyes off Jesse. "Which way are we going?"

"Up to the top of the hill," Thomas pointed as he gave perfect directions. "Take a right, another right at the intersection just past the pool, third road on the left. You can't miss it."

"Don't wait up guys," Hack said as he and Recon started to walk up the hill towards the garage.

"Don't worry and hey, Recon!" Jesse shouted. "Don't go over there empty handed. Take what you're gonna drink."

"Drink your Scotch, Commander," Recon hollered back. "We've already got that taken care of."

A red Yamaha golf cart with a suspension lift kit, oversized off-road tires, one-piece roof and lights went up the hill with the three SEALs who were out seeking a little fun.

"Thanks, Tom. They'll have a good time."

"At Leslie's? They'll have a great time!"

Chapter 74

The hours passed and the sun had tucked itself behind the treelined hills off in the distance. Jesse and Tom continued to sit by the campfire and sip their Scotch, reminiscing and catching up, completely forgetting that Karma and Savannah had left in Thomas's Corvette, and not realizing that they'd been gone for hours until they saw the flashing lights reflecting off the treelined campground roads.

"What's with those flashing lights coming down the hill?" Jesse asked as he pointed them out to Thomas.

"White and yellow," Thomas replied. "It's not a cop car."

"Hear that?" Jesse asked a little concerned, getting up from his chair. "It's a diesel engine, that's a tow truck."

"No way."

"This can't be good, buddy."

Just then the flatbed tow truck came into view and stopped in front of Jesse's place. What was left of Tom's 71 Corvette was strapped to the back. All the neighbors started to gather around at a distance to watch and listen as Karma and Savannah sheepishly exited from the passenger's side of the flatbed hauler.

"Are you kidding me?" Thomas muttered under his breath in disbelief.

"Karma, Savannah!" Jesse hollered. "Are you two all right?"

"What happened?" Thomas asked immediately.

"Where do y'all want this pile of scrap dropped?" The tow truck driver asked coming around the front of the vehicle.

Karma just shook her head as she got closer to Jesse. Before she could get her arms around him for a hug, tears started falling.

"Hey, Karma. It's okay," Jesse told her.

"You girls okay?" Thomas asked again, softly, giving Savannah a hug. "Don't worry about the car. Is either of you hurt?" Thomas shot Jesse a glare of frustration without the women noticing. Jesse knew he was not happy about the severely damaged, ultra-rare Corvette.

"No, we're okay." Savannah answered softly.

"I've got another call to get to," the tow truck driver snapped. "Where do you want this mess?"

"Hey, buddy," Jesse fired right back to the tow truck driver. "Can it. Three more minutes isn't going to break you."

"Hey, buddy," the tow truck driver sassed back to Jesse, "if you don't tell me…"

"Just leave it right here in the driveway," Karma told the tow truck driver. "We'll take care of it from here." The group of four moved to the side and watched the car roll off the flatbed and into the driveway. The tow truck driver left immediately, leaving the group staring at the mess.

Once word got out that there were no injuries sustained to Karma or Savannah, a few campers started clapping, just to make light of the situation.

"The headlights went out and before I could get the car stopped, we went off the road."

343

"Mr. Waddell," Savannah spoke up, "Karma didn't wreck your car. I did. I was the one driving."

"Ladies, it doesn't matter who was driving. I figured you'd both drive it," Thomas replied sincerely. "I'm sure this was not intentional. You said the headlights went out?"

"Yes!" Both women admitted with sincerity, sticking to their story.

Without saying a word, Thomas pulled a little flashlight from his pocket. It was not much bigger than a triple "A" battery and illuminated a single LED bulb. He leaned over into the passenger side of the wrecked Corvette and pulled out a fuse. He lifted the fuse up and shined the light onto it. Without saying a word, he handed the fuse and the flashlight over to Jesse.

"Doesn't look blown to me," Jesse said, handing it over to Karma with the flashlight. She snatched them out of his hands and held them up to see for herself.

"Really, Buck?" Karma shouted when she saw the fuse *was* actually blown. "Now is not the time!"

"I'm glad you both are okay," Thomas offered sincerely. "How fast were you going?" Jesse asked, betting it was much faster than the posted speed limit of 55 MPH. "We were moving pretty good," Savannah admitted. "C'mon, it's a Corvette."

"This is my fault ladies," Thomas apologized. "I upgraded the headlights and never stopped to think about putting in a bigger fuse. I'm sorry and I'm really glad you're both okay." Karma and Savannah both walked over and gave Thomas a hug, letting him know that there were no hard feelings. When the hug was over, Thomas walked around to the other side of the Corvette where the front fender was completely missing. He reached down and pulled the dipstick out of the engine to check the oil.

"Huh," he commented to himself and put the dipstick back in place. "It doesn't appear to be leaking oil." He then climbed into the wrecked Corvette and turned the key. To everyone's amazement, it fired right up."

"The damage might just be cosmetic." Thomas said with just a bit of relief.

"It's a little more than cosmetic," Karma told him with a solemn voice.

"If I can drive it back to my campsite, it can't be that bad." Thomas said with a grin. "Jesse!"

"Yeah, Tom."

"You get to help me fix this."

Jesse just stood there and smiled while Thomas limped the wrecked Corvette out of the drive and out of sight.

"Savannah," Jesse said while reaching down to hold Karma's hand. "You just wrecked a..."

"A very rare Corvette, I know," Savannah interrupted. "I'm not real proud of myself right now, Jesse. You didn't have to go there."

"I was going to say a half-a-million-dollar car."

"The damage is just cosmetic, remember?"

Chapter 75

The sun was peeking up over the trees when Jesse and Karma stepped out onto the deck for some coffee and bagels.

"Savannah still in bed?" Jesse asked.

"How would I know, Buck?" Karma fired back with sass. "I slept with you last night, not her."

"Did Recon and the guys come back?"

"Jesse, really?" Karma questioned as if Jesse was losing his mind. "We went to bed together, we got up together, we showered together. At what point in time do you think I was keeping track of your team?"

"I just thought you might…"

"Here come the three stooges right now," Karma interrupted as she pointed down the hill. Jesse turned around to see Recon, Doc and Hack stumbling up the gravel road after what appeared to be a long night of drinking with some newly found friends. Jesse and Karma just watched until they got close enough to have a conversation.

"Get lost, did you?" Karma asked the men with the same sass she fired at Jesse earlier.

"Nope," Recon fired right back.

"Didn't you guys leave in the golf cart?" Jesse asked remembering that he had thrown the key to Doc.

"Yup," Hack replied

"Well," Jesse asked very sarcastically, "Where is it?"

"In the woods," Doc replied tossing the ignition key back to Jesse.

"Right next to Thomas's Corvette!" Recon shouted out, immediately sending the three men into hysterical laughter. Jesse and Karma just looked at each other.

"I don't find that the least bit funny," Savannah said as she walked onto the deck wearing nothing but a long t-shirt, obviously just out of bed.

"Guys," Jesse asked again, "Where is the golf cart?"

"In the woods, Commander," Doc answered again, "We can't get it out."

"Right next to, actually underneath, Thomas's Corvette," Recon confirmed. The three men burst into laughter again, slapping their knees and holding their guts from laughing so hard.

"What in the hell is so funny?" Jesse demanded, starting to lose his patience. "I'm not seeing the humor in this."

"Apparently," Recon started to tell the story, "Savannah drove your buddy's ZR-2 off the road last night. Is that true, baby?" Savannah sheepishly nodded her head.

"Well," Doc continued to tell the story, "Thomas was limping his Corvette home last night and he stopped at Leslie's to have a drink with us and to see how we were getting along with everyone."

"And?" Jesse asked. "This story is going where?"

"When Thomas left a couple of hours later," Hack started, but couldn't finish because he started to laugh so hard.

"The brakes went out on his Corvette and it went down the hill into the woods," Recon added, bursting into laughter again.

"It took your golf cart with it!" Doc finally finished, also laughing hysterically.

"Why was my golf cart parked at the bottom of the hill?" Jesse asked, still not finding the humor in the story.

"There were so many people over there that there was no place else to park, so we parked at the bottom of the road Leslie lives on and we hiked up to her place," Recon answered, finally getting control of his laughter.

"Is Tom okay?" Jesse asked, wondering if he should have.

"We think so," Hack answered, containing his laughter. "He got out of the car and walked away."

"Yeah, he didn't say anything to anyone. He just left," Doc added.

"Jesse," Recon said changing the gears of the conversation, "you and Thomas might go back a ways, but there are some people here at your campground that think he's, well, a little *off* shall we say?"

"Recon," Jesse replied, defending his long-time friend, "they just don't know him like I do."

"I'm not judging, I'm just sharing."

"Tom might be a little off, from where I'm sitting, we're all a little off, are we not?"

"C'mon guys!" Karma intervened, clapping her hands together. "Let's get breakfast out of the way and go get the toys out of the woods."

Chapter 76

It didn't take long during breakfast for the silence to be broken. Everyone at the table was wondering *what* the next step was going to be, but no one had the gumption to ask until Recon finally did.

"Commander," Recon spoke respectfully, while making eye contact with Jesse sitting across the table, "What's the plan?"

"After breakfast?" Jesse questioned before reiterating. "We're going to go clean up that mess you guys made in the woods last night."

"Not the short-term plan Commander, the long-term plan."

"That's a great question, Recon." Desi responded as she and Erin popped out from around the corner and stepped onto the deck.

"Recon!" Jesse spoke with commanding authority, "you obviously failed to check the Hummer for a GPS tracker!"

"Here's the tracker, Jesse," Erin said as she handed the smashed device over to Jesse. "We're the only ones who know where you are."

"For now." Desi added.

"Pastor thought…" Erin started but was immediately interrupted by Jesse.

"I don't care about Pastor."

"Well you should," Desi fired back aggressively.

"Why is that, exactly?" Jesse made direct eye contact with Desi and spoke sternly, all while maintaining composure and keeping his cool.

"He's the only one who's keeping you out of prison right now for smashing the President's face in."

"He had that coming."

"Jesse!" Desi shouted, "this is serious!"

"She's right." Erin added, "this is serious."

"How do I get my name cleared?" Jesse asked. "What needs to be done?"

"I don't know if that's going to happen, especially not right away," Desi told him honestly. "You screwed the pooch this time, Jesse."

"Commander," Recon butted into the conversation, "forget about the President right now. What's our plan?"

"You all want to know what the plan is?" Jesse said getting up from the table. "Here's the plan." Jesse moved over and put his arm around Karma before he continued, giving her a gentle squeeze as if to say, "this is for you."

"We have the whereabouts for all of the kingpins trafficking humans in the Unites States and abroad. We know who they are and where they are. We're going to break off into teams of two and take them out. First in the U.S. then overseas. Knowing what I know now, when we've completed our mission, we're going to ask Pastor to inform the President of our accomplishment and gracefully request a pardon."

"Good luck with that," Desi snapped sarcastically. "You beat him up pretty good, Jesse."

"I need to know who's with me. From this day forward. Who's in and who's out. Speak up," Jesse ordered, ignoring Desi's comment.

"I'm in," Erin answered immediately, being the first to give an answer.

"You know I'm in, Buck," Karma replied right after.

"I believe I speak for the team," Doc replied, getting head nods from the other SEALs. "We're all in."

"Savannah?" Jesse asked.

"Hell yes, I'm in!" Savannah replied excitedly. "There's no way I'm missing out on this!"

"Team," Jesse addressed the group with a stern tone and a sharp eye. He suddenly went into SEAL mode. "We're going to break up into groups of two and scatter. Our mission is to take out the kingpins in the U.S. first, then travel abroad and take them out over there. When our mission is completed, we'll meet in Fiji and lay low. That's where we'll bring Pastor in and request our pardon. Questions?"

"Wouldn't we be safer hiding out in a non-extradition country?" Doc asked.

"I thought about that," Jesse replied with a calculated response. "That's where everyone will be looking for us. There are over 300 islands in Fiji, many of which are not inhabited. Karma and I noted that Fiji would be a great place to hide if we ever needed to."

"Needle in a haystack," Karma added.

"Who are the teams," Doc asked "and why are we separating?

"Teams are as follows," Karma replied. "Recon and Savannah, you two are Bravo team. Doc and Erin, you'll pair up as Charlie team, and Hack and Desi, you two are team Delta."

"I suppose you and Karma are the Alpha team?" Desi asked with a little sarcasm.

"Alpha leaders, that is correct."

"The reason we're separating," Jesse stated, taking over the conversation again, "is because we'll be operating on a truncated timeline. We must strike twice, hard and fast. Then we'll fly to our overseas destinations and do it again. Thirty hours, four hits per team, meet in Fiji."

"How are we doing all of this?" Erin asked cautiously, wanting clarification.

"We're posing as couples. No one will suspect a couple on vacation to be a threat. We'll be using .22 caliber pistols with silencers. One shot folks, make it clean, don't miss."

"What is our means of transportation?" Erin asked. "How are we flying?"

"We'll be flying on our own private jets."

"Our own private jets?" Desi questioned. "What private jets?"

"The private jets we seized from Camper," Jesse replied with a smirk.

"Is that safe?" Savannah asked, not crazy about the idea. "When our targets learn that his jets are heading in their direction…"

"…it'll make them easier targets," Desi interrupted, nodding her head with approval. "We're not posing as couples on vacation, we're posing as buyers."

"To the general public, we'll look like couples. To the kingpins, we'll look like buyers, no one sees this coming."

"When do we leave?" Recon asked while eyeballing Savannah. "How do we keep in touch?"

"We don't," Jesse replied after a long pause. "Every team has a SEAL; the SEAL leads the team. Every team is on their own until we get to Fiji."

"That's a dangerous game, Commander." Doc addressed the group with a little concern. "What's with the urgent urgency to start and complete this mission without proper planning and training?"

"We are properly trained, remember Vegas? That was our test."

"It's the only way to surprise everyone without being discovered," Jesse replied as he started to pace back and forth. "There is no reason for us to stay in contact. We can't help each other for starters, and we don't need our mobile phones pinging off cell towers while we're on our mission. We don't want to be tracked."

"Won't the flight logs track us?" asked Erin.

"The flight logs will track the flights; we'll manipulate the manifest," Hack answered. "Fake ID's."

"We're all on our own mission," Jesse continued. "Movement by human traffickers is done in the late evening and overnight. We strike here in the U.S. first, catch a plane overseas and strike again, then fly to Fiji. We strike so hard and so fast that no one sees us coming and no one has time to react. Enough time has passed that they feel Camper was an isolated incident, and they need to move the people they have backed up. Now is the time to finish the job."

"We're in, we're out, we're done," Karma stated, now seeing what Jesse was thinking. "We give the President all of the credit for disabling human trafficking on a global level, and we, hopefully, get pardoned."

"This seems a little too simplistic, Commander." Recon spoke to Jesse but was really addressing the entire group."

"You guys have gotten soft! Simplicity is its power!" Jesse shouted at the group. "Don't overthink this!"

"What do you know that you're not telling us, Commander?" Desi asked, not being the only one who wasn't connecting all of the dots.

"Hack, do it." Jesse fired back immediately, almost a bit overzealous."

"The weak link for the bad guys is their schedule," Hack announced to the group as he got up out of his chair. "Because what they are doing is so risky, the plan for moving humans needs to be laid out months in advance. There is zero margin for error here."

"The plans for moving the shipments were on the disk, weren't they?" Doc asked, seeing right through the smoke screen.

"Yes, they were," Hack admitted with a smirk. "That's why we're leaving tomorrow."

"Tomorrow?" Karma asked, shocked with Hack's response. "Jesse! There is no way you planned this in fifteen minutes."

"Hack and I have been working on this together since we got back."

"When were you going to tell the rest of us?" Karma asked. "I'm a little peeved with you for not sharing this with anyone until now."

"I have to agree, Commander. What's up with that?" Recon added.

"Anyone else want to get diarrhea of the mouth?" Jesse asked sarcastically.

"I knew about it," Doc chimed in.

"Yeah, Erin and I kind of knew about it as well," Desi admitted. "Just not all of the details."

"No diarrhea from me, Jesse." Savannah popped off with a smirk. "But I can't wait to watch you dig yourself out of this one."

"There's nothing to dig out," Jesse fired back casually. "You two were planning your wedding," he said pointing to Recon and Savannah "and you, Karma, have been getting reacquainted with your parents. I wasn't going to take that time away from either of you."

"Are you finally getting married?" Karma asked excitedly, clapping her hands together. "When? Tell us when, Savannah!"

"Ten days ago, we were getting married tomorrow," Savannah said looking at Recon. "That was back in Eureka. Now I don't know if it'll ever happen."

"Savannah, my love," Recon said to her while picking up her hand in his, "I don't know what's going to happen tomorrow, so I think we need to make this happen tonight."

Chapter 77

Once again, the group of tightknit friends scurried together to have a crash wedding. The clubhouse on the campground didn't have any scheduled events that afternoon or evening, so it was available for the ceremony. The women broke off in one direction and the men in another, completely forgetting about the mess in the woods that needed to be cleaned up. In just a few hours, the group had reconvened at the clubhouse, along with some fellow campers, including Thomas who jumped right in to help with the decorating frenzy.

Balloons and streamers were hung everywhere. White tablecloths covered folding tables and each table had its own unique centerpiece that was loaned by a different camper. For an impromptu country wedding, the clubhouse looked quite amazing and, of course, everyone at the campground was invited to the celebration.

"Jesse!" Desi shouted coming through the door excitedly. "Erin and I found a winery down the road a piece. We have wine and Champagne for tonight, enough for anyone who wants to come."

"There's a winery around here?" Jesse asked, not remembering there being one.

"Raven's Glenn," Erin answered coming through the door with a case of wine in her arms. "There chardonnay is fantastic!"

"We're in the middle of nowhere, yet, why am I not surprised that you and Desi could sniff out a winery?"

"And do a little wine tasting," Erin replied with a wink.

"C'mon, Buck!" Karma said with a poke as she walked up to her man. "Don't rain on their parade. You should be happy about their find."

"I hope you bought enough." Jesse replied with a chuckle.

"No doubt," Thomas added. "Once our fellow campers find out there's free wine and Champagne up here, there'll all come running!"

"The more the merrier." Recon said, walking into the conversation. "I want the whole world to know how much I love this woman."

"She's a looker, I'll tell you that," Thomas said to Recon as they shook hands.

"Jesse!" Doc shouted from the other side of the room. "We're about done here. Why don't we clean up our mess while we have the chance?"

"That's a great idea Doc," Jesse said, tossing him a set of vehicle keys. "You and Hack go get the Hummer and we'll pull them out of the woods."

Chapter 78

Thomas's Corvette was dragged back to his campsite, and what was left of the golf cart was pulled from the trees and placed in its garage to be dealt with at a later date. Jesse gave Thomas the keys to the Cadillac CTS-V as collateral, no strings attached, until they had the time to make the repairs to his wrecked Corvette.

Savannah was dressed in a white sundress. It was sleeveless and above the knee. She had on a white choker for a necklace and white sandals on her feet. Recon wore black denim shorts with a black polo. Black sneakers without socks completed his attire. It was a campground wedding, with Jesse officiating. Nothing fancy, lots of love. Recon and Savannah's wedding turned out to be the best time most people have had in a long time. Their wedding was proof that you don't have to break the bank to celebrate one of life's greatest moments.

The wedding was a great time. Lots of campers stopped in for a drink and to wish Recon and Savannah the very best with their new life together. The evening was over sooner than anyone wanted it to be, and Recon promised Savannah a real honeymoon once they made it to Fiji, just a few short days away.

Chapter 79

At ten o'clock on the nose the next morning, Kurtis was pulling up outside with a brand-new black Cadillac limousine, much like the last one that was involved in the accident.

"Kurtis!" Jesse shouted as Kurtis exited the car in front of the campsite. "It's damn good to see you!"

"It's damn good to see you too brother," Kurtis replied while giving Jesse a man hug,

"Hey!" Karma shouted coming down the stairs off the deck. "I thought you weren't playing in our sandbox anymore!"

"Hi, Karma" Kurtis replied, walking over to give her hug. "Funny thing about your sandbox, it always seems so inviting at first."

"Got lured in, didn't you?"

"Jesse needed me," he told her. "Besides, how much risk could there possibly be in taking you all to the airport?" Kurtis asked laughing. "What could *possibly* go wrong?"

"That's a question we'd rather not address," Jesse mentioned.

"Kurtis!" Doc shouted with his big booming voice. "You drove all the way up here from Virginia to take us to a municipal airport thirty minutes away?"

"It's damn nice to see you too, Doc." Kurtis replied with a man hug. "Call it crazy."

"We're not flying out of Cambridge." Hack told him, stunned that he didn't make the connection. "We're flying out of Pittsburg."

Before another ten minutes had passed the entire group was headed to Pittsburg International Airport, which was not much more than a two-hour drive away. Each team of two was leaving on their own private jet that would take them to their five stops, with the final destination being Fiji.

"Team," Jesse announced to the group, "everyone here is very well trained. There is no margin for error. You get in, you make the kill, you get out, you hit your next stop. Are there any questions?"

"Yeah," Recon questioned delicately. "After our last kill, we do what?"

"Any questions *other* than Recon's?" Jesse asked while the group shared a light chuckle.

The group was silent. There were no questions to be asked, no answers to be given. Every team knew the drill. Every team knew what was expected of them. The limo pulled up to the private charter area of the airport where there were four jets standing by. It was 'go time.'

"Before we head in our own directions," Jesse insisted. "I want you to pray with me."

The group held hands and bowed their heads while Jesse said a prayer.

"Dear Jesus, our Lord and Savior, please forgive us of our sins, as we forgive those who have sinned against us. The people that I love dearly are heading in their own directions to eliminate a global threat amongst your people. We ask that you give us the courage to complete this

360

mission, the knowledge to keep us safe and the wisdom to make wise choices. Please bring us all back together safely in Fiji, in just a few days. In your name we pray, Jesus. Amen."

"Amen."

Made in the USA
Monee, IL
29 February 2020